Hope you
Peter i

# WHEN THE BOAT COMES IN
# BOOK IV

# Jack High

by Peter Mitchell

First published in Great Britain as a softback original in 2018

Copyright © Peter Mitchell

The moral right of this author has been asserted.

Typeset in Iowan Old Style

Typesetting and publishing by UK Book Publishing

www.ukbookpublishing.com

ISBN: 978-1-912183-40-1

This book is dedicated to my father, the novelist and screenwriter, James Mitchell, without whom there would have been no 'Boat' in the first place.

James, a heavy drinker all his adult life, died of Liver Cancer in 2002. Unlike me, he never encountered an opportunity to enter 12-step, abstinence-based recovery. In his memory, a share of the proceeds from the sales of this work in all formats will be donated to the Newcastle-based charity, The Road To Recovery Trust.

# WHEN THE BOAT COMES IN
# BOOK IV

## Jack High

# PREFACE

I grew up with When The Boat Comes In. Written and created by my father, James Mitchell, it was instantly a nationwide success as a BBC television drama when it was first screened in January, 1976. Set in the mythical town of Gallowshield in industrial North East England, it was set during the Interwar Years and examined that period of great social, economic and political change through the lives of working class people.

There were three successful series, then a hiatus before a fourth was released in 1981. There were books, too – three of them, in all – and, like the TV series, they covered the trials and tribulations of the ambitious protagonist, Jack Ford and his turbulent relationship with the Seaton family during the early part of the 1920s. They ended with Jack doing what he always managed to do, overcoming the obstacle that stood in his way. In this case, the obstacle in question was an exquisite historic building which he demolished without a second thought.

When the television series came back to the screens in the early eighties, we found Jack returning from America five years later having made a fortune then inevitably losing it in the Wall Street Crash. But what happened in the intervening years has always remained a mystery.

From a practical perspective, I wrote Jack High (more than forty years after the publication of the first books) to try to begin to fill in some of the gaps. But there were other reasons, too. For a start, because of its immense popularity, the series has become a part of North East media culture. It was a substantial hit all over the UK and in other parts of the world, too (especially, Australia). But the region in which 'The Boat' was set, really took it to their hearts.

What made me think I could become the 'keeper of the flame'?

Well, the truth is I don't and I'm not. I simply started writing and thoroughly enjoyed it. In fact, I felt closer and closer to Dad, the further I got into the book. I imagine that the process of placing the characters in new scenarios was a bit like using your father's old chisel or playing his violin. The creative output is your own but the process has been made easier because it is so familiar. Better still, even though he has been dead for fifteen years, I had many a fascinating chat with him along the way.

I hope you enjoy it.

Many thanks and I hope your boat comes in.

*Peter Mitchell*
**January 2018**

# CHAPTER 1

Jack Ford was used to losing things: losing jobs, losing friends, losing face. In the War, he'd almost lost his life - several times. But somehow, he'd survived and with every defeat there was a lesson learned and a score to be settled. The Army had taught him that, it was what got him through it. Picking yourself up after a knock down took time, effort and the irresistible energy of deep-seated resentment. He knew that. He was used to it.

But what on earth did you do when you'd won the last battle and the war was over?

There was a knock on the door and he put down his newspaper. 'Come.'

'Tidy your room sir?'

Ford beckoned the maid inside as she pulled the rattling trolley into his suite. The uniform was smart and crisp and its contents were young, athletic and pretty. As he watched her work, Ford even managed to appal himself by the thought that this innocent interruption was likely to be the highlight of his day. She started clearing away his breakfast dishes.

'Was everything all right for you, sir?'

'I should think it was – at these prices.'

That threw her. Guests at The Connaught rarely talked about

1

money and they never ever talked about it to the staff. She glanced over to him and was relieved to see he was smiling.

'And what about you?' he said.

'Is everything all right with you today?'

By now she had the tin of polish out and was vigorously buffing the wooden table top until it gleamed in the mid-morning sun.

'Oh yes, sir. I'm always all right. After all, I'm working, aren't I?'

It was her turn to smile then and Ford couldn't quite work out whether or not she was being sardonic. In the end, he decided he hoped she was.

It was a fresh Spring day and the wind chopped up the surface of the Serpentine as Ford took his afternoon stroll through Hyde Park. Strolling was new to him. In the Army he had marched everywhere, obviously. And he'd never really lost that rhythmic, purposeful stride when he'd been discharged. It was different then, though, back in Gallowshield. He casually flicked a pebble into the water with the toe of his shoe as he thought about his home town. A boil on the backside of Britain – it was nowhere, really. Just another grim industrial town clinging onto life like the sea-gulls cling to the cliffs when the wind blows in Winter. There, you had to keep moving as briskly as possible just to take the edge off the knife-like wind hurled down from the Arctic Circle. Generations ago, Gallowshield had been nothing but a fishing village on the North East coast but the industrial revolution had changed all that. Coal, steel and ships had brought the peasants flocking from the fields to the Promised Land where regular wages meant full bellies and a place to live. The town grew bigger and with it the mines and shipyards prospered. But nobody got fat – nobody that Jack knew anyway. To get fat you had to own things: factories, houses, banks, land, mines. No-one that Jack knew ever owned anything of any real value – a few sticks of furniture maybe, the clothes on their back, a few tools. Nothing substantial, nothing you could build on. They were all caught like rats in a trap. You worked a ten-hour shift at a coal face or in a freezing yard to earn money to buy food in someone else's shop and pay rent for a house that someone else owned. A decent, honest living, they called it. But Jack didn't think so – it was far too much effort just to stand still. When War broke out and the opportunity came for him to enlist, he didn't think twice and that was when the marching started.

When the fighting was over, Ford was still No-one and he went straight back to Nowhere. But he'd learned a lot – a lot about staying alive and getting on. He'd joined up in 1914 as Private Ford, a bright-eyed teenager, innocent as a lamb and dumb as a coal scuttle. Six years later by the time he got home, he had three stripes, an eye for the main chance and a box full of treasures. And he'd only just begun. Jack had fought his way to a medal and now he was going to work his way to the top.

But that was yesterday and the urgency had gone now and with it the point of getting anywhere in a hurry. The stiff cord work trousers with coarse woollen coat and hobnail boots had been replaced by a blue Saville Row suit in light tweed with quarter-brogue Oxfords over silk socks. The transformation had brought undoubted comfort to the body but it had achieved bugger all for the restlessness of his mind.

Ford settled himself down on a bench to watch the ducks and the nannies and the messengers and the businessmen and the tramp snoring like Billy-oh on the seat next door. What on earth could possibly be wrong with him? He'd done the deal and made the money – tons of it. He'd turned his back on the grubby old northern town and rented a suite at The Connaught. He dined where he liked, drank what he liked, did what he liked. His boat had come in, well and truly.

He thought of the mischievous maid who'd tidied his room.

'Of course, I'm all right. I'm working, aren't I?'

She was a smart lass. She knew the score. Not like the maid Jack had married. Not like Dolly. Dolly wouldn't have known the score if she'd read it in the papers. And she was a bonny one an' all. Even bonnier than the maid in The Connaught. But she was long gone – ran off with his mate, Tom Seaton. Ran off to play Happy Families on three fifths of bugger all. Happy? Jack Ford would bet his life on it.

He opened his Newcastle Journal and Daily Star. 'Red Paradise,' the paper announced with its usual fistful of sarcasm. A delegation from the British Trades Union Congress were visiting their revolutionary friends in Russia where wages were said to have trebled since before the war. Really? I bet they're celebrating all the way to the bread queue, thought Ford.

After a melancholic sort of day, his spirits rose when the lights of evening flickered into action. Night-time in London was a sparkling place to be when you had money. Ford had a dinner date with an old acquaintance. Sir Horatio Manners wasn't exactly what you could call a friend. Over the years he'd been a rival, an enemy, an associate and even a co-conspirator. Tonight, he'd be a dinner companion. Ford knew him through his son – Capt. Peter James Bertram Manners, MC. The officer commanding Ford's Company at Ypres. Manners had died in his arms after being wounded in a shell burst. That had been a decade ago but as Ford straightened his white tie he remembered it as if it were yesterday.

'What am I doing here, Sergeant? I said I'd dine at the Savile.'

Ford would never forget the final utterance of his young commanding officer. Why should he? Over the years those final whisperings had become his most successful chat up line by far. The list of impressionable young conquests who had yielded under the full onslaught of Captain Manners' poetic departure was long and distinguished – unerringly attractive, too.

'You're a blackguard and a scoundrel, Jack Ford.' He admonished himself for the fond memories and threw a conspiratorial wink to the mirror.

In 1920, when Ford had eventually returned to Gallowshield to hang up his uniform, times had been tough but there was still work to be had for skilled men – still plenty of torpedoed Merchant Ships to be replaced. Manners Senior was a wealthy and well-connected businessman so Ford had tracked him down, sought an audience and told the story of the death of the grieving man's son. The two of them had been crossing swords in one way or another ever since. But tonight, there'd be a truce – there had to be. They were going to dine at the Savile.

The food was good but the company was a trifle sour. Hory Manners looked at Jack Ford and saw a younger version of himself: competitive, ruthless, quick-witted but more agile and better looking. That was never good for his temper.

'Bloody steak's overdone.' A grumpy Manners prodded at it with his knife.

'Can't be…if it's still bloody.'

Ford grinned and took another swig at his claret.

'Very funny. You know your problem?' Manners was in no mood to back away.

'I know you're going to be kind enough to tell me.'

'Too clever by half.'

'Yes, and if I was any sharper, I'd cut myself. Come on Manners, what's really the matter? You look like you've lost a shillin' and found a farthin'.'

'Well it's funny you should say that – but I rather think I have?'

Ford started to laugh.

'You? You don't even know what a farthing looks like. You spilled more than a florin's worth on your shirt tonight.'

But Manners wasn't finding it funny.

'This return to the Gold Standard. It's costing us a damned fortune.'

'When you say us...?'

'I mean the manufacturers, Ford, and you damned well know it.'

Hory Manners was chairman and a major shareholder of Lewis Bishop – the largest shipbuilding yard on the Tyne.

'Exchange rate pricing you out of the market is it?''

'It is. And it's not just the yards, Jack. Every manufacturer is feeling the pinch – and it's going to get worse. There'll be closures. You mark my words.'

The old man punctuated the sentence by jabbing his fork in the direction of his dinner companion, the lines on his brow deepening into concerned furrows.

'Hey, steady on Sir Horatio. My mam always told me it was rude to point.'

Manners lowered the cutlery.

'Yes, and she was right. I'm sorry. But things are going to get pretty grim up there, I can promise you that. It was boom time when the war ended, but not now. Wages have remained high while the working week has been cut. Our productivity is poor, Ford. We're not competitive.'

Ford listened and got stuck into his fig tart while Manners explained the tomfoolery of allowing politicians the authority to meddle in something as important as economics.

'Of course, the German market is completely gone – reparations saw to that. One of our best customers before the war and now they're on their knees and undercutting us – building ships at a loss for anybody who wants them – even rebel nations. We haven't a cat in Hell's chance.'

Not a hint of sentiment or feeling. No malice or forgiveness either. Four years of pain and agony and millions of dead including his only son but to Sir Horatio Manners, the overriding conclusion on the entire catastrophe was that the peace settlement was bad for business.

At least Jack understood the problem. He was a time-served fitter himself and, in leaner times, had done his fair share of graft in Lewis Bishops. He'd been glad of the opportunity, too. Newly married to Dolly and with a child on the way – he'd needed the work. But then she lost the baby and there was emptiness so he filled the void with ambition, saw an opportunity in the union and landed the top job: Regional Secretary. And that was when Jack Ford started to learn something about economics.

'Of course, it'll be all your pals who will suffer,'

Manners dabbed at the remnants of béarnaise sauce on his chin with a linen napkin.

He didn't look as though he was about to shed any tears.

'They're not my members any more, Hory. Can't we just enjoy the bloody dinner? There'll be cognac and cigars afterwards if you eat up all your pudding.'

His chauffeur-driven Bentley arrived at 9.30pm and Ford was happy to see Sir Horatio Manners off into the evening – the older man's engine was still running as he grunted a dismissive farewell – miserable old codger.

Jack was just a two-minute walk from his hotel but it was too early for him to call it a night. The club's bar resembled a reading room for the over-privileged and under-employed all of them younger versions of Hory Manners – all share-price, interest rates and despondency. Self-pity was a trait that Jack avoided at all costs so he decided to step out into London and find something more uplifting. All this talk of shipyards and impending poverty had reminded him where he had come from and the people that he knew. Did he miss them? A few, maybe; one, in particular. If he was going to find some of his own kind, Mayfair wasn't a good place to start. But Soho was just a fifteen-minute walk and the West End was definitely more interesting on foot.

Winter had only recently begun to retreat after a steady, three-month onslaught and the dry night had enticed people out in large numbers.

At the top of Bruton Street he crossed Regent Street and immediately detected a different scent in the air – he savoured it with relish. It was the unmistakeable whiff of illicit behaviour. He'd been told that once you crossed the border into Soho, the titled grandeur and formality of Mayfair gave way to a much more free-thinking, free-wheeling world of jazz clubs and cosmopolitan cafes, unlicensed drinking dens and dangerous conversations. Ford felt quite excited at the prospect – one thing you could be in London was anonymous. No-one really cared who you were provided you could settle the bill. It wasn't that he had anything against wealth and formality, in fact quite the contrary, he liked everything it offered and he wanted as much of it as he could get. But it wouldn't be enough. Not for Jack.

His first port of call was the Royal Oak. He'd been tempted by the dim lighting and the drunk outside chasing his cigarette end with a lighted match. But as he leaned against the chipped marble-topped bar he could see he'd made a mistake. And as things turned out, he wasn't exactly anonymous either - he attracted more than a couple of curious glances as he lifted his pint of bitter to his lips in full evening suit and patent leather shoes. The piano player was manfully competing against the rowdy clientele and you could just about make out the depressing melody of The Roses of Picardy in there somewhere. But after about 10 minutes of bad beer in a choking tobacco fog, Ford decided to try to find somewhere more stimulating. Something with a little more spice.

He'd turned into Gerrard Street when he stumbled upon it quite by accident.

There, on the other side of the road, was a tall, slim man surrounded by three other fellers. And, despite his obvious objections, they appeared to be dragging him down the steps of a building. Then, they seemed awfully determined that he should accompany them around a corner and down into a dingy back lane. Ford eased himself into the shadow of a greengrocer's shop and settled himself to observe. He'd done a lot of observing in the army – he'd done a lot of fighting too. But it was always safer to watch first, see how the land lay. That's how Ford learned to stay alive. He saw a punch thrown and heard a groan as the unwilling object of their attentions received a heavy blow to his body. The victim – a middle-aged man, by the look of him - then seemed less able to resist as his attackers succeeded in hauling him off around the corner of the building and out of sight.

Whatever it was this man had done, he was about to pay a high price for it. Ford looked at the building from which the men had emerged. There was a brass plaque on the door which read '1917 Club.'

He knew the fight was none of his business – he didn't even know the people involved but he couldn't help himself. Three against one – it just wasn't fair. But he wasn't going to intervene out of a sense of fair play – that would be ridiculous. No, there was something else. Something about the tall, slim man who'd been punched in the ribs, something familiar. Ford sensed it and he acted.

First, he looked around for a makeshift weapon. All he could find was the greengrocer's dustbin, so he picked that up and emptied the assortment of rotting vegetables onto the pavement before crossing the road and turning into the lane.

Even in the gloom Ford could see the victim being pinned against the wall by a man either side. The third bloke had already got in a couple of telling blows to the face and he was setting himself to deliver another.

Ford ran up behind him with the bin in both hands and rammed it down over the man's head. He took two steps back before shoulder-charging man and bin and sending them both to the ground with a clash, a groan and a clatter. While the other two were still trying to work out what was happening, Ford grabbed the second man by the lapels and butted him full in the face, smashing his spectacles and his nose simultaneously. The third man was trying to run off when he tripped over the bloke in the bin.

'Howay, marrer – we're off!'

Ford grabbed the victim's wrist and yanked him back up the lane towards the street lights and safety.

The entire rescue had taken less than fifteen seconds but the pair didn't stop running until they'd reached Shaftesbury Avenue. Eventually the injured man gestured that he had to stop and was bent almost double as he tried to get his breath back. He was also holding his side where the thug had landed the first blow.

'Are you all right, bonny lad? I think we'd better get you to a hospital.'

The man looked up at him and shook his head.

'No. Not necessary. I know a place. Just give me a minute.'

Ford could see the extent of his injuries. On top of whatever damage had been done to his ribs, he'd suffered a bash in the mouth which had burst his bottom lip and from the swelling around his right eye, the cheekbone might be broken. But he could also see from the quality of his leather shoes and the cut of his clothes, this man was no street ruffian. So why didn't he want to go to hospital?

'We haven't been introduced. My name's Ford – Jack Ford.'

Still bent over, the stranger grabbed Ford's proffered hand and looked up at his rescuer.

'I owe you a great deal Mr Ford. Thank you. I'm Charles Needham.'

As they shook, Ford took a closer look at the other man's face.

'Are you indeed? Well come along Mr Needham, you show me where we're headed and when we get there, you can tell me why a former Cabinet Minister is spending his evenings getting duffed up in a Soho back street.'

# CHAPTER 2

Needham was right – it wasn't far to the Ham Bone Club but the door was locked tight shut.

'It's a little early for them just yet. There'll be someone inside – just keep knocking.'

Ford did just that and about twenty thumps later, a woman more pre-occupied with her make-up than her visitors, reluctantly opened the door.

Her irritated glare was immediately transformed into a look of utter compassion the moment her eyes fixed on Needham.

'Charlie! – What on earth's happened to you? Come in, come in.'

Ford helped Needham into the entrance of the club and down a long corridor.

'I'm so sorry about this, Rose.'

She wasn't in the mood for apologies – not right now. This young woman was genuinely concerned.

'Straight on to the very end – the door on your right.'

Needham had run out of energy and Ford almost carried him the last few steps.

Once inside, he helped the man on to an old, leather couch while Rose lit the lamps.

They cleaned him up as best they could and Ford stretched a length of cotton torn from a bed sheet tightly round his middle to support his ribs. Needham winced as Ford gave the sheet an extra tug.

'Right. I think we could all do with a drink now.' Rose returned with a decanter of Scotch, two glasses and a small brown bottle with no label which Ford viewed with suspicion.

'That's for Charlie. The whisky is for us.'

'What's in that one, then?'

'Laudanum.'

'Really? I thought that went out with Queen Victoria.'

'Well strictly speaking it is illegal to have it on the premises. But then again, strictly speaking the whisky isn't exactly genuine either. We distil it ourselves, in Croydon.'

She poured some laudanum on to a large serving spoon.

'Open wide darling!'

Rose held Needham's nose while she poured it down.

'It's awfully bitter. But it bloody well takes the pain away.'

'You do that awfully well. Are you a nurse?'

She turned to face Ford.

'Certainly not but I have taken an awful lot of medication in my time. Right - who are you and why have you done this to Charlie?'

But it was Needham who answered.

'It wasn't him. On the contrary. Rose Milne, this gentleman is Jack Ford. He came to my rescue when I was attacked outside the 1917 Club.'

'What?'

She started to laugh.

'You were attacked outside the 1917 Club?'

'What the Hell's so funny?'

For the life of him, Jack couldn't see anything amusing and all

13

Needham could do was dab at his bloodied lip and stare at the ceiling in agony.

'Oh, but it is funny, don't you get it?'

Ford shook his head, still mystified.

'The 1917 Club is a political talking shop for a bunch of intellectual socialist do-gooders who want to save the world.'

'So?' said Ford.

'The Ham Bone – where you are now – is one of the most notorious cabaret clubs in London. Anything goes here. Straight, queer, drink, drugs. We take hedonism to new heights and we open all night. This is a den of iniquity. Charlie, here, is a member of both. But guess which one put him in this condition?'

'Dangerous thing, politics,' said Ford.

'Too right, Jack – let's drink to that.'

She refilled their glasses.

'But you're a member of another exclusive club, aren't you Mr Needham, or may I call you Charles?'

Needham smiled and nodded at Ford.

'You know I am.'

'The Rt Hon Charles Needham, Labour MP for Jesmond.'

'Correct. And if I don't mistake that accent of yours, Jack – not too far away from where you were born.'

'Gallowshield. What gave it away?'

'When you pulled me away from those thugs you said 'Howay marrer.'

Rose Milne thought she was listening to a foreign language.

'Howay Marrer? What on earth does that mean?'

'It's a Tyneside term,' explained Jack.

'Howay means "come along" or something along those lines and your marrer is a close friend.'

'As far as I was concerned, hearing you speak meant I was safe,' said Needham.

14

'Thanks again Jack, you were a sight for sore eyes when you showed up.'

'But why were those blokes duffing you up? What had you done to them?'

Needham shrugged.

'Nothing in particular. Problem is I'm not exactly what you'd call a popular chap.'

'I'm not buying that, Needham. Those blokes would have given you a damn good hiding. Maybe worse. I've seen blackleg miners get off more lightly.'

'I'm sure you have. Well let's see...'

He propped himself up on his elbow to go through the list of his alleged shortcomings.

'I was a Liberal but joined the Labour Party. Then I was part of Ramsay McDonald's first Government which practically everybody detested.

'I'm born into an extremely privileged aristocratic family and we own a big stately pile on a vast estate in Northumberland.

'I'm constantly banging on about the underprivileged poor and strongly believe that education is the key to equality

'How am I doing so far?'

'Sounds like some people may have got reasons not to like you, but not enough to give a belting, surely.'

'I'm committed Jack. That means I'm vocal. If you're in politics and not on my side, you have plenty of reasons to hate Charles Needham.'

'All that may be true. But that attack wasn't out of the blue. It was planned. And, I could be wrong, but in the kerfuffle, I'm sure I heard someone shout the word 'Sympathiser', at you.'

'Ah. Did they? Well that explains it,' said Needham.

'On top of all my other failings I spoke out against the war. Worse still I campaigned against it.

15

'I also believe the Versailles Treaty to be ridiculously harsh. Germany was beaten – it didn't need to be humiliated. These aren't popular views to hold in Britain today, Jack. So many have died or suffered a loss because they believed they were fighting for democracy. They wanted something more – a better life. Tonight's episode wasn't an isolated incident. It has happened before and will probably happen again.'

'I see,' said Jack.

'Well my war is over now bonny lad and I for one don't want to fight about it anymore.'

'Who did you serve with?'

'I was a Sergeant in the Royal Northumberland Fusiliers.'

'Did you see much action?' The question was asked with a note of genuine sympathy.

'All the way through,' said Ford. 'And then after Armistice I went looking for a bit more.'

Rose was puzzled.

'More? After the ceasefire? I didn't know there was any more.'

'I volunteered for the NREF.'

That took Charles Needham by surprise.

'Really? The Russian Front?'

Ford shrugged it off.

'Well the war was over and there was nothing much left for me at home. I'd never heard of Murmansk so I thought, what the Hell?'

Rose was becoming confused.

'What on earth was the NREF?'

Needham answered.

'It was the North Russian Expeditionary Force. Set up by the Government to keep the Russian Baltic ports open. By 1919, they were fighting against the Bolsheviks – the Russian revolutionaries. Did you kill Bolsheviks too, Jack?

Ford kept his gaze steady and his features still.

'I was in Intelligence – after a year, they pulled us all out.'

'Do you wish you hadn't stepped in to help me, Jack? I am a Socialist, after all.'

'Not at all. I don't do causes but I still enjoy a good fight. Two against three – them's canny odds.'

'Two men and a dustbin, Jack – don't forget your secret weapon.'

Rose Milne didn't need to know the details.

'I really don't want to hear any more. The whisky's there and I've got to get ready for tonight – we'll be open in half an hour. Jack, you're more than welcome to stay but if it's too risqué for your blood, I'll understand. And thank you for looking after Charlie. You're a sweetie.'

'I doubt it'll be too much for me bonny lass but I might make a tactical withdrawal tonight if you don't mind – it's been an eventful evening and I need my beauty sleep.'

She looked him up and down, scrutinising every inch.

'Not from where I'm standing, Jack. Another time then. Don't leave it too long, will you? Goodnight.'

# CHAPTER 3

'That was four-pence well spent eh, Billy? Eh, Da?'

Tom Seaton had nearly turned professional himself and nothing gave him greater pleasure than a rare day out at the football.

Billy just grinned back at him as he pushed his father's wheelchair through the crowds and over the cobbles towards Central Station but Bill senior still managed to be grumpy despite the 3-0 win.

'Four-pence? To go to a football match? I could hardly believe the lad had the gall to tak' the money. It's bloody theft.'

'Howay Dad. We won didn't we?' Billy had never shown his brother's talent but like most folk from Gallowshield, he was a sound judge of the game.

Much against his better judgment, Bill had to agree with his youngest.

'Aye. And that second goal was a belter! Come on then you two, if we put a spurt on to the station we can stop at the Bluebell for a swift one on the way home.'

The train was packed as it always was on match day but consideration for Bill's wheelchair meant that the crowds parted in biblical fashion to allow them through to a space between the carriages. All the talk was of the diminutive goal-scoring wizard, Nobby Tate and the faint possibility of a championship for the first time since 1909.

Just ninety seconds after the train pulled away from the platform, the air was thick with grey smoke as pipes and tabs were lit to pay due tribute to the serious and weighty matters under discussion.

The train headed east along the river towards the sea and the heavy industrial boiler-house of Tyneside revealed itself in all its soot-stained glory as they left the commercial centre behind. Arms factories, engine makers, timber stores, metal works and shipyards glided in and out of view. Not one of the Seatons worked on the river and yet they could all name every single manufacturer: Armstrongs, Palmer's, Swans, Redhead's. A busy Tyne meant a thriving town and nobody ever forgot it. As each station passed, standing, sitting and breathing became just a little easier as their fellow travellers slipped out to their own favoured watering holes along the way.

Ever since the subject of beer had been mentioned, the Seaton men couldn't think of anything else and the Bluebell couldn't come soon enough. Sadly for them, they were going all the way to the end of the line and their thirsts grew more urgent with every stop: Pelaw, Hebburn, Jarrow, Tyne Dock, High Shields, Low Shields, Gallowshield.

Before the train had even come to its final halt, the door was opened and Tom was down on the platform reaching for his Dad's chair.

'Howay you two – I'm gaggin'.'

'Push us oot man, Billy.'

His father, never the most patient of men, was becoming frustrated.

'Steady on Dad – you're no lightweight, you know.'

19

Bill held on to all three caps in his lap as they careered down Mile End Road and they nearly spilled him altogether when Tom had to swerve to avoid a paperboy on the corner but they reached the oasis of the Bluebell in less than ten minutes.

A table was found in the corner and there was just a moment's reverend pause as the pints were lifted and ceremonially relished before the first sip was taken. The ritual now observed, Billy and Tom launched straight into the relative strengths and weaknesses of the United side. And while Bill would never admit such a thing, he allowed himself a feeling of pride as he watched his two sons enjoy one another's company after what had been, for once, an utterly successful day out.

There was Billy, a university lad, a graduate – the first one of the Seatons to get a degree. It had been a family achievement, of course. They'd all gone without to make sure Billy could pay his way through college. God knew it hadn't been easy and Billy could have helped to pay the loans back quicker if he'd got himself a proper job in a proper practise. But no, not him. He chose to spend most of his time at that paupers' clinic in Wellesley Street looking after the waifs and strays who couldn't afford to pay.

And then there was Tom – big, daft Tom. A pitman, like himself, his first-born could have been a professional sportsman but he turned his back on that to marry Mary and bring a wage in. But Mary had contracted TB and Tom had gone thieving to make sure she got the fresh milk and eggs that she needed. Well, where had that got him? Mary had died anyway and he'd gone to prison. And now that he was out, Tom had taken up with Dolly, the ex-wife of Jack Ford. And Jack was not a man you'd want to cross. He had always been clever and ruthless and conniving but now he was rich an' all. What chance did Tom have against that lot? At least Jack and Tom were marrers. They'd spent time in Durham Jail together and looked after each other. And now Jack was safely 250 miles away in London. Bill Seaton hoped it would stay that way.

Right on cue, just as he was thinking about Jack Ford, the man's best friend came over. Matt Headley had been thick as thieves with Jack during and after the war. He served under him in the same platoon as his corporal and then Jack had made him his assistant when he'd become regional secretary for the fitters' union. And when Jack moved on to greener pastures, Matt slid smoothly into the top job at the union and his smart house on Lavender Avenue.

'Evening Mr Seaton, Tom, Billy.'

'What fettle Matt? Did you hear the score?'

'I did, Tom. Three bonny goals apparently.'

'They were, man. Three little beauties. Could have been four or five. We've just called in for a quick one on the way home.'

'Family outing, eh? Have you seen 'owt of Les Mallow? There's a meeting here tonight – union business.'

'I haven't seen Les come in yet, Matt. Looks like you're first here. Trouble brewing?' Billy was a big admirer of Les Mallow – a fellow socialist, a hardliner.

'We can't be sure yet, Billy but there's a rumour coming down from the Clyde that the bosses want to cut the rate again.'

'What?' That got Bill's attention.

'They can't do that. They lopped half a crown a day off last month.'

'Aye I know Bill. If they cut much more we'll be back to pre-war rates.'

'Well what are you going to do about it?' Bill looked appalled at the prospect.

'I told you. We're having a meeting.'

Les Mallow arrived then with Malcolm Poskett and he and Matt disappeared into the back room.

'What's wrong Dad. You look like you've seen a ghost.'

He knew his sons were laughing at him and he knew why. Bill had been a pitman all his working life and a strong union man, too but a rock fall had broken his back and finished him. He'd lost his livelihood along with the use of his legs. The mine-owners had tried to trick him out of his compensation and if it hadn't been for Jack Ford, they would have got away with it, too. But Jack had set them straight and with the compensation money from the accident, Bill had opened a shop in the front room of their terraced house. He and his wife, Bella worked hard and the shop was so successful that he opened another in Cobbett Street. And Bill wasn't going to stop there either. He had his heart set on a chain of grocery stores – each one with his name above the door. But that wouldn't happen if the employers kept cutting the men's wages – their wives would have much less to spend.

'It's a bloody disgrace,' he said.

''Come on Mr Selfridge,' said Tom.

'It's home time.'

Economics continued to be the main topic of conversation around the dinner table in the back kitchen of Bill's house that night – not the balance of payments, the relative merits of the Gold Standard or the deflationary effects of the exchange rate. No – this was the economics of Gallowshield – a job or the dole; butter or scrape; replace or make-do. These were the big issues raised by yet another cut in the hourly rate.

Bill's wife, Bella, had conjured her usual magic trick of turning lamb scrag, carrots, potatoes and stock into a culinary delight but that everyday miracle went by the board when the Seatons engaged in political debate. And Jessie was there, too to add a little spice. Jessie was Tom and Billy's sister. A former schoolteacher, she was even brighter than Billy and even braver than Tom. And she was strong, too. A strong socialist (much to her husband's dismay): she was informed, articulate and headstrong.

'And are the bosses taking a cut in their profits, too? No - I wouldn't think so.'

'There's nowt wrong with making a bit money Jessie.' That was her father's capitalist streak.

'Maybe not. But there's nowt wrong with them feeling the pinch along with everybody else, either.'

Tom could see where this was going and he didn't like the direction of travel.

'Maybe things will take a turn for the better. There's always been ups and downs in shipbuilding.'

'But it's not just shipbuilding, is it?' Billy would always side with his sister.

'It's everywhere man. The pits are the same and the railways. Even the council workers. I saw Jackie Gregg at the clinic the other day, you know, the one with angina. He's down a quid a week from this time last year. How's a man supposed to feed and clothe a family on three pounds a week? Can you tell me that? The system's broken Tom. It's time we all woke up to it.'

Ten years ago, Bill might have stood up and applauded but not now. The system was paying his bills and putting food on the table.

'Aye. Simple as that, is it? Well, you're eating the profits of that system right now. And if you don't like it, you can go hungry like Jackie Gregg and his seven bairns.'

Jessie was about to rise to Billy's defence but her Mam had had more than enough.

'Can you all not just hold your tongues for a minute?'

Bill was about to interrupt but one look at Bella's face made him think again.

'Don't you dare, Bill Seaton!' she glared at him and the entire family fell silent.

'Right then. This doesn't happen often, but just for once I've got my family around the kitchen table on a Saturday afternoon. And what do you all do? Start sniping and fighting – first chance you get. Well I've had enough of it. Surely to goodness it can't be beyond the wit of everybody in this room to be civil to one another – at least until after the pudding.'

'I won't be shushed in me own back kitchen, Bella. If I wasn't in this wheelchair...'

But she cut him off.

'If you weren't in that wheelchair you'd be under the ground Bill. So just thank your lucky stars you're not.

'Tom, there's beer and gin in that cupboard – you know where the glasses are. Jessie, you can help me with the crumble. And you two...', she growled at Bill and Billy and brandished her wooden serving spoon.

'Not another peep out of the pair of you unless it's civil.'

And it was more than civil. Bella's demand for peaceful enjoyment backed up with the threat of sanctions in the form of cooking utensils wielded like cudgels made for the kind of family gathering the Seatons had forgotten they were capable of creating. And just when they remembered why it was they were so fond of each other, Jessie rose and reached for her coat.

'That's enough fun for one day. I have to get home to Arthur.'

'Now Jessie – that's no way to talk about your man. You make him sound like a real misery.'

'No Mam he's not that. But he's not exactly Charlie Chaplin either. Arthur's no vaudeville act but he's a good man and he's looked after the bairn for long enough.'

Bill was outraged.

'You've left that poor man with Baby Arthur all this time? You should be ashamed.'

'Ashamed Dad? To let a father look after his son. I don't think so. But now his Mam wants her turn.'

'About bloody time an' all,' said Bill.

Billy immediately offered to walk his sister home before the terms of the Peace Treaty were broken irretrievably.

It was a brisk twenty-minute walk to Jessie's: across the park and through the cut by the cemetery. They both enjoyed these times together. They afforded them the chance to be honest without fear of contradiction or causing offence. Jessie and Billy were the closest in age and in intellect. They were also the closest in their politics. Social justice was something that had to be fought for and socialism had to be organised if it was ever going to be effective.

'Sometimes Billy it seems as if we're going backwards.'

'You mean the wage cuts?'

'I mean the wage cuts and the poverty and the squalor and the lack of education. Even the war didn't achieve anything. We're almost back where we started.'

'I don't think so, you know. The unions are stronger now, there's more Labour MPs. Things are changing – it's just that sometimes we get so close to it that we can't see it.'

'You know Billy? When I was a teacher, I saw it every day. Every time Class 4B trudged into the classroom I saw what the bosses had done to them. No shoes, empty bellies, bad teeth, rags for clothes – it was a downright disgrace. My Arthur is headmaster at that school and it's still the same, nothing's changed. But what does he see Billy? England's green and pleasant land? A land fit for heroes?'

'I know Jess. The clinic is the same. There's little that comes through the door that couldn't be cured by decent housing and a living wage. I don't know how the middle classes sleep at nights.'

'Like Dad, you mean?'

That stopped Billy in his tracks.

'Dad? Middle class? You must be joking.'

But Jessie was sure of her ground.

'Oh yes. Arthur's been teaching him double-entry book-keeping. So he's seen the takings. In this last year, our Dad has earned more money than a head teacher - a lot more.'

'Good God – I'd no idea. Is this what happens Jess? We get a bit richer so we want a bit extra. Then we get a lot richer so we want a lot extra. He's changed his bloody tune.'

'And there's more. He's been thinking about moving house, too.'

'No.'

'Mam told me. They've been looking at Lavender Avenue.'

'Isn't that where Jack Ford's place was?'

He regretted mentioning Jack's name as soon as he said it. He quickly glanced at his sister and saw that the memory of the broken engagement still hurt. But she swallowed hard and moved on.

'It is. Matt Headley's in there now. And Mam told me they'd looked at a place just a few doors down.'

'And Dad wants me to stop working at the clinic while he's rolling in it?'

'No Billy. That's so you can pay him what you owe him. And me. And our Tom. That's different.'

But Billy wasn't convinced.

'But you and Tom aren't earning a king's ransom on the backs of the poor, are you? Dad is – at least that's how it looks from where I'm standing.'

'You know how it is with us Seatons, Billy. Debts are there to be cleared and they won't be forgotten until the last penny is paid back in full.'

'How could I forget it? I'm reminded of it often enough.'

'So, Jack, how did you get rich? Piracy, was it?'

Jack met Charles Needham at the St Stephen's entrance to the Palace of Westminster and they walked together up Tothill Street to the Adam and Eve pub just around the corner in Petty France. They'd been together three times since the incident outside the 1917 Club - a drink in the Stranger's Bar, dinner at the Needham family's Park Lane home and breakfast at Pellici's in Bethnal Green followed by a protest rally in favour of equal suffrage for women. Charles Needham got around.

'I used to be a bit of a privateer – but that was under orders in Murmansk after the war. These days I'm not even an entrepreneur.'

Needham was still curious.

'But you haven't answered the question.'

'Get away.'

'Come on Jack. I've opened up to being a privileged aristocrat, whose family have grown fat on the labours of the workers. Don't fob me off. I can't see you maintaining your Connaught lifestyle on the wages of a union official.'

Ford raised his arms in surrender.

'All right, I give in. I made a modest sum on a land deal then I invested the lot through an old pal of mine in the United States. Met him in France in the Spring of 1918. He was lost and about to go blundering into enemy lines. Me and my corporal - Matt Headley - set him straight. Now he's setting me straight. He's a stock broker.'

'What sort of investments?'

'What they call household goods: radios, washing machines, that sort of thing. They're flying out of the factories and people are queuing up to buy them on tick.'

'Tick?'

'On credit. Buy now pay later.'

'Are you paid in dollars?'

'Who are you? The customs and excise man?' Ford was joking but also warning Needham not to probe too deeply. Nevertheless, Ford relented and told him what he wanted to know.

'I was, until recently.'

'And now?'

'Now the Gold Standard has pegged sterling too high. My mate is keeping my dollars for me and when my money runs out here, I'll go over there and get them.'

Needham stubbed out his cigarette.

'You must trust this old chum of yours.'

Ford smiled, remembering.

'Well when I said he was lost on the Front, what I neglected to say was that he'd been captured. Me and Matt were hiding in a fox-hole after a night trench raid and we saw this squad of Jerries carting him off into the mist. We knew he wouldn't survive it, so we wandered over and brought him back.'

'That was shockingly brave.'

'We were shockingly drunk!'

Needham remembered the three strangers who'd given him a beating outside the 1917 Club.

'You obviously make a habit of rescuing complete strangers in the dark.'

'I wouldn't say it was a habit, Charlie. More of an occupational hazard.'

They finished their beer and Needham ordered a quick sandwich lunch before he had to return to the House for Education Questions.

'What about tonight? Are you busy?'

'I'm never busy, these days,' said Ford.

There was a hint of boredom with just a tinge of regret in his voice.

'Well Beatrice has gone back up to Northumberland early so I'm on my own. Why don't we go back to the Ham Bone Club. You did promise Rose you'd pay her another visit.'

'Sounds good. Wouldn't do to let a lady down.' And even as he was saying the words he was thinking to himself, especially a young lady as pretty as Rose Milne.

Needham had to vote in a late division so they met at the club at what Rose would have regarded as the much more civilised hour of quarter to midnight.

'Oh, it won't get warmed up until 3.30am but by then you won't be able to hear yourself drink.'

Rose looked stunning in a knee-length pink dress trimmed with fur and a spectacularly sparkling, diamante headdress incorporating purple feathers. The ensemble was finished off with a pearl brooch and a smile that could raise the Titanic.

Her hair was cropped short in the latest page-boy style and her bold, blue eye make-up was almost theatrical in its impact. But Ford saw through the trends of the latest fashions to appreciate the natural prettiness that positively refused to hide in the corner. The make-up was Rose Milne's armour plating, her defence against the world. Ford knew he would have his work cut out to breech those defences.

She gave Needham a playful poke in the tummy.

'I can see your health's improved, Charlie. How are you Jack?'

'Never better,' he said.

She was more confident tonight – louder and funnier, too.

'Good. Come through boys. Keep your hands off the waitresses – they bite. And don't swallow anything you haven't tried before.'

'I bet you say that to all the boys.'

'Why would I?' she asked.

'That's how I usually make my money.'

She led them once again down the dark corridor but instead of turning right into the room where Charlie had received his unorthodox pain medication, they entered through the double doors on the left.

There was a tiny lobby with a young woman clad head to toe in dark red taffeta hanging on to a clothes rail. Her lips were painted black and her face matte white.

'Coats,' she explained in sleepy monotone.

Needham and Ford obliged and got a ticket in exchange for the shillings they dropped in her black-gloved hand.

They couldn't see much. The room was lit by about two dozen gas table lamps which appeared to be randomly spread about the place offering little pools of yellow light to warm the shadows. The atmosphere reminded Ford of the foggy winter's days in France just after sunrise, when the light was so thin that colours became pastels and shapes no more than mere suggestions. Back then, danger had lurked in those murky depths but not anymore.

There was a raised area in one corner where a clarinet player hesitantly swayed to his own mediocrity while a man on the double bass struggled to keep up. A gentleman in his sixties and a lady of far fresher vintage, who appeared to have been hard at the celebrations since lunchtime, staggered around the dancefloor in a funereal stomp holding on to each other defiantly in case they fell in a heap on floor.

Rose steered her friends to the opposite corner where there was a polished wooden bar with what appeared to be an ample supply of Croydon whisky.

'I hope you've eaten,' said Rose. 'I can't vouch for the food.'

'I can,' said Needham. 'It's an abomination.'

Ford took the hint. 'Let's just drink then, shall we? Whisky, is it?'

Rose nodded but just then Needham spotted someone he

knew entering through the sickly gloom.

'That's Mabel Wallas – her father's an old pal of mine. She went to Newnham College, you know. Like her mother. Won't be long.'

As he wondered off to greet the young woman, Ford noticed that the club had begun to fill up substantially. The clarinettist had given way to a quartet of piano, drums, sax and bass and they didn't know the meaning of the word mediocrity. Half a dozen bars into the first number, the dance floor was packed and the place was jumping.

Ford was about to pay for the drinks he had ordered when Rose told him to put his money away.

'This is my place and you two are my guests.'

There was a determination in her voice and a 'don't-you-dare' glare in her eyes.

'That's very kind,' said Ford. He made an effort to say it as gently as possible.

'I am very kind. If I like the look of someone.'

He logged the compliment but did not react.

'Tell me something, Rose Milne.' Ford had to raise his voice to a yell to make himself heard over the band.

'Yes?'

'Now don't get me wrong. I have no wish to upset you – especially when you're being kind enough to pay for the drinks. But what on earth does the fifty-something-year-old former Cabinet Minister, the Rt. Hon. Charles Needham find remotely appealing about the Ham Bone Club?'

'How insulting,' she said, 'I'm mortally offended.'

She grabbed his lapel and drew him closer towards her before kissing him on the cheek.

'Can you keep a secret, Jack Ford?'

'I think I can, yes.'

31

'Well the Rt Hon Charles Needham is not exactly all that he seems.'

She dragged Ford out into the corridor so they could hear themselves talk.

She'd known Needham for years – since childhood – and he'd been a close friend of her mother's.

'When I grew up we had a family home near Stratford-upon-Avon and Daddy made a jolly decent living from farming and had a large interest in the local auction mart. Unfortunately, he also had a particularly healthy interest in wines and spirits and he drank himself to death when I was thirteen. Mummy had to sell the farm and the Mart and we had to live off the proceeds. She died of Spanish Flu in 1919 so after several romantic disasters and a year of illness, I decided to put what was left of my inheritance into this place.'

'You own it?'

'I own half of it. I do front of house, keep the books, pay the bills and try to keep track of what laws we might be breaking. My business partner books the acts, hires the staff, takes care of marketing and promotion and generally has a good time. That's him there with Sir Broderick Hogg.'

Ford looked over to see an extremely well-polished young man leading an older gentleman by the hand on to the dance floor before going on to give a highly-accomplished performance of The Shimmy.

'A handsome couple,' said Ford.

'Hilarious isn't it. Well that's my partner – Lansing Bell.'

'I see,' said Ford. 'But you still haven't told me why Needham keeps coming here.'

'I haven't, have I? I'm always doing that – straying off the point – sometimes I can't seem to be able to concentrate. Well at first, I'm fairly certain that he came here to keep an eye on me - as a favour to Mama, I suppose. But now I get the general impression that he comes to let his hair down and see how the other half lives. The ones who don't hang out at the miserable old 1917 Club. Like Mabel Wallas over there for one. Her father was something or other political. But she just loves the music so she comes with her friends and dodges the bullets like the rest of us. The world is changing, Mr Ford.'

'It is, isn't it? But that suits me. I like change.'

They went back inside and Needham joined them. They drank scotch and enjoyed the floor show.

Just after 1am the quartet was joined by Jazz Tap Dancer King 'Rastus' Brown from New York. With limitless energy and a commendable never-say-die attitude he combined his complex repertoire of numbers with an audience participation technique which involved him impersonating animals or objects on request. He then incorporated them into his dance moves. Horses, tractors, steam trains and elephants were all suggested and duly interpreted by the 'King' while Ford and Needham stood utterly open-mouthed at the diminutive man's staying power.

'He's amazing, isn't he?' said Rose. 'And he's not expensive really. The only problem is, he doesn't know when to stop.'

Eventually Lansing did the dirty work and, with a little physical help from the portly Sir Broderick, managed to man-handle King Rastus from the floor with offers of money and alcohol.

With the main attraction now relieved of his duties, the Ham Bone clientele settled themselves down for the serious business of the night – indulging themselves with whatever was to hand. The place was heaving now and what with the number of bodies, the lamps, the tobacco, the hashish and the enclosed space – the heat generated in the club became unbearable. People paired off according to their preference and disappeared under tables or through doors to other rooms. Bottles were relieved of their contents, the cigarette smoke was replaced by a headier scent and in one corner, Ford could see, even in the lamplight, that it had started snowing with a vengeance.

Rose poured a large chunk of Croydon into a glass and gulped it down as if she were thirsty. She swallowed hard and strode off to take up her sentinel station on a three-legged stool by the main door. It paid to be on the lookout for any curious Coppers who might wander into the yard. At least that's what she told the people who asked and it was true, some of the time. Mostly she liked to get away from the heat and the sweat. There was a reek of sadness and desperation when things really got going and that could be frightening. How she envied people who were confident enough to let themselves go in public. She preferred to be alone when the pot began boiling. She'd rather retreat and let the cool air drift over her skin. It was soothing, cleansing.

She leaned against the door frame, crossed her arms and eagerly gulped large quantities of vintage London into her lungs. There was a bitterness to it but it was better than the sickly sourness of the club. She checked her handbag. God bless Lansing! He never forgot. The little packet would keep her going until morning.

The band prepared for yet another set and Ford looked at his friend.

'Are you ready to admit defeat?'

'Yes, I think so. I'm definitely getting too old for this,' said Needham. A smile of unabashed relief was playing on his lips.

'Watch your step!'

Ford steered the MP around two pairs of legs that had become entangled on the floor. Their owners' heads were with their bodies, embracing under a table.

'Thanks Jack. I can manage this only about once a month these days even then I have to take a few days off to recuperate.

34

I'm going back up to Northumberland this weekend as a matter of fact. I've been invited to speak in Gallowshield on Saturday night – Education Policy. You don't fancy a trip down Memory Lane, do you? Welcome to stay with us, of course.'

Jack paused for thought. He'd never even thought of going back there. There was nothing left for him in Gallowshield but memories of an unhappy childhood, a lost love and a broken marriage. He'd spent all his life trying to work out how to escape the place. Why on earth should he go back?

Then he thought of Jessie.

'Do you know what, Charles? I'd be delighted. Although I'll make my own sleeping arrangements if that's all right with you. I'll visit, of course.'

'That's settled. I'll be off home now, then. Why don't you stay here for a while and keep Rose company? Get to know her better, Jack. She's had her problems but she's a lovely girl. I knew her mother rather well. I worry about her sometimes. There's a sadness...around the eyes.'

It was just after 5am when the last of the revellers was persuaded that the evening had definitely come to an end. Rose kissed and cajoled the last wobbly customer, bagged up the takings, reminded the barman to lock up and casually took Ford's arm. Lansing had left an hour earlier to drink Champagne with Sir Broderick and settle his account. The city was still asleep and their footsteps echoed off the pavements as they strode down Piccadilly, past Green Park and on to Hyde Park Corner. The West End had an eerie emptiness about it and fine rain coated their clothes and faces. There was an impatient swelling of bird song from the early risers anticipating dawn, but signs of human life were scarce.

'Your place or mine?' said Ford.

There was never any suggestion that they wouldn't be spending the day together – apparently the only matter to be settled was the geography.

'I really need my own bed,' she said.

'Tired?'

'Certainly not – I just want to be in my own bed.'

'Your place it is, then.'

She squeezed his arm as they crossed over at Hyde Park Corner just as the rain started.

Rose's flat was a tiny one-bedroomed attic affair on Kinnerton Street. They negotiated the three flights of narrow stairs and Rose was still breathless from the climb when they stepped inside her hallway and shook themselves dry.

'I think I'm getting worse with these stairs – I must be hideously unfit,' she said.

She took off her hat and coat and kept on undressing.

'There's no rush, you know,' said Ford.

'Oh, but there is. Experience has taught me the first time is always the worst so it's best to get that one over with as quickly as possible. All that fumbling. All that fear. Don't you agree? Won't be a mo – just powder my nose, as they say.'

When she walked out of the loo, she was completely naked. She sneezed as he struggled with his laces.

'Allergies?' he asked.

'Blind terror,' she replied.

In the end, the shoes were kicked off in frustration and he joined her under the covers.


She was determinedly willing and robotically compliant for the next half an hour.

'Well if that's as bad as it gets, then I think I'm going to enjoy the times we spend together, Jack.'

Ford wasn't convinced. You're still wearing the armour plating, he thought. You know what to say, you know what to do, you just don't know what to feel.

'If that's a compliment, I'll take it,' he said.

At her suggestion, they got up to eat and he cooked omelettes while she made coffee and fussed over the untidy state of the kitchen. The longer she had to think about what had just happened, the more tense and anxious she became.

Ford watched her trying and failing to work through her awkwardness. In the end, he said nothing at all, walked over to her and hugged her.

'Enough,' he said.

They ate two omelettes with two forks from the one clean plate and went back to bed. They dozed and played and dozed and joked and played and then, at last, he slept. But still her mind played host to all her demons. She looked at Jack. He was stone out, sleeping the sleep of a man without torment. She liked Jack. She liked him a lot because he was strong and capable and witty and gentle. But still she didn't feel safe. Rose leaned over to her bed-side cabinet for her medication. She looked at the box and remembered the warning words of the doctor.

'It's a hypnotic. Just pop the powders into a glass of water and you'll be out like a light.'

That phrase had stuck in her mind. 'Out like a light.'

'Be careful with the dosage,' he'd said. 'Medinal is a superb sleeping draught but it can be dangerous if you take too much – so just one sachet in any 24 hours.

She counted the sachets left in the box. There were five. Her fingertips raked up and down the paper containers making a rhythmic scratching sound. Ford was breathing steadily and deeply beside her. Perhaps he could be reassuring – if he stayed. She decided to obey doctor's orders.

It was mid-afternoon when Rose came out of the bedroom and

found Ford brewing tea in a sparkling, orderly kitchen.

'You don't entertain much, do you?' he said.

Rose was still groggy from the drug.

'No, not much.'

She yawned and stretched to consider the matter further.

'In fact, under normal circumstances I don't entertain at all – unless Lansing's had his heart broken and he wants to come around to cry on my shoulder.'

'Does that happen often?'

'No. He's usually the one who does the breaking. Then it's the guilt he can't cope with.'

'I imagine your social life is pretty hectic?'

He warmed the pot before adding the boiling water.

'You'd think so, wouldn't you? But the Ham Bone is pretty tying. I'm there six nights out of seven and sleep all day Sunday. There's sometimes a chap – now and again - but they don't stick around for long.'

Ford remembered the conversation they'd had earlier at the club.

'You said before that you'd been ill. What was the matter?'

'Nothing, really. The doctors called it Melancholia or Reactive Depression. It just seemed to come out of the blue. Suddenly I had no energy, I couldn't be bothered to do anything. I'd moved in here after Mama died, but as small as it is, I couldn't bring myself to go outside.'

'So, what happened?'

'They tried various potions and pills – one of them even recommended a head operation but I screamed bloody murder. In the end, it just seemed to leave me. I've no idea why. Peculiar, isn't it? Maybe the pills started working.'

'Terrifying, I should think.'

She looked away and her gaze fell to her feet.

'I was scared. I thought about doing away with myself for a while. That was wrong of me.'

'Understandable. Parents both dead, no-one else close to you in the world. You're sick, you're frightened. I wouldn't be too hard on yourself.'

Then she looked back up at him, clasped her hands behind her back and put on a little girl's voice.

'I had a little bird,
Its name was Enza,
I opened a window
And in flew Enza.'

Ford looked at her.

'What was that for?'

'Oh, you know – just feeling sorry for myself. I heard some children chanting that rhyme in Green Park the day Mama died. They sounded so sweet and yet they seemed to be taunting me. It hurt. It still hurts.'

'Children can be cruel without realising they're doing it.' he said.

'The world can be cruel. And it knows what it's doing'

But she reached for him and put her arms around his neck.

'But not today. There's no grey blanket today.'

She smiled a smile that spread sadness.

'Let's celebrate. You can take me to dinner. I want to go somewhere hideously expensive.'

He lifted his cup of tea.

'I'll drink to that.'

# CHAPTER 4

L es Mallow's highly polished work boots crunched along the cinder path that ran alongside the cemetery. It was a bright and blustery day and the nipping north easterly wind made his eyes stream in the glaring sunlight. Through his tears he could see the Gallowshield Cenotaph standing tallest among the monuments to the dead. He stood and stared. The grey monolith towered over the grave stones just as it towered over him. How Les despised the Cenotaph. It was mocking him. It wasn't a tribute to the fallen, it was a glorification of war – a bosses' war that he'd refused to fight.

A man of principle was Les, a man of honour. When conscription came in 1916, Les Mallow, a Quaker, had claimed a conscientious objection and was called before a tribunal. The chairman had dismissed his objection but instead ruled that, as a shipyard fitter, he was in a reserved occupation. His conscience was an irrelevance. From that day, his dislike of the middle classes transformed into a deep, burning resentment.

He walked on and began to console himself with the progress that he'd made. With the help of comrades, he'd learned to read and he'd begun to educate himself. He'd joined the Fitters' Union and never missed a payment. He'd travelled the country to hear his leaders speak – seen Keir Hardie on the platform, attended rallies with Tom Mann, cheered with the Brothers and Sisters when the Romanov Dynasty fell and helped the Labour movement grow into a political force for change. These were the things of real importance. These were the proofs that victory was in sight.

Strengthened by this memory of self- satisfaction and achievement, Les Mallow's even humour was gradually restored by the time he opened Jessie Ashton's gate and knocked on the door. He knew this would be a good time. Her husband, Arthur, would be dutifully flying the flag of Empire at the Warrior Street School where he was the head teacher. Why, oh why had a wonderful, Socialist woman like Jessie Ashton married a man like that? A Tory! While he, a self-educated, man of morals, sound ethics and high values, lived alone. There was simply no justice in the world.

She greeted him with a handshake and led him through to the parlour where they had sat together so often before. This was the place where she had introduced him to Shelley, Morris, Marx and Shaw. This was the place where he had grown to become so familiar with words that he no longer had to mouth them as he read. This was the place where Les Mallow had fallen in love. But as they sat now, separated at either side of the fireplace by the mid-morning sunbeam, he had to endure the presence of the small child that symbolised the unfathomable truth, that the fantasy in his head was just that – fantasy. Les Mallow would have to make do with Socialism.

'How have you been, Les?'

'I won't keep you long Jessie, I can see you have your hands full these days.'

She ran a hand through the child's blond locks.

'Oh, this one's no bother. He's calm – like his father.'

'I've brought you this. I thought you might be interested.'

He produced from his pocket a folded sheet.

'Mikhail Bukanin is the leader of the trade union movement in Russia.'

She didn't look up from reading the letter.

'I know who he is, Les.'

'Of course, you do. But he's coming here, Jessie – to Gallowshield.'

'Really? Don't let Arthur know, for goodness sake. He'll call the authorities.'

'This is no joke. He's leading a delegation to Britain and he's going to address the North East Trades Union Council. He's visiting Labour Clubs and Trade Union offices all over the place but he's making only four keynote speeches: London, Manchester, Glasgow and here, in Gallowshield.

'It's a great honour for us, Jessie.'

He was puffed up with pride.

'I suppose it is. But what's it got to do with me, Les?'

'He's a huge figure in the Red International, a political leader, he can help us, Jessie, in the struggle.'

'He's a Bolshevik. He believes in bloodshed and revolution. He believes in taking. Don't we stand for different things?'

But Les was ready for her.

'In the end, we share the same goals: jobs for all, education for all, healthcare for all. This is happening today, right now in Russia. Why shouldn't it happen here? Will you help me Jessie?'

She was confused then.

'Help you? Help you with what? I thought it was a TUC thing? You're the union man, Les. Not me.'

'I know. But he's coming here for two days. We can't just leave him in a hotel and pick him up when we want him to speak for us. He'll need to be entertained, shown around, looked after.'

She smiled at him.

'I thought he was a great revolutionary, Les - a working class hero. Surely, he can look after himself. Sounds to me like you want him to be treated like a toff!'

That riled him.

'Come on Jessie. That's not what I meant at all – and you know it.'

Then he softened.

'Please. I'm no good at organising.'

That made her laugh out loud.

'No good at organising? Lord help us, you're the Regional Convenor!'

Yet again Les Mallow was defeated. He looked down at his polished boots and what she saw was utter dejection.

'Arthur would be dead against it,' she said.

But he could tell from her tone that she was weighing it up.

'You would be in the background Jessie. I just need help planning the visit, contacting the right people, inviting folk. What do you say?'

'I'll do what I can on the quiet, Les, but keep it to yourself. If Arthur finds out he'll be livid. You can do me a favour in return.'

'Name it.'

'Charles Needham, the Jesmond MP, is coming to Gallowshield to talk about Education Policy.'

'I know that. I'll be there,' said Les.

'Yes. I know that you'll be there, Les, because you're always there. So will Billy, so will I. But how many others are going to turn up, eh? As a gesture of good faith, I want to see the hall full. Full of your members.'

He let out a sigh.

'It's a Saturday, isn't it?'

'Yes, Les. It's this Saturday coming at the Memorial Hall.'

'But it's their drinking night, Jessie.'

'Every night is their drinking night when they're in work. If we know there's enough coming we'll be able to put a bar on and a raffle to raise some extra money. So now we do. Problem solved.'

Jack Ford had been around for a couple of days. He knew Gallowshield like the back of his hand – he knew where to go to find people and where to go to avoid them. The Royal Saracen Hotel wasn't exactly The Connaught but it wasn't exactly Garibaldi Street, either. The rooms were spacious and the staff were courteous and attentive. And the Royal Saracen was convenient, too. The rear of the building backed on to the railway station and if you wandered out of the front doors you were just a three-minute walk from the centre of town. But the locals went there only for functions. The bar prices were far too inflated for regular drinkers. The other guests were mostly there on business: senior sales people and company directors, lawyers and doctors, army officers and civil servants.

Despite the majesty of the coastline, Gallowshield didn't feature on the tourist trail – the climate saw to that. And once you ventured inland, you'd begin to wonder why anybody stayed there at all. It was a hard place. Cramped back-to-backs were huddled together in irregular rows, each one housing families of eight or more with just two bedrooms, a scullery and a draughty netty out the back. Malnutrition, TB, rickets, infestations, dreadful sanitation and scant medical care all plagued many of the residents. As far as Jack Ford was concerned, the place was a dump.

So why, he wondered to himself, when he was offered the chance to come back, did he jump at it. Even though he knew the answer was Jessie, he also knew she was married to someone else - Arthur Ashton. But to Jack she was and would forever be

Jessie Seaton – the girl he'd made angry at the picture house when they'd first met; the girl he'd persuaded to fall in love with him when he'd rustled sheep to feed the poor; the girl he'd betrayed when he'd slept with Matt Headley's sister and made her pregnant. And even now, after all that, he knew that he still loved her and she still loved him. All they could share now was disappointment and sadness. But even that was better than nothing. So, he'd accepted Charles Needham's invitation to come to Gallowshield because, in the end, he had no choice in the matter. Jessie lived there and that was all there was to it.

He joined the queue at the Telegraph Office in the railway station and shuffled his way up to the grille. Ahead of him was an excitable group of Spanish seamen who seemed so anxious not to miss any drinking time while sending their message that they'd brought the contents of the pub with them and were now offering free swigs from the neck of the rum bottle to irritated members of the queue. Eventually the drunken Armada weighed anchor and Ford found himself at the front and the operator was more than a little relieved as he accepted Ford's handwritten message and discovered that it was in English.

'I've had nowt but bloody foreigners all day,' he protested.

From Gallowshield to Manhattan, via the Geordie Post Office and Western Union. Ford smiled as he handed over his shilling to complete the transaction.

'Next please,' said the operator.

Ford turned and his smile grew broader as he heard the man behind him in the queue address the window in a thick Russian accent.

But then the smile disappeared as quickly as it had arrived.

Standing next to the Russian man was a woman whose eyes engaged Ford's in equal surprise. Ford halted, just for a moment as he scanned the features, just to check. It couldn't be her – not here. But the eyes told him there was no mistake. Gathering himself, he edged towards her ever so slightly but her eyebrows rose and her chin jerked back an inch, as if to say 'Stay away. Say nothing. Please'

Ford got the picture in an instant. Telegrams weren't the fastest method of communication by a long chalk. He touched the brim of his hat with his forefinger, acknowledged the woman with a nod of the head and marched out of the office without looking back.

He walked swiftly along the station concourse and in through the back door of the Royal Saracen. He took the half flight two steps at a time, weaved his way past the guests queuing at reception and breezed into the lounge bar.

'Get us a whisky Joe – make it a large one,' he said as he walked straight to the bay windows to his left. He folded back the net curtain. If he was lucky enough, he might see the couple leaving the station from the front.

His whisky arrived and he reached down to pick up the glass without taking his eyes from the street for a second. Just when he thought they must have caught a train or left by a different route, he saw the man and the woman again – plain as day.

She was a beauty all right. Tall, elegant, graceful as a thoroughbred racehorse. He'd seen her better dressed, mind. The brown woollen coat was clean and practical but there was no finesse, no style – not like there had been. And who was the Russian gentleman accompanying her? He had a long, heavy, black beard and was wearing a thick tweed suit which tested his tight-fitting overcoat to the limit. He was thick set but on the short side – certainly shorter than her. Their arms were linked and they moved closely together – almost in unison. Was that through affection? Not on her part, he decided. Not from the discontented look on her face. Ford let the curtain fall and took another sip of his drink just as the couple approached the hotel. Once they had passed the window he walked over to the other side of the bay and picked up a rear view of them strolling down the broad pavement before disappearing into the imposing stone building on the corner of Armstrong Street. But what on earth were they doing visiting the Northern Institute of Mining? The last time he'd seen her she was in Murmansk, waiting to board a train while stuffing a diamond necklace inside the lining of her mink coat.

# CHAPTER 5

It was true that Jack was keeping a low profile but he couldn't not see his best mate, Matt Headley. Matt had been his Corporal in the War, his assistant at the union and the best man at his wedding. They had been through a lot together and an exception must be made. Besides, Matt was useful. He was a slow but steady kind of feller and loyal as the day was long. People trusted Matt, so they told him things. He soaked up information like a sponge and yet he seldom knew its value.

It was a dry evening so Jack chanced a walk to Matt's local, the Bluebell. He wasn't disappointed. His old marrer was in his familiar spot at the bar sucking at a beer glass as if it were a baby's comforter.

'What fettle, Matt?'

'Bloody Hell, I don't believe it. Jack Ford.'

After the greetings and the order, Jack ushered Matt through to the snug where they could be less conspicuous.

'What's your news, Matt?'

'Bugger all, marrer. You know how it is round here, nothing ever changes.'

'Don't believe you. How's Dolly?'

'She's fine Jack. She and Tom are fine. And the little one.'

Matt looked away when he mentioned the baby. His sister's inability to bear children had been a constant source of pain when she'd been married to Jack. And then as soon as the marriage ended and she ran off with Tom Seaton, she had a flawless pregnancy as if by magic.

Matt knew that wound would never heal but Jack didn't flinch.

'Good man. Good. And your Sarah?'

Sarah Lytton was the sharpest pin in the cushion. She'd arrived in Lavender Avenue as a housekeeper after Dolly departed. But once Jack had decided to move away, it took only a dinner dance and a new hat for Matt to persuade her to become Mrs Headley. Which was the best idea Sarah Lytton had ever had.

'Sarah's just fine, Jack. Keeps me right, anyway. I've got a seat on the council now as well. That was Sarah's idea.'

'I bet it was. She'll be Lady Mayoress before you can say policy and resources committee.'

Jack was playing the politics of friendship and he would have to go through the niceties whether he was interested or not. In fact, he was, just a little. By the time the second pint arrived with the whisky chasers, Jack found he could steer his friend to more fertile ground.

'Do you see anything of the Seatons? Apart from Tom, obviously.'

'Round and about, Jack. Old Bill's got a canny few shops now – seems to be going well. Bella's just the same and, as you know, Billy's fully qualified – a proper doctor. He's doing some compensation assessments for the union now.'

'That's grand,' said Jack. 'Really grand.'

'But that's not who you're really interested in, is it Jack?' There was the merest hint of an accusation in his voice.

He looked down, drank the whisky and looked Matt square in the eye.

'Have you seen her?'

'Jessie? As a matter of fact, I have. Saw her today funnily enough with another old mate of yours.'

'Who?'

Matt lowered his voice, said the name and then waited for the reaction.

'Les Mallow.'

'Les Mallow? Is that bugger still breathing? What on earth is she doing with him?'

'Nothing, man. He's a Socialist, isn't he? She's a Socialist. They're on committees and things together.'

'Very cosy. And what does Arthur Ashton think about that?'

'I think Jessie works on the assumption that the less her husband knows about her politics, the better it is for the both of them. It's totally innocent, Jack.'

'I know that, man. It's just the injustice of it. She gets to spend time with a Left-wing loser like Les Mallow. It's almost enough to put you off your beer.'

'Don't tempt fate Jack. Anyway, they came to see me about a Russian.'

'Oh aye?'

Jack stood and gestured to the barmaid for more drinks.

'Aye,' said Matt, 'He's a bloke called Mikhail Bukanin. Leader of the Russian Trade Union Council.'

'What about him?'

'He's visiting Gallowshield.'

'Bukanin is coming here? Really? Why?'

'He's addressing the Trade Union movement. He's going to London, Glasgow and Gallowshield.'

Matt was enjoying the moment.

'You see, Jack. We're on the map. Les Mallow and Jessie Seaton are organising his visit. And that's why they came to see me.

I represent the fitters union and they want me to organise a reception for him.'

'I wouldn't have put you down as a revolutionary, Matt.'

'Hands across the water, bonny lad.'

'I see. I'm impressed. Mikhail Bukanin, eh? Is he coming on his own?'

'No man, there'll be about ten of them altogether. Some of them are here now – kind of advance party, if you like. Just making sure the natives are friendly and sorting out the arrangements.'

'Is that so, Matt? Where are they staying?'

Suddenly the penny dropped.

'Now, Jack – we don't want any trouble.'

'What on earth do you mean, bonny lad?'

'I haven't forgotten what you did after the War.'

'What are you talking about, you daft beggar?'

'Murmansk, Jack. That's what I'm talking about.'

'But that was years ago. It's different now. I've got no interest in visiting Russian Trade Unionists. How could I have? I'm just curious, that's all.'

Matt was quiet. He took a drink and concentrated. He turned the question over and over in his mind. No. Jack was right. Russia was a big place – a huge place. What possible connection could there be. He owed an apology.

'Ee, I'm sorry, Jack. But I know what you were like in the old days. Always making connections. And there's a lot of opposition to Bukanin's visit. The papers are saying he's only here to stir up trouble.'

'I know – I've read some of it,' said Jack.

'I am truly sorry though. I should know better but I always get a feeling you're up to something.

'Forget it, bonny lad.'

And then he winked at his friend over the top of his glass.

Yet even while he was doing it he thought, but you have no bloody idea what I got up to in Murmansk, have you, Matt? Because you weren't there.

'Anybody in?'

Bella was in the kitchen prodding expertly at the coals. She nearly dropped the poker when she heard his voice.

'Ee, Jack? Is that you? Come away in, lad. Let's have a look at you.'

This was the love affair that never was and always would be. Bella Seaton adored Jack Ford and when he split up with her daughter it was hard to tell who was the most cut up about it, Jessie or her mother.

'I'm not interrupting anything, am I?'

He walked through the scullery and popped his head around the kitchen door.

'You are not, lad. And even if you were, I wouldn't give two hoots.'

He looked shiftily around the room.

'Is the coast clear, Madam?'

She nodded mischievously with an excited glint in her eye like a five-year-old at Christmas.

'They're all out. Tom's giving Bill a push up to Tyne Bank. It's just me.'

'I come bearing gifts.'

He winked as he spoke and dug in the pockets of his Crombie coat and produced a half bottle of gin from one side and whisky from the other.

'Ee, look at that. You're a very naughty man, Jack Ford. Sit down here by the fire. I'll get the glasses.'

There were few people in the world for whom Jack felt deep affection. Jessie was one and her mother was another. She was the Mam he didn't have and if she doted on him, the feeling was entirely mutual.

The bottles were cracked open, the liquor was poured and the interrogation began.

How was he? He looked thinner – in need of some home cooking. How was London? Busy and full people – a filthy, dirty place, no doubt. Was it all parties and dinners and posh folk? All well and good but he'd be missing home, likely.

Bella could have the entire conversation all by herself. All Jack had to do was smile, nod and refill the glasses. This was the ritual of Bella's kitchen. This was her world, her domain and everything about the room told you everything you needed to know about Bella. The smell was wholesome – a powerful mixture of coal fire, drying laundry and pork chops. The room was full but not cluttered: seats by the fender, a sofa under the window, table in the middle and a clock on the wall.

The range was never out – even in summer. After all, this was a pitman's house and it didn't matter that her husband, Bill, had been invalided out of the mine long since. You needed heat to cook, to boil water, to wash, to doze in front of. A cold house was a lonely house, a frightening place – it felt like poverty, disease. To Bella, it felt like death itself.

But there was no thought of that today, not with the fire on and Jack sat there right in front of her eyes while she nursed a glass of gin. This was heaven on earth.

'How long are you stopping?'

'I don't know, Mrs Seaton. A week or so maybe or perhaps a bit longer. I'll just have to see.'

'Cagey, Jack. Always cagey - restless.'

She looked into the fire in warm recollection.

'Does our Jessie know you're here?'

'I haven't told anyone I'm back. I had a drink at the Bluebell with Matt last night but no-one else knows I'm in Gallowshield.'

'And you'd like to keep it that way an' all.'

'We both know you can't keep secrets around here, Mrs Seaton. Too many loose tongues and nosey neighbours.'

'Hah! You're right there, bonny lad. Their nets is never still. I'll tell Jessie then. Just so she's not...you know.'

'Taken by surprise?'

'Yes. She doesn't like to be knocked off her guard. You know that.'

'Tell her what you like. She's doing well, I hear?'

'I'm not so sure about that, now. She has her bairn, little Arthur, and he's a right smasher. But that's not enough for our Jessie – never would be. You know that.'

'Is she still fighting the good fight?'

'Politics? Oh yes. She's twice as bad now that Billy's home full time. I don't think it's right, Jack – not for a woman. And Arthur's not too happy about it either.'

'But he puts up with it.'

'Oh, she doesn't tell him the half. The poor man's at the school every day – weekends, too sometimes. Jessie's policy is simple. What he doesn't know won't hurt him.'

'Well at least she's not lying to him.'

'She's not telling the truth neither.'

Even the sound of the word took her by surprise. Bella was being honest but she was betraying a trust. Jack had been Jessie's fiancé. They had loved each other. Still did love each other as far as Bella could tell. But Jack had done the dirty and Jessie was married to someone else now.

'Now mind, Jack. I've spoken out of turn. Please, don't repeat this to anyone. I'm just rambling on.'

Ford smiled, licked his index finger and pointed it formally to the ceiling.

'See this wet and see this dry,
Cross my heart and hope to die.'
She gave him a playful slap on the leg.
'Give over, you big bairn and pour us another gin.'
He slipped away before the family returned. He couldn't face them – not en masse – he had neither the energy or the inclination. The Seatons were a pugnacious bunch – even their affection was exhausting. When he got back to the hotel there was a message. It read:
'A little bird called Enza telephoned. Please don't close the window.'

The hotel was deserted on Saturdays because the businessmen returned home to re-introduce themselves to their wives and families. The town, too, had a distinctly different air. The men who had spent the working week either down pits or in draughty shipyards suddenly had the freedom of the pavements. They gathered on street corners for 'a bit crack' before the pubs opened, or popped to get a haircut before planning the domestic repair jobs which never quite seemed to be completed. Jack felt it as soon as he left the hotel. On Saturday mornings, a man could walk about without feeling guilty because he didn't have a job to go to, or over-privileged because he didn't have to work. He immediately felt better.

The Northern Institute of Mining was a stone's throw from the hotel. It stood rather uncomfortably on a corner but once inside, the building was undoubtedly impressive. A chequered stone floor with high ceilings created an atmosphere of reverence, of studious intent. Oak panels and polished brass fittings encouraged due respect from all visitors and there were two retired pit deputies on the door to filter out the riff raff before they made it as far as reception.

Confident that the Savile Row suit would deter any potential interference, Ford removed his hat and nodded benignly at them before walking straight past them.

The slight, balding man behind the desk peered at him over the top of his half-moon spectacles.

'Can I help you, Sir?'

'I do hope so,' said Ford. 'My name is Ford. I wish to see Mr Cecil Fitzpatrick. I'm sorry, I don't have an appointment.'

'Oh, I'm not sure I....,' the man was spluttering. 'I don't think we...I can't recall...Mr Fitzpatrick, you say?'

Jack smiled.

'That's right. As I said, I'm sorry but I didn't have time to make an appointment. I do hope it's not inconvenient.'

The man swallowed hard.

'But Mr Ford, the only Fitzpatrick we have here at the Institute, is our, er...'

'That's right. Your caretaker. I wonder if you could send someone to see if he would be so kind as to spare me a few minutes of his time.'

Ford threw the man his sergeant's stare. The look that had sent grown men over the top to oblivion. The diminutive receptionist obeyed without question.

'Mr Bowyer!'

He summoned the larger of the two pit deputies on guard duty.

'Yes, Mr Scrope.'

'This gentleman would like to see Mr Fitzpatrick. Would you see if he's available, please?'

'Who?'

'Mr Fitzpatrick.'

Nothing.

'Cecil Fitzpatrick.'

Nothing.

'Ces the caretaker?'

'Really? Oh.' Mr Bowyer could hardly believe his ears and stood there transfixed.

'Some time soon, Mr Bowyer?' suggested Mr Scrope.

'Oh. Right,' said Mr Bowyer and waddled along the corridor, his feet sliding, scraping and echoing on the marble floor. He disappeared down a winding iron staircase, dangerously narrow for his girth.

A few minutes later Ford could hear two sets of footsteps and two sets of heaving lungs wearily climbing the stairs back up to ground level. They were accompanied by a low-pitched murmur of wheezy disbelief.

Mr Bowyer appeared first. He stood to one side to reveal Ces Fitzpatrick in all his grease-smeared glory.

'Visitor for you, Mr Fitzpatrick,' said Scrope, gesturing towards Jack.

Ces stood and squinted as he rubbed his oily spectacles on his overalls. He put them on and leaned forward. A huge grin created an enormous gash on his flabby, toothless face.

'Bugger me,' he shouted. 'It's Sergeant Ford!'

The words 'Bugger me' and 'Ford' reverberated for what appeared to be a full minute around the hallowed chambers of the Northern Institute of Mining. Mr Scrope looked desperately in need of a restorative.

'Fitzy – how are you doing, man?'

Jack strode forward with his hand outstretched.

'Bugger me, bugger me. BUGGER ME!' said Mr Fitzpatrick.

Scrope could bear it no longer.

'Perhaps you two gentlemen would like to use the lecture theatre. It's empty this morning. No...I insist! Please just go on through. Just...go.'

The institute was home to all the documents, plans, contracts and designs relating to the Durham and Northumberland coal fields. They were housed in the vast reading room which was shelved from floor to ceiling and accessed by cantilevered step-ladders that ran up and down the length of the cavernous space on rubber wheels. For engineers, mine-owners, historians and researchers this place was unique. The North East of England was a region built on coal: entire communites had grown up on it; entire towns had thrived on it and often the cemeteries were prematurely full because of it. But this building housed the paper that turned the ideas into heritage. This was the focal point. Here was the evidence of an industry that measured its costs in more than pounds, shillings and pence. Behind every dusty document lay countless struggles and controversies, numerous disasters and celebrations. And tucked behind the Archive Hall was a small, sunken lecture room with green leather benches where invited engineers, academics, trade unionists, politicians and enthusiasts the world over gathered to listen and to learn.

Jack Ford was in the learning business.

Fitzy had just about recovered his poise. He pulled an oily rag from his pocket and blew his nose, royally.

'How long's it been, Jack? Passchendaele, was it?'

'It was, Fitz, Autumn, 1917. Here, did you ever get that tank moving again?'

'No, we bloody didn't. Sunk six foot into the mud she was. Still there as far as I know. What a bloody foul up, that was. A right circus.'

'Well there were plenty of clowns, I know that much.'

'Too bloody right. What brings you here, Jack? I'm not daft. I know you're not one for old time's sake. Not you.'

Jack grinned.

'Aye, your right marrer. I want some information. I could ask that poisonous oaf on reception but I don't think he'd be too helpful. It's sensitive, you see.'

'Fire away, Jack – I'll help if I can.'

'Well there were two Russians came here on Wednesday morning. There was a man and a woman. They were working for another Russian feller called Bukanin, Mikhail Bukanin. He's big in the unions over there and he's coming to Gallowshield for a visit.'

'He is Jack, later in the year. There's a right song and dance about him in here, I can tell you. Half of them think he's the devil incarnate and the other half think the sun shines out of his derriere. He's speaking at a rally right here in this very room. That's why I'm up to me armpits in grease. I've been servicing the boiler.'

'But what about these other two. Do you know who they are or where I can find them?'

Fitzy shook his head.

'Jack man – I'm just the caretaker. I don't know who anybody is. I just make sure the netty works when they spend a penny. I could find out though.'

Jack's eyes lit up.

'Could you? Could you do that for me, Fitzy?'

'Easy as pie. You see yon numbskull on reception? Well, Scrope's secretary is my niece, Violet. I'll see her Monday. She always brings her bait down to the boiler-room at dinner-time. Nice and warm there, see. She knows everything that goes on. Where are you staying, Jack?'

'I'm at the Royal Saracen, Fitzy. Come and see me there and I'll buy you a pint. If I'm not around, leave us a note and I'll see you right.'

'No bother, Jack. Consider it done. You did me a hell of a favour in France, Jack. I'll not forget it. Not ever.'

'Thanks, bonny lad.'

The Memorial Hall was nothing like the institute. More welcoming than imposing, it was clean and functional with a raised stage at one end and ladies and gents loos at the other. The floor was bare boards and the kitchen housed the giant urn which provided endless cups of tea served from an endless supply of trestle tables.

There were only three tables in use tonight and they were on the stage to provide suitably elevated accommodation for Charles Needham and the Labour Party Area Committee who had invited him to speak.

The body of the hall was filled with hard, low wooden benches which would serve those members of the masses who would rather not loiter in the doorway or along the sidewall where beer, kindly provided by the Fitters Union, was being distributed in china mugs. By the time Jack arrived the benches were half full but the standing areas were tightly packed. Matt was holding court by his beer barrel, young Billy Seaton was discussing Scarlet Fever with a young couple concerned about their daughter's temperature and Jessie Seaton and Les Mallow flanked the Rt Hon Charles Needham at the top table. He looked around and caught her eye. Suddenly it was Jessie who appeared to be struck down by her own version of scarlet fever which appeared to restrict itself to her cheeks and upper neck. He removed his hat and held his smile just a few seconds more than he should.

By the time Needham got to his feet the place was packed. Free beer and a cast iron pledge that the meeting would be over by 9pm had guaranteed a healthy attendance.

Ford watched his friend as he wooed his audience. Needham was a man of undoubted wealth, rank and privilege. At first glance, this man was the enemy. Yet there he was arguing passionately, without notes, that the school leaving age be raised to 15, that entrance into grammar schools should be made more accessible and that more public money should be ploughed into an education system that should be free to all.

When he'd finished, the audience seemed to forget that he looked and sounded like a toff. They stood up and applauded with genuine vigour. One of their number applauded much less enthusiastically than the rest and while she did so, Jessie Seaton damned Jack Ford for turning his back on her, on Gallowshield and on politics'

It didn't take long for the hordes to clear. The free ale had been enough to whet the appetites and now the men wanted a proper drink – after all, it was Saturday night.

Needham led his hosts over to where Jack was standing with Matt. The adrenalin was still charging through him after his speech.

'And this, ladies and gentlemen is my good friend, Jack Ford. Jack, this....'

But Jack smoothly interrupted him.

'Les Mallow, Billy Seaton and his sister, Jessie Ashton. How are you, Mrs Ashton?'

'I'm well, thank you, Jack.' Her voice was nipped, the handshake, limp.

'Do you know everyone in this town, Jack?'

'Not quite, Charles. But I do want you to meet this fellow here, Matt Headley. He's the one man who ensured a full house tonight.'

Les Mallow frowned.

'Oh,' said Needham, 'How come?'

'He supplied the beer, didn't you Matt?'

Matt shuffled with embarrassment.

'It was Les's idea but the union was only too happy to put on a barrel for the men and I'm sure they were only too pleased that they came, once they heard you speak, Mr Needham.'

'You're too kind, Mr Headley.'

And Ford looked at Matt, astonished.

'Bloody hell marrer, you're getting good at this politics stuff, aren't you?'

Les Mallow refused to believe that the presence of free alcohol was the sole reason for the healthy audience.

'Some of us care more about poverty than we do about beer, Ford.'

Jack looked at him, grinning.

'Of course, you do Les. You don't drink alcohol at all.'

But he was swift to change the subject.

'I think this calls for a real celebration. What say we all go back to the Royal Saracen for supper and a nightcap?'

'Splendid idea, Jack,' said Needham.

'I'm game,' added Billy, 'if it's all right with you, sis?'

'The Royal Saracen, eh? Funny kind of socialism at those prices. I promised Arthur I'd be home by half ten. I'll come if we're quick.'

'What about you, Les? Will you join us? Or will your cocoa get cold?'

'I'll come. I want to hear some more from Mr Needham, here. And I don't need beer to enjoy myself.'

No, you don't thought Ford. All you need is the presence of Jessie Ashton.

'I'll get your coat Mr Needham, it's hanging in the office.'

'Thank you, Mrs Ashton. What about you, Mr Headley?'

'I'll decline if you don't mind. Mrs Headley will have supper prepared and I don't like to disappoint.'

'And anyway, the lads down the Blue Bell will think war's broken out if you're not there for last orders, eh Matt?'

'I'm not like that, now Jack. You're looking at a changed man. That's not to say I won't pop me head in to say thank you to the lads for their support this evening.' He threw Jack a wink.

'Get away with you. I'll see you through the week.

Jessie returned with Needham's herringbone overcoat and he slipped it over his arm.

'Lead on then, Jack. I have a thirst – most inconvenient when the free beer has run dry.'

When they arrived back at the hotel, Jack was intrigued to see the result of watching his two worlds collide. In truth, he was slightly uncomfortable about it. Sat around the circular table in the lounge with coffee and brandies were the representatives of his old life. And they all had reasons to hate his guts.

There was Jessie, the woman he had betrayed. He'd cheated on Jessie because sex before marriage was simply something that nice girls didn't indulge in. Jack didn't want to play nicely and Matt's sister had been only too willing to do the aiding and abetting.

Next to Jessie was Billy – her self-appointed protector. Jessie had paid for most of his medical training, made sure he kept up with his studies and shielded him from their parents. When Jack broke his sister's heart, he had become Billy's sworn enemy.

Then there was Les Mallow. He'd been trotting after Jessie like a love-sick puppy for years. But he'd hated Jack even before that. Les was a tee-total pacifist - a self-educated man but not a very bright one. Jack was a thug, a streetfighter who knew how to persuade, to influence, to pull strings. Jack Ford had possessed the two things in life that Les Mallow coveted: Jessie was one and the office of Secretary of the regional branch of the Fitters Union was the other.

Jack Ford sat and watched each of them in turn. It might have been the brandy or perhaps it was the warm, soothing tones of

Charles Needham's supportive voice, but they all appeared to be passive enough.

'Do you know we've never had one,' Billy was proud as punch. 'This constituency was created after the Great Reform Act of 1832, and since then we've never ever had a Tory MP.'

'Well I'll be blowed,' said Needham.

'It's true,' said Mallow. 'We've had plenty of Liberals. Do you remember old Pinner?'

'How could I forget?' said Jack. 'We all stood and threw our medals at him. Oh, not you, Les. You never joined up, did you?'

'He had his reasons – you know he did.' Jessie bared her teeth and it was Needham who stepped in.

'Why was that?' he asked.

'Because Pinner did nothing for the working man,' said Mallow, flatly.

'That's not why we threw our medals at him, though,' said Ford.

'Really, why then?' Needham was intrigued.

'We staged a protest because Pinner was Chairman of the Bench when one of our comrades was committed for trial. He'd beaten a child with a stick while he was suffering from shell shock. That man had been buried alive in the Somme. It's no wonder he went barmy. That's right, isn't it, Jessie?'

He stared at her – challenging her to contradict him. The Pinner protest hadn't been about poverty. It was about justice.

She turned away and faced Les.

'It was about a lot of things. People had had enough. It was time to do something about it.'

The tone was dismissive – final.

'So, it's Labour from now on, eh?'

'Not necessarily, Mr Needham.'

Billy baulked at that.

'Why do you say that, Les? We're all Labour – always have been, always will.'

'Proper Socialism. That's the answer for me, Billy. Ramsay Macdonald's effort at a Labour Government was an embarrassment, an insult to working men and women. I'm sorry Mr Needham. I know you mean well but it's clear to me that you're not one of us and there can be no compromises. If change doesn't happen at the ballot box, the way I see it, the workers have to take matters into their own hands.'

Needham kept his head low and tapped his fingertips together. He understood the frustration – the desperate desire for change.

'Will you be going along to hear Bukanin speak, Mr Mallow?'

'I should think I will, Mr Needham. I'm organising the visit. That is, with the help of Mrs Ashton, here.'

Jack feigned amazement.

'Really Jessie? Bolshevism? I'm surprised.'

'Things change, Jack. People change. I think leaders like Mr Bukanin should be listened to. At least they have a Socialist system in place. We might all learn something. Don't you agree, Mr Needham?'

'I agree with the listening part, Mrs Ashton.'

'You'll be coming to the meeting, then?'

'I'm afraid I can't. It would be a gift for the Tories. Ever since the Daily Mail published that Zinoviev Letter, we have to be extra careful about which we meetings we attend and which platforms we share in case it is misinterpreted in the Press. Perhaps you can tell me about it afterwards.'

'She won't be your spy.'

Trust Les to take it so bloody seriously.

'I wouldn't expect anything of the sort, Mr Mallow.'

'All right then. But we can't be too careful. Mr Bukanin is going to be a guest of the working people of Tyneside – an honoured guest. We've all read the lies in the papers, Mr Needham we don't need any more establishment propaganda.'

'Now listen, Mallow –'

But Jessie stood up before Jack could finish the sentence.

'It's late gentlemen and I'm expected at home. Billy, Les, will you walk with me?'

When they'd gone, Needham said: 'Impressive woman, Mrs Ashton. Attentive, attractive, bright. Are you still besotted with her, Jack?'

'I'm not sure. Like she said, people change.'

Needham took a room and retired for the night and Ford remembered the message from Rose. He popped into one of the kiosks in the hotel lobby and the operator put him through to the Ham Bone Club.

Rose Milne wasn't there but Ford recognised the voice of the gothic looking woman who collected the coats.

'Do you know what time she'll be in?'

'No idea. She's never been late before.'

# CHAPTER 6

Jessie Ashton didn't feel like Jessie Ashton. She didn't even know how Jessie Ashton was supposed to feel. She felt like Jessie Seaton only in an unfamiliar place – as if she was on an enormously long holiday and staying in a moderately upmarket hotel where she was the only guest. People popped in to visit – Mam, Dad, Billy, Les Mallow, even Arthur felt like a visitor – but she remained there with a beautiful baby that had been given to her for her to look after.

She missed home dreadfully. Not so much the actual building, after all, her Mam and Dad and Billy lived there and when the time came for Jessie to leave, she had felt that was right. No – Jessie missed the essence of a home. She missed the unconditional warmth and comfort, its safety and its strength against the world outside. Poor Arthur, he'd thought quite innocently, that when he had provided this four-bedroomed detached house, he had given her the opportunity to create such a home for themselves and their children. But that wasn't how Jessie saw it. To Jessie this was Arthur's house and it was her duty to run it on his behalf – despite the fact that its apparent opulence made her restless with guilt. And for all its space and status, she felt hemmed in by it, restricted and restrained. She discovered that, when the chores were done and little Arthur was put down for his regular naps, she had taken to pacing the floors.

It hadn't been so bad before the baby had come along because she was still working. She had found some relevance in the daily classroom contact with the children whose lives she'd been trained to enhance. There was a point to that – a purpose. She was making a contribution, however small.

Arthur had been right, of course. Warrior Street School was a jungle and there was enough wildlife living on the average child to fill a biology book. No. She would have to give up her career and look after little Arthur. It wasn't as if they couldn't afford it.

And for all her education, her quick wits and her competence, she couldn't come up with a single practical reason why this was not a good idea. Except one: she didn't want to stop teaching. She immediately condemned herself for such selfish thinking and got on with it – just as Jessie Ashton should.

Saturday night hadn't done anything to ease her torment. Why did she always let him get to her? It wasn't as if she hadn't been forewarned. Her Mam had told her straight.

'Now mind, Jessie. Jack's back from London. I'm just telling you because…well, you know.'

Jack Ford – the engineer of all her pain. This was a man who could do things, change things, turn the world on its head and then set it right again. He'd been her man and she'd loved him so much she could hardly bear it. But there'd been a principle: no sex before a wedding. She laughed out loud at the irony of it. Jessie Seaton had tried to hold Jack Ford to a principle. Jack – the most unprincipled man who'd ever walked the stone flags of Gallowshield. What a bloody fool you were, Jessie Seaton.

She gazed through the parlour window and the branches of the cherry tree bobbed up and down in sardonic agreement.

She'd told her Mam not to worry. Her and Jack were finished

long ago. She had Arthur now and the bairn. She was a different woman – she was Jessie Ashton.

But on Saturday night Jack had walked into the Memorial Hall with that familiar easy stride. Still marching, Jack? Still soldier, Jack?

'My wars is over, bonny lass.' That's what he used to say. That's what he always said whenever she wanted him to do something to help her in the struggle to put men in work, or shoes on bairns' feet, or food in hungry bellies. Lord knows what they could have achieved if he'd lifted a finger. But no, not unprincipled Jack.

When she'd seen him, she'd felt herself blush - felt the sweaty warmth edge up her back, over her neck and across her cheeks – like the spreading of a disease. She never heard a word of Charles Needham's speech – not one word! It took her all her strength to fasten her eyes in a rigid stare on to the fading coronation print of George V which hung on the tilt on the back wall above the broken cupboard where the brass band stored their sheet music.

But from that fixed position she managed to witness his every flinch, every flicker of movement. Physically, he was unchanged: still tall, still wiry. He was better dressed obviously: pressed shirt immaculately white, Oxford shoes shined to perfection. Jessie wondered if Ford had given even a passing thought to the breadline wages of the laundress or the miserably squalid life of the vulnerable shoe-shine boy. Obviously not and why would she wonder such a thing? More important to consider why he had come back at all. What was in it for Jack? Did he really need to escort his friend? Surely Needham knew how to handle himself. He ought to. Rich beyond measure, educated, privileged, landed. He hadn't always been Labour, either. Needham was the epitome of a fair-weather Socialist.

That evening before the rally, Les Mallow had gone further and labelled Needham an infiltrator. What was it he'd said?

'He's the worst of his class. He sees which way the wind is blowing and joins the other side to protect his interests. Once a boss, always a boss.'

Any doubts she had were dispelled the moment Jack Ford had entered the hall.

She concluded that he had come back to Gallowshield to gloat. He and Needham were two peas in a pod. They were both infiltrators.

'Anyone at home? Jess?'

The voice from the hallway jolted her back to the present.

'I'm in the parlour, Billy. Hang up your coat and come on through.'

He was early. Much too early, she hadn't even tidied up.

She gave the cushions a token plump as he came through the door.

'I got your note. I had a house call in Marigold Avenue so I thought I'd drop in now. Is anything wrong?'

'Wrong? No. I don't think so.'

She tried to clear a path through the emotional tangle of her mind. The presence of a real voice was intrusive even though its owner was her little brother.

'I wanted to talk to you about Saturday night.'

'What about it?'

She hesitated to get the question right.

'Impressions. What were your impressions?'

He sat back and undid the bottom two buttons of his waistcoat. Now that Billy was earning money and eating regular meals at his Mam's, there was slightly more of him than there used to be.

'Oh, I made plenty of those. There was a good turn-out but that was down to the free beer. I thought Needham was a decent enough chap – for a toff. He spoke well enough and he talked a lot of sense but I didn't get the feeling we could expect anything

much to change any time soon. That's the problem – it all takes
so long.'

'You sound like Les Mallow.'

'Do I?'

'Yes, you do. Les was saying the other day that he's looking
forward to meeting Bukanin. Wants to hear how the Russians
managed it.'

'All of a sudden Les wants to man the barricades. He always
told us he was a pacifist.'

'That was when it was a Capitalists' war.'

'Well he won't be short of support around here. There's many
a family fed up to the back teeth with rhetoric, Jess. Ramshackle
Mac has no-one to blame but himself.'

'Is that what they call Ramsey Macdonald? Ramshackle Mac?'

'It's what the more diplomatic Brothers and Sisters call him in
Scotland. I won't mention his other monikers.'

But Jessie's attention had drifted off to the cherry tree again.

'Jessie. Jess!'

He had to raise his voice to attract her attention.

'You didn't ask me round to talk about Les Mallow, did you?
What's bothering you? It's Jack, isn't it?'

He knew his sister well. Billy had been there when she and Jack
had parted but he was all too aware that the agony she suffered
was yet another injury he could add to his list of incurable
maladies. She turned around, faced him and plonked her clasped
hands on her lap.

'In a way, it is. I admit it.'

'Well? What about Jack?'

'How did he appear to you?'

'He appeared like Jack: arrogant, smug, self-satisfied. What
more do you want?'

She pointed at her brother.

71

'That's it!' she said. 'Smug. He waltzed in there like he was king of the walk. I was so angry, Billy.'

She stood up.

'So angry.'

'Yes?'

'So angry that I, I couldn't help it.'

Now Billy was utterly confused.

'Couldn't help what? What have you done?'

Jessie sat down again.

'Now you won't tell anyone, will you?'

The hands weren't clasped now, she was wringing them and biting on her lip – the same way she did when she admitted stealing money from her Mam's purse to give to poor Elsie Manners when she'd snapped the head off her dolly.

'Jess. It's me. Your brother. What on earth have you done? Tell me.'

# CHAPTER 7

There were a couple of moments of silence while Jessie searched to find the words that would explain how it was that she had done something so completely out of character, that she had shocked even herself. She swallowed hard, gathered herself, took a deep breath and then it all came out in a rush.

'Well you remember I went to get Needham's coat from the office.'

'I remember that, yes. So?'

'Well when I picked it up from the back of the chair, this fell out of an inside pocket.'

She handed Billy an envelope and he reached inside and pulled out a hand-written note.

'Jess, this is a Privy Council document.'

'I know that.'

'It's marked Highly Confidential.'

'That's what it says.'

'You stole it?'

'It fell out of his pocket.'

'But you took it?'

'Yes.'

'Why?'

'I saw the House of Commons seal on it and I thought it might be important.'

Billy couldn't believe his ears.

'So?'

'So, I took it Billy. I took it and I read it. Enough is enough, Billy. Les is right. We're fighting a war and we need all the ammunition we can get.'

'Bloody hell, sis. You know you could go to prison for this?'

'I assumed so, yes. No – I mean, I assume so, now. But at the time, I didn't think.'

'What are you going to do with it?'

'I'm not sure. I don't know yet.'

'You must give it back.'

'No. I'm not sure.'

Her voice was beginning to crack.

'Why on earth did you do it?'

She blushed once more and her neck and cheeks glowed like hot coals.

'It was the principle of the thing.'

Sarah Lytton had always been a grafter. Her father was a waster, her mother was a hypochondriac, her brother was a criminal but Sarah was a grafter and the best day's work she ever did was when she persuaded Matt Headley to propose.

She took nothing for granted, either. She may have a house on Lavender Avenue, two china dinner services and an account at Chapman's Department Store but all of that meant nothing if Matt were to lose his seat on the council or – even more unthinkable – he failed to secure re-election as Regional Secretary of the Fitters Union.

Now Matt was a good man – everybody said so – but he was no high-flyer. A bit too gullible perhaps, a little naïve, sometimes.

It was just possible that some ambitious, underhand individuals might get the idea that he was vulnerable. If they did, they would do well not to under-estimate the finely tuned antennae of his wife. Sarah could smell trouble a mile off and when her nose twitched, she wouldn't rest until the source of the danger had been well and truly snuffed out.

She fired an accusatory glare at her husband.

'Another sausage?'

'But I'm still hungry, pet.'

'That makes three, Matt Hedley. You'll be the size of a house end if you carry on like this and then you won't even be able to climb the stairs to that office of yours.'

They'd been married long enough for Matt to learn the difference between Angry Sarah and Teasing Sarah – a bit like the difference between a Howitzer and a pop gun.

Today he was in luck. It was the latter.

'I have to keep my strength up today, Sarah. Meeting at Lewis Bishops with Sir Horatio Manners, no less.'

'Ooh, the big, bad boss. Trouble?'

'Bound to be – more lay-offs, most likely. The cranes are idle, the men are idle, half the bloody town's idle.'

'I'll have no bad language over the breakfast table, our Matt. Well if everyone's idle, you better show them how it's done. Shape yourself and get cracking bonny lad, I want you out the road. Unless you want me to set about you with the carpet beater.'

'Chance would be a fine thing.'

He ducked to avoid the flying dish cloth on his way out.

It was one of those Tyneside days when the weather looked fine from the kitchen table - blue, bright and fluffy. Matt decided to dispense with the overcoat and marched out confidently in his best suit. At the end of the street he turned the corner and the wind wrapped its arms around him in a bone-chilling embrace.

The north-easterly came straight from the sea and felt like it was being chased by Vikings. Before long, his eyes were streaming and his cap was demoted to his jacket pocket for safety's sake.

On top of the new road bridge he stood and looked down over the great bend of the river. The yards lay stretched out in front of him like a giant riverbank tapestry. Almost all the berths were empty. The herring gulls and the kittiwakes caw-cawed above him and swooped down over the water in great, predatory arcs. He stood and listened to them. The sound of their call was a precise indicator of the economic gloom. When the yards were busy, the blast from the furnaces, the clang of cranes, the chatter of the rivet hammers all combined to silence the sea birds. Today they were as clear as a cathedral choir, taunting his every step.

Matt walked on, past the Mile End pub, through the cut and along the cobbles to the surprisingly forlorn-looking double gates that signalled the entrance to the river's biggest employer, Lewis Bishop and Co. Ltd.

'Have a seat, Mr Headley.'

Matt pulled back the heavy leather chair and sat down. Unlike the entrance gates, the office of the chairman fulfilled all expectations with room to spare. It appeared to be large enough to house a corvette. The boardroom table, like the desk, the chairs, the shelving, the window sills – even the hat stand - was crafted out of Burmese rosewood left over from the fitting out of a luxury liner christened and launched before the war. Along the walls were pictures of just a selection of the yard's numerous offspring: HMS Goliath, HMS Gabriel, HMS Courage. The armoured fleet had siblings of a more refined, civilian lineage: SS Celestial, SS Majestic, SS Fantasia. Every craft built by skilled tradesmen. There was more to ships than steel plate and drunken sailors.

'Thanks, Sir Horatio.' Matt always felt stupid saying that name out loud. No matter how many times he tried it, he always felt it sounded servile.

'I won't beat about the bush, Headley. You're a reasonable sort of fellow – we've had dealings in the past.'

'We have and I'm sure you'll agree that my members have stood by Lewis Bishop.'

'We've rubbed along, haven't we, thus far. But things have changed.'

'We know that. We're not fools, Sir Horatio – we can see the river's not busy. That's why we agreed to the 500 lay-offs. Under protest, yes. But we agreed. Not a day of action as a result.'

Manners started to look out of his window at the yard below. A sure sign that the bad news was about to come.

'It's not enough,' I'm afraid.' There was a calmness to his tone – a resignation.

'There was a meeting here yesterday. The directors have decided to shut up shop.'

'I'm sorry?'

Matt had been prepared to take a belting but this sounded catastrophic.

'What do you mean? Shut up shop.'

'You're a reasonable man, Mr Headley, and there is no sense in prevarication. Let me lay out some hard facts for you.'

Manners took a deep breath, turned and faced Headley and leaned forward behind his desk.

'Before the war, and while it lasted, we couldn't build ships fast enough. The order book was full to overflowing and completed vessels were sold on for, on average, £24 a ton.

'For a year or two afterwards, we did all right. The merchant fleet needed to be built back up again. Today, the order books are empty – even the Government persists in this crazy disarmament policy – and the best worldwide price we can get is £9 a ton. The shareholders can't bear the cost any longer. Yesterday they came to a decision. We're closing the yard.'

Matt was stunned and it took a few seconds for him even to react with any kind of appropriate response.

'Permanently?' There was no hiding it. He couldn't halt the tremor in his voice.

'We believe there might be an upturn. Maybe next year or the year after that.'

'But what about the men?'

Manners raised his hands to demonstrate a condition of utter hopelessness.

'We'll have to lay them off. There's no alternative. Surely, you can see that.'

Matt could not believe it. His voice had ceased faltering. Now it was strengthening in protest.

'What? All fifteen hundred of them?'

'Blame Mr Churchill. There's no demand at home, Mr Headley and, with the exchange rate being what it is, we're too expensive to sell abroad. Even the Germans are more competitive than we are.'

'So, you're closing the operation down?'

'Yes.'

'Locking the doors?'

'That's right.'

'A bloody lock-out!'

'What choice do we have?'

'Surely, you can do something - lay off a few more, look at rates, reduce hours.'

'We've done our sums, Mr Headley.'

Manners wasn't posturing. This was no negotiating stance.

'We're telling you first because the fitters make up the biggest proportion of the staff here but all the unions will be informed before the end of the day.'

But Matt wasn't finished.

'What about suppliers. Can they not reduce costs?'

Manners sighed. He was being patient only because Matt Headley was one of the more likeable union leaders he had the misfortune to deal with.

'The price of steel is less than half what it was a year ago – makes no difference. The Sunderland Engineering Works has stopped building engines. Nobody, I repeat, nobody wants to buy our ships at the present time. This yard closes on Friday at four o'clock. And mark this, Mr Headley: we won't be the last.'

Matt had one last bullet to fire.

'But there'll have to be maintenance. If you want to protect your investment and re-open in a few months, the yard and the equipment will have to be maintained. Surely that'll save a few hundred jobs at least?'

But Manners had that covered too.

'Supervisors and Under Managers. All taken care of, thank you.'

'But that's against the agreement. Demarcation, Sir Horatio –'

Manners got to his feet. The meeting was over.

'No yard. No agreement. Good day, Mr Headley.'

Five minutes later, Matt was stood back on the bridge overlooking the river. The gulls were still carving up the sky and the lazy wind clawed and nipped at his flesh. His eyes were streaming again but this time the tears had nothing to do with the weather. His mind was racing as he tried to process what he had just been told. Closure was not an outcome he had even considered. He knew his members well – many of them by name. These were the people he grew up with, served with, worked with, drank with. They didn't have the resources to last 12 days without wages, never mind 12 months. Then there were the wives and the bairns. Even in good times they lived on little more than suet and hope. What the hell was he going to do? What would Jack have done?

'Well lad, what do you think?'

Tom looked at the dilapidated frontage on the corner of Trevelyan Street and Wharton Terrace and contrasted it with the fulsome glow of optimism expressed on his father's face.

'Needs a lot of work, da'.'

'Bool us round to the side, son.'

'If I must.'

Tom was already breathless. Trevelyan Street consisted of a steep bank that ran due north from the river up to the main road that lead directly into the town centre. It was a stiff walk for any man but a definite slog if you had the additional misfortune of having to propel a 12-stone relative in an oak and cane wheelchair.

'All it needs is a lick of paint and a new bit signage. Be good as new.'

'Is that so?'

Try as he might, Tom had never been able to share his father's enthusiasm for the retail trade. He could think of few things worse than being stuck behind a shop counter all day. And he was wary of making the same mistake he'd made as a boy – following in his father's footsteps. Young Tom had been an outstanding footballer – some said he could have gone all the way. But his dad returned from shift one day and said there was the chance of an opening down by. He'd had a word with Digger Prentiss, the deputy at the pit, and Tom could get a start as a Putter.

'What would I have to do?' he'd asked.

Bill had explained it to the boy right enough – he'd made it sound simple, too. Shovel the coal into a tub, shove the tub along the tunnel to a wagon. Then empty the coal into the wagon and come back and do it again.

He'd neglected to mention that you did this in the pitch black, through seams so narrow there was barely room to crouch. He didn't mention, the rats, or the silt, or the heat, or the foul air that clogged up your lungs and stung your eyes. He didn't mention the risks either. Accidents down the pit were commonplace and Tom had seen his share: heads, torsos and limbs fractured and shattered between heavy trams and faulty gear, bodies burnt and torn apart in explosions, men crushed and smothered by falling stone. All of these accompanied by chilling screams in the darkness and the frantic efforts of colleagues desperate to save a life.

Tom was never going to play football for a living. The look on his father's face told him that loud and clear. There was rent to pay and food to be put on the table. Tom was a man now. He was 14. He had to earn his keep.

He worked side by side with his father for more than 10 years. It came to an end only when Tom had blacklegged. He broke a strike solely to buy eggs and milk for his first wife, Mary, who was dying of TB. When the strike was over, Tom could never work underground again even if he'd wanted to go back. Miners had long memories and you had to be able to trust the man digging next to you. Tom had betrayed that trust and would never be forgiven.

Tom found burglary far more lucrative but that, too, had its risks. Inevitably, Mary died anyway but he didn't stop thieving. Tom spent 18 months in Durham jail – six of them with Jack Ford for company. That's where they became firm friends.

When he came out, Tom found his dream job – gardening. After years below ground and a spell in prison, what could be better than to spend your life in the outdoors. Tending, growing, cultivating – that was more Tom's nature. He was good at it too and he was building up a steady client list when his father had suffered a broken back in a roof fall.

Bill used his compensation payment to turn the front room of their terraced home into a shop and Tom was needed to hump the crates to fill the shelves. More donkey-work for his Da'.

Then Dolly came along. She'd been Jack's wife but his friend didn't cut up rough when she left him for Tom. Jack had his sights set on getting on and Dolly would have never understood him in a month of Sundays. But she and Tom got on just fine and when Bill wanted to open another shop in Cobbett Street who better to put in charge than Dolly. And Tom's world was closing in on him yet again and that knot in his stomach was beginning to tighten.

But none of that was Bill's way. Bill was a 'head down and keep swinging' kind of man. If he had to dig coal, give him a seam and a pick and he'd keep smashing that wall until you said stop. If he had to run shops, the attitude was exactly the same. Everything in life entailed pain and all pain could be endured.

'All you need is a bit imagination, man. It's a perfect spot. Right on the corner – you can see it from the bottom of the hill and all the way along Wharton Terrace. There'll be no need for folk to walk all the way into town, see. They can buy all their groceries from us.'

'Us? Don't drag me into it.'

'You ungrateful bugger! Who do you think I'm doing all this for? When I'm gone, all this will be yours.'

Bill's hair-trigger temper was lost on Tom and he grinned at his father.

'I'm not interested. You'd be better off talking to Dolly.'

'Aye well, she's a grand lass – and a good head for business, too. At least somebody appreciates what it takes. But I've seen enough. The landlord's asking a king ransom for the lease but we'll take it.'

Tom couldn't believe his ears.

'It's greed, that's all. Sheer greed. And who's going to be pushing you up the bank thrice a week to watch your empire grow? Me! That's who. I hope you know what you're doing. Mam's got her heart set on a house in Lavender Avenue. Are you going to be able to afford that if you take on another shop? Why can't you just be satisfied with what you've got? You're doing all right, aren't you?'

'You've got to speculate to accumulate, Tom. I thought we were doing all right when I was down the pit. You never know what's around the corner. Your mam might have to wait a year or two for Lavender Avenue, that's all. She'll understand. Right, I'm ready. Push us to Jowett's – I'm going to sign that lease.'

'Do you not think you should mention it to Mam first?'

'I do not. Your Mam's trusted me all these years to do what's best. She'll not falter, you'll see.'

'You've done what?'

Bella was more than faltering. She was positively incandescent.

Bill could see things were not going go as smoothly as he'd hoped so he did what he always did – he got his retaliation in first.

'Now don't you start questioning me in my own house. I'll spend my money how I want.'

Bill and Bella Seaton had been married for more than thirty-five years and Tom watched in wonderment as they fought like two prize-fighters slugging it out, toe to toe.

'Your money? Your house? Your shops? Your future? – Is there no-one else in your world, Bill, except you?'

Bill swung his pick again – he knew no other way.

'Is that what you think? That I'm doing this for me? Why should I? My life's over – it ended when I lost the use of me bloody legs! I'm doing this for you. And I don't see much gratitude, lady!'

Bella stood and raised herself to the fullest extent of her four feet and eleven inches. She spoke quietly and Tom knew that things were about to take a turn for the worse.

'Gratitude, Bill? I'm afraid to say you don't know the meaning of the word. Pass my hat and coat, Tom. I'm going out.'

Tom did as he was told but Bill was still at the coal face.

'Out? No, you're bloody not. What about me dinner?'

Bella stood in front of the mirror to adjust her hat. She was swallowing hard and trying to stem the tide of emotion that would inevitably overflow the second she left the room. She walked over to Bill and bent down, inches from his face and whispered softly in his ear.

'You're a selfish, cruel, lying, old bastard. Get your own bloody dinner.'

Tom didn't hear what she said to his father but he witnessed the result.

Bill's arm moved, the blow was struck and Bella fell to the floor.

'Da'! No!'

Tom moved towards his mother but she was already wriggling away.

'Stay back Tom. I'll get up me'self.'

Still struggling on the floor, she put a hand out to halt him in his tracks.

Bill sat silent in the chair – arms hanging down by the wheels.

'Mam, I – '

'Quiet, Tom. There's nowt to say.'

Bella rolled on to her side and managed to get to a sitting position on the rug. She reached up to a chair and pulled herself back on her feet. Panting with the effort she returned to the mirror to re-adjust her hat with as much dignity as she could salvage.

Tom wanted to look away but he saw her face in the mirror. An angry weal was spreading across his mother's eye and down her cheekbone. Bella felt her knees give way momentarily and she held out a hand to the wall to steady herself.

'Like I said, I'm going out.'

She walked out of the kitchen, through the scullery and out into the yard. They heard the back- door open as she stepped out into the lane and away.

Tom leaned against the kitchen table and listened to the clock working steady away as it had always done. He turned to his father.

'I ought to knock your bloody block off,' he said.

# CHAPTER 8

'Do you miss me, Jack?'

He had to admit that he did miss her. Rose Milne, he decided, was one of the more attractive things that London had to offer.

True she was a bit broken. But who wasn't?

'Of course, I miss you. I've been trying to call you at the club. Where were you?'

Her voice sounded like it was coming from the bottom of a crumb-ridden biscuit tin but he could just about make her out.

'I know I'm sorry. I slept in. I've never done that before.'

'You slept in? But you don't start work until midnight. How can that even happen?'

Rose explained that she had been feeling a bit low. That meant her demons had paid her a visit.

'You know how I am, Jack. I told you. It happens, sometimes. You do believe me, don't you?'

'Of course, I believe you. So why did you sleep in?'

'I came in from work and had a few drinks. But I wasn't tired – not at all. Then I took some of my pills and decided to try to get my head down. At first my mind was racing and racing and then I must have dropped off. When I woke up, I'd slept for 23 hours. I'd lost nearly a whole day. Lansing was furious with me, I can tell you. He said I was being.....'

As she was speaking, Ford moved the receiver away from his ear. Rose was talking at a hundred miles an hour and what with the biscuit tin and the crumbs and her voice coming and going, he was finding it difficult to keep any kind of track of the conversation.

When he tried to re-engage, she was still taking.

'Rose – '

'...said I needed to buck up my ideas and that the club wasn't profitable yet and...'

He decided to yell.

'Rose!'

'Yes, Jack?'

'Are you eating? Proper meals? Are you being sensible?'

He didn't know how else to ask it.

'I grab something when I need to. Don't worry about me. I'm absolutely fine. Really, I am. Tip top.'

'Are you sure?.'

She was talking so quickly she was actually forgetting when to breathe.'

'Actually, I've never felt better. My mind is as clear as crystal. Lansing's been looking after me. Honestly, don't concern yourself. I'm raring to go. I – '

He got in just before she gathered another lung full.

'For goodness sake, can you slow down, I –'

'Got to go darling, there's someone banging on the kiosk door. I'll call you sometime.'

Then the line buzzed at him and she was gone.

Damn Lansing Bell and damn his medical advice.

As he stood up to leave the hotel phone booth, he noticed the concierge loitering.

'Are you free now sir?'

'Yes, I'm finished. What is it?'

'A message from a Mr Fitzpatrick, sir. He awaits you in the bar.'

Fitzy could hardly have been more of a contrast to Rose Milne – in fact it was difficult to believe that the two individuals belonged to the same species. Where Rose was like a thoroughbred filly - terribly fragile and highly strung - Ces Fitzpatrick was like a great big, grinning, cuddly panda. As individuals, they both shared a complete and utter lack of malice but there the similarities ended.

Jack strode into the hotel bar, saw his old friend nursing his pint pot in a giant paw and immediately felt the stress of his conversation with Rose, dissipate.

'Fitzy lad. Good to see you.'

Ford meant it. Dealing with other people's misery was a frustrating business – especially when you cared for them, especially when they were two hundred and fifty miles away. What Ford needed was 'a good bit crack' – a harmless conversation with an old mate; the opportunity to share pointless jokes and nostalgic stories over a pint or two. London had its charms – Rose Milne included – but it didn't have this particular brand of therapy readily available on tap.

'You finished your shift?'

Jack pushed a fresh pint in front of his friend and, without even pausing between swallows, the giant paw embraced it before launching its contents in the same direction as its predecessor.

'Aye Jack. Yon Scrope's mighty appetites have been sated for another day.'

'You must be a comfort to you,' said Jack, with a seriousness laced with irony.

'Oh, but it is. I wouldn't be able to sleep at night if I thought I hadn't done right by that upright and charitable man.'

Fitzy dug deep into his left trouser pocket and pulled out a crushed packet of Park Drive.

Jack took one and straightened it out before sealing one end by tapping it on the bar.

'You have any joy with your Violet?'

Fitzy grinned his toothless smile.

'You know what it is, Jack? I love our Violet. Do you know why?'

'I don't. Why?'

'Because she does things properly.'

Fitzy reached into his hip pocket and produced a cream envelope in good quality paper. He slid it along the polished top of the bar. On the front was written: 'For the attention of: Mr J Ford.'

'She's a formal sort of girl your Violet, isn't she?'

'She is Jack. She watches her 'Ps' and 'Qs' – even when she's committing a sackable offence.'

'You must be very proud.'

Fitzy offered a serene nod of agreement while Jack opened the letter. He took the note out and read it:

*'Dear Mr Ford*

*As requested by Uncle Cecil, I enclose the details of the two representatives of Mr Bukanin's delegation:*

*1.   Mr Igor Toblinski*

*2.   Miss Irena Kuznetsova*

*Currently residing at the Balancing Eel Inn, Gallowshield but due to leave for London on the 14th. They will return with Mr Bukanin in the Autumn (precise date as yet undecided) when he will deliver his address at the Northern Mining Institute.*

*Your obedient servant,*
*Violet Casey*
*(Niece)*

The note told him everything he needed to know.
'Has she been of any help?'
For once in his life, Fitz looked anxious.
Ford smiled and took a fiver out of his wallet and put it into the empty envelope.
'She has – a big help. Give her this and tell her I'm extremely grateful. What's today's date?
'It's the twelfth, Jack.'
'Good. I've got all the time in the world. Shall we make an evening of it?'
'I cleared my diary in anticipation of just such a development. My turn, I think.'
'Before you do that, Fitzy – do you mind if we change location? I'd like to see what the world looks like outside of this hotel. I haven't been out all day.'
They decided to take a tram Whiteburn – a fishing village on the outskirts of Gallowshield - and then work their way back pausing for refreshment at some favourite watering holes along the way. First stop was The Crab and Lobster best known for its longest serving regular – a gloriously pink Galah Cockatoo called Albert. Nobody knew exactly how old Albert was but he'd been through at least three sets of bar owners and the present landlord had been in place for over fifteen years. Albert had a large metal cage suspended from the ceiling at one end of the bar, but the door was left ajar during opening hours and the colourful old bird had the freedom of the place until closing time. Albert didn't talk

exactly but he did scream a lot and when he wasn't doing that, he amused himself by sneaking under tables and untying the boot laces of unsuspecting drinkers. Eventually, the screeching became too much and they caught a motorbus down the coast road to the Smugglers Inn – a cosy pub which was literally carved into the cliff face above Spaniard's Bay. It was accessed via a set of rickety wooden steps which lowered the intrepid customer over one hundred feet down towards the beach below. At about half way, a steel walkway with a handrail had been bolted into the sandstone which lead into the upstairs lounge bar of the pub. Inside there was no panelling or wallpaper. Instead the bare rock walls had been painted with a clear deck varnish to give the impression that the entire place was glistening like a wet fish. The ambience was more impressive than the beer, so Fitz and Jack decided to strike for a final watering hole closer to home. The Blue Bell was the benchmark for quality and they agreed to walk the two-and-a-half miles from the sea front in order to work up a thirst worthy of the ale.

Ford found Fitzpatrick's conversation fascinating. A night out with an adult male from Gallowshield generally consisted of a fairly limited range of discussion topics – pay rates, football and the war. But Fitzpatrick was an engineer. That in itself was not unusual – Ford was something of an engineer himself. Like hundreds of other men in the town he was a fully-skilled fitter and turner. He could cut metal to patterns with incredible precision. Whether that metal be a simple cog for a machine part or a majestically curved turbine blade. In a sense, all the time-served fitters were proud, capable engineers – they rested at the pinnacle of the hierarchy of the shipbuilding trades. But Fitzpatrick wasn't typical – he was phenomenal. He saw the world in a different way. He spent his life looking for problems that engineering could solve. He could take other designs apart, improve them and put them together again without the drawings. Instinctively he would know the torque of this or the stress-limit of that. Fitzpatrick turned engineering into a living science.

He knew absolutely nothing about football and cared not a jot what he earned provided it kept him in copper slip and feeler gauges.

Like his peers, he was happy to discuss the war. But to Fitz, the entire period was seen in terms of technological development. And because of that, when he talked of it, he became expansive and excited, rather than anxious and appalled. It was refreshing for Jack to share just a little of that perspective. In that sense, he and Fitz had much in common – even more than Ford had with Matt Headley. The fact was that both men, in their different ways, felt quite at home in wartime. It wasn't that they enjoyed it exactly, it was more that they didn't know quite what to do with themselves when it all came to an end.

They turned left at the bandstand and began the gentle uphill slog into town while Jack listened, captivated by Fitzpatrick's explanation of an article he had read concerning the workings of a camera that could develop its own printed images.

Eventually, Ford could stand it no longer.

'I'm sorry Fitz, but I have to ask. How on earth has a bloke like you ended up as a caretaker at the Mining Institute?'

'What do you mean, Jack? Do you not think I'm up to the job?'

The light was fading and Ford had to look closely to see that Fitz was teasing him.

'The truth is that they haven't got a clue what I do. All they know is that I can fix their boiler. To be honest I'm the only person in the world that can fix that boiler. The original was so clapped out that I've had to re-design and re-build half the workings from odds and sods I had in the shed. I pity the poor bugger who gets the job when I go.'

He started to chuckle to himself.

'What's so funny?'

'I've been working on something else, too.'

'Oh aye?'

'Yes. It's a new type of gearing for a propeller system I've designed for the aeroplane. There's a feller down in Birmingham interested. With a bit of luck the Institute will have to find someone else to unblock their netties.'

'Oh dear. Poor old Scrope – however will he cope?'

They were both laughing at the thought as they walked through the doors of the Blue Bell.

'I'll make this one my last Jack, if you don't mind. I would have gone home after the Smugglers only the beer was so bad I needed to come here to take the taste away. I'm not much of a drinker.'

'No problem Fitzy. I've enjoyed the night though. It's been good to see you. Cheers.'

As they raised their glasses to toast each other, the barman rushed past Jack and knocked his arm.

'Oi! Careful bonny lad.'

The beer slopped lazily down the front of Ford's jacket and he was brushing it off with a bar towel when he clocked the reason for the commotion. A woman in the snug was singing what Ford thought might just possibly be a rather inebriated but persistent rendition of The Indian Love Call. The barman was trying as best he could to quieten her down while discreetly escorting her from the premises. She, on the other hand, was expressing a fervent desire to stay where she was.

'Hang on Fitzy – I know that lady. What on earth?'

He moved towards them and then he was sure.

'Mrs Seaton?'

Bella heard her name and stopped singing.

'Jack? Is that you Jack?'

She stumbled towards him, put her arms around his neck and burst into tears.

Cecil Fitzpatrick was still sober enough to know when to make his excuses.

'I can see you've got your hands full, Jack. I'll just slip away now. Leave you to it.'

Jack held on to his sobbing bundle and nodded at him as Fitz diplomatically eased his way out between the curious drinkers who had gathered to watch the floor show.

'Come in here and we'll get ourselves a seat.'

He ushered Bella back into the snug but the barman wasn't satisfied.

'Nothing more to drink mind, Jack. I want her out – she should be at home. What a state she's in. It's disgraceful. We keep a decent house here.'

'You bloody hypocrite. In twenty minutes time, every man in this pub will be shovelling beer down their gullet as if they're on piece work. So, she's had too much to drink – so what? Maybe she's got good reason. Give me five minutes to settle her and I'll take her home.'

'See that you do. No respectable woman would allow herself to get into that state.'

He carried on muttering to himself as Jack turned to face Bella. Something must be terribly wrong for her to be out in public and drunk out of her mind.

'Now then, bonny lass. What's all this about, eh?'

That was when he noticed the swelling on her face which was now turning blue and green around the eye. Gently he put his hand under Bell's chin and turned her head to face him.

'You didn't get that from a bottle of gin, did you?'

She didn't speak but tears appeared. In a few seconds her face glistened in the lamplight and Bella reached into her coat pocket for a hankie and winced as she wiped them away.

They sat and talked but Jack was none the wiser at the end of it. When he asked her a question she looked into his eyes with a twisted grin on her face. She stroked his cheek and repeated his name; she turned away and her head lolled forward as if she'd lost control of the muscles in her neck; she threw her head back and took in a huge breath as if about to launch into song once more. Bella Seaton wasn't drunk, she was paralytic.

The only words he could make out that made any sense was when he offered to take her home.

'Haven't got a home,' she informed him.

'Got plenty shops though.'

Bella considered that comment to be hilarious but Jack soon found a way to put a stop to the laughter when he suggested they should find her husband.

'Huh! Bastard Bill? Don't want him. What would I want him for? Bastard Bill!'

There was nothing else for it, Jack thought. He'd have to run the gauntlet and take her to Jessie's.

The Ashton house was no more than half a mile away from the Blue Bell, between the park and the cemetery. But it took Jack forty minutes to get her there. It wasn't as though Bella had lost the use of her legs absolutely. Sometimes the feeling would come back and she'd try to disentangle herself from his grip and run back to the pub. To make matters worse it had started to rain – a real Summer shower with heavy drops that soaked on impact.

'Ee, look at us Jack. We're drenched.'

Grinning inanely, she pulled off her hat, thrust her face to the sky and shook her cheeks vigorously while making a wobbling sound at the back of her throat.

'Very clever, Mrs Seaton. Just one more corner.'

Jack had always known that Bella Seaton liked a drink. The

first time he'd met her when Jessie had asked him back home after the pictures, he'd had the sense not to come empty-handed. But he'd never seen her like this. What would Jessie and Arthur make of it? He wouldn't have to wait long to find out.

Jack opened the gate and edged her along the path. It was at that precise moment that Bella decided to announce their arrival in song.

'When I'm calling you....oo-oo-oo-oo-oo-oo.'

'Oh for God's sake – sssh.'

'Will you answer too....oo-oo-oo-oo.'

'Bella, man – you'll wake the street.'

She peered at him lovingly and expressed her feelings with a wink and a hiccup of pure juniper.

He managed to prop her against the wall and held her there firmly with one hand pressed against her chestbone.

He took a deep breath. Right, he thought, ready, aim, fire!

Jack pulled the bell.

There was no need – the door opened as he did so and the impossibly tall, drainpipe-thin, perfectly groomed figure of Arthur Ashton looked down on him wearing his headmaster's face.

'Good evening Ashton – '

Jack was about to launch into a vague attempt at an explanation when Bella wriggled free, brushed past them both and rolled down the hallway.

'Where is she then? Jessie? Jessie? Howay lass – it's your Mam!'

Ashton raised an inquisitive eyebrow at Jack. Then said with immaculate politeness, 'Please come inside. I see it's raining.

'Let me take your coat – you must be soaked.'

'I'm sorry it's so late. I was having a drink with a pal in the Blue Bell when we bumped into Bella. I thought it best to bring her home safely.'

Ashton looked at Ford with open eyes and a placid smile. He was completely un-phased by the situation. As if entertaining roaring drunks who rang on his doorbell late at night was commonplace.

'You did absolutely the right thing to bring her here. I'm terribly grateful. I'm sure Jessie will be, too.'

Ford scrutinised him again. Nope – there was still was no flicker of bad feeling.

'Come along through. There are some people here that you know.'

Oh no, thought Ford. She's entertaining. This just keeps getting better and better.

Ashton announced him.

'It's Jack Ford, Jessie. He kindly walked Mum home from the Blue Bell.'

Jack scanned the room.

'Hello Jessie, Billy. How are you Les? Matt lad, good to see you marrer.'

There was an eerie silence as everyone watched Bella attempt to negotiate identifying, turning, then reversing into an armchair.

Billy got to his feet.

'Why the hell did you get her into this state?'

Jack took a step back.

'Wait a minute bonny lad – don't jump to any conclusions.'

But Billy had done his sums and filled in the answer.

'Did it for a laugh, did you? Let's see how much the old woman can handle.'

'Shut your mouth Seaton or I'll belt you. As I said to Arthur, she was three sheets when I walked into the pub with Ces Fitzpatrick. All I did was escort her here.'

The silence fell again like a cold cleaver. Eventually Billy turned away and went back to his seat.

'Pack up all my cares and woe, feeling low, here I go, bye, bye blackbird.'

Bella was feeling musical again and she was rocking back and forth in time to the music and clapping her hands in rhythm.

'Oh shut up Mam. You're drunk.'

Even when Billy was angry, nobody really took him seriously. Bella giggled like a little girl.

'Ee, did you hear that, Jack? The doctor says I'm drunk.'

'I heard him Mrs Seaton. I think he's right an' all.'

Billy got up again.

'Right. Let's get you home.'

She looked at him as if the very sight of his face turned her stomach.

'Take one more step Billy Seaton and you and me's finished. I'm sick to the back teeth with you.'

The venom in her voice stopped him dead but Bella hadn't finished. She raised her finger and pointed it at Jessie.

'And I'm sick to the back teeth with you an' all.'

Les Mallow hadn't heard the sound of his own voice for a while so he thought it best if he chipped in.

'Come on Mrs Seaton, you don't mean that. It's just the drink talking.'

She threw him a glare of the deepest disdain.

'And how the Hell would you know – holier than thou, too-good-to-live Les Mallow. I know all about you. Jealous. Jealous of the world. Bugger you an' all.'

'I don't think that's fair –'

'Leave it Les,' said Jack. 'I don't know what all this is about but I don't think it's about anyone in this room. Not really. Come on lads, let's get away and let the family take care of their Mam. Jessie, Arthur, I'll bid you good night.'

'Aye,' said Matt. 'You're right Jack. Come on, Les. Let's go.'

All the time Jack had been in the room Jessie hadn't spoken, but as he got to the door she said.

'Tell me this, Jack. Why did it have to be you?'

'Jessie!' Arthur couldn't stand rudeness – it was the one thing liable to make him angry.

'It's all right Arthur, lad,' said Ford. 'It had to be me, Jessie, because I was there.'

'Yes,' she said. 'You're always there, aren't you, Jack? Just waiting for an opportunity.'

He walked down the hall followed by Matt and Les. When they got outside, they could still hear Bella.

'No one here can love and understand me,

Oh, what hard luck stories they all hand me...'

They trudged on through the downpour until Les peeled off down the cut towards the park. Jack and Matt turned into Lavender Avenue.

'Poor old Les. He hates my guts, doesn't he, Matt?'

'Les hates everybody tonight. I don't see why you should be any different.'

'Why tonight? Has something else happened besides Bella going berserk in the Blue Bell?'

'Aye, Jack, it has.'

'Spit it out then, marrer.'

'I went to see your mate this morning. Sir Horatio Manners.'

'Oh aye? What did he have to say for himself?'

'Quite a lot. He told me they've decided to mothball Lewis Bishops. They're closing the whole thing down until the orders pick up. Everybody's being laid off. Everybody – apart from the managers.'

Ford whistled. No-one knew better than him what a massive blow this would be to Gallowshield.

'Did he say why? No, wait – let me guess. Exchange rate?'

'He said if we wanted to blame somebody we should blame Churchill.'

'Manners was banging on about the Gold Standard last time we had dinner. In a right old state, he was.'

'Well he's taking it out on us.'

'Is he Matt? Strikes me that if no-one's buying ships, there's little point in building them.'

'Trust you, Jack. Trust you to take the bosses' side.'

'I'm not man. I'm just pointing out the flaming obvious.'

'It gets worse an' all. I've had messages from the Venus Yard and the Robson Works this afternoon. They've called me in for meetings as well. And they won't be about upping the hourly rate.'

'No, Matt – they won't.'

They stopped at Matt's gate.

'What am I going to do, Jack? We've bloody had it, this time.'

'Ride it out. There's nowt else you can do.'

'Les Mallow says we should fight.'

'Does he now? Well I've never seen Les fight, so I could be wrong. But ask yourself this - how many times has he been on the winning side?'

'That's why he hates you, Jack.'

'Aye marrer. Truth hurts. Give my love to Sarah.'

# CHAPTER 9

The truth was on Jack's mind the following morning. The kernel of the problem was Irena Kuznetsova. How on earth did she find her way to Gallowshield? When he'd left her at the Railway Station in Murmansk she'd been known as Countess Irena Olga Goliksyn. Now she'd mysteriously reappeared in Gallowshield and changed her name to Kuznetsova – which, if Ford remembered correctly from his days as an army interrogator - roughly translates as Smith. He'd been with her the night before she left and he'd personally put her on the train to Kuolajarvi, just over the border in Finland. She'd left with all she could carry. What she couldn't carry, she'd given to Ford. It wasn't much – by her standards - just a few trinkets she'd flung into a handmade wooden box: a pouch of uncut diamonds, an 18-carat gold watch, an emerald bracelet and a diamond tiara of all things that had belonged to her Aunt. The haul rested on a bed of banknotes that Ford didn't even bother to count. They were already worthless like all pre-revolutionary roubles.

Before 1917, the Goliksyns were a family of enormous wealth with estates the size of countries. But all of that came to a brutal end and the aristocracy was hunted down and shot, imprisoned, or, perhaps worse, re-educated – a peculiarly Bolshevik form of barbaric retribution.

Sgt Jack Ford had joined the North Russia Expeditionary Force in 1918 and, because of his frontline experience, was awarded the rank of Warrant Officer First Class. Stationed in Murmansk and attached to the Intelligence Corps, he'd found himself billeted to a Dacha belonging to the Goliksyn family four miles outside of town. He knew that he had landed on his feet as soon as he got there. He didn't know how soft that landing was until he met Irena. Their brief affair was made all the more highly charged by the spread of revolutionary success and the utter failure of the White Russian forces. When it was Irena's turn to run for her life, she had turned to him for help. Fortunately for her, Warrant Officer Ford signed the travel orders.

And yet there she was in Gallowshield, as large as life and an honoured representative of the Russian Trades Union Council – spreading Socialism and solidarity to working classes everywhere.

That was one Hell of a conjuring trick, he thought as he slid the wooden box out from the bottom of the wardrobe. He took the tiny key from his pocket and opened the padlock that he had fitted himself. Everything was just as it had been when she'd handed it to him on the platform. Even during the tough times - and there had been plenty of them - it had never crossed his mind to sell the treasures given to him by a Countess. Ford untied the velvet pouch and emptied the uncut stones onto the palm of his hand. He selected one – the smallest – and slipped it into an envelope with a short note.

Charming the barmaid in the Balancing Eel was simple enough. For a start, she didn't like the look of Igor Toblinski.

'Miserable old goat and that beard of his needs a good scrub!'
Thankfully her opinion of Irena was somewhat different.
'Lovely gentle voice she has. And beautiful hands.'
Ford wondered how she'd managed to slide those feather soft

fingers past the Cheka.

She teased him when he gave her the envelope.

'Billet-doux, is it?'

'What? No pet that's just an invitation.'

'I've been all over the world and Gallowshield girls are the best of the lot.'

He winked at her.

'Get away with you.'

But she was smiling at him.

'I'll pop up now and slide it under her door. He's at the other end of the corridor. Anyway, he'll still be snoring his head off, most like.'

Twenty minutes later he watched her walk into the park. She glanced at him as she passed his bench overlooking the bowling green. After a few seconds he got up and followed her around the lake. There was a small wooden pavilion to the left and she nestled herself in the corner. Ford sat down next to her. There was no make-up and the clothes were plain and functional – long calf-length brown woollen skirt to laced black boots. But she smelled warm and sweet and her gestures were as feminine as they had been when she'd had the benefit of a fortune's worth of enhancements. She could quieten her beauty from a distance but from close-up it would have the final say.

'You got the note, then?'

'Yes. I knew you'd come.'

'Irena Kuznetsova?'

'It was all I could think of.'

Ford laughed. He'd interrogated dozens of Kuznetsovas during his time with Army Intelligence in Murmansk, and none of them was a true identity.

'What did you expect? Once I saw you I had to know what the Hell was going on. You should be in Berlin or New York or wherever it is your lot disappeared to.'

'Ha – most of them just disappeared. But you're right – things didn't quite go to plan.'

As she told the tale she began to relax just a little although her eyes seldom stopped scanning the entrance to the park which was just visible through the trees. The delivery of her English barely faltered. The accent had always been irresistible.

But as she recounted the events following her departure from Murmansk, he could see the fear return to her face.

Her train had been stopped ten kilometres from the border by a Bolshevik patrol. When the soldiers searched the train, the driver had hidden her under a pile of mail sacks. The soldiers took everything on board, luggage, parcels even some of the passengers. The coal was shovelled onto wagons and the train was just left in the middle of nowhere. But the driver took care of her for a price she wouldn't discuss and they found refuge at the home of one of his cousins. She never made it to Finland.

'You want to hear something funny, Jack?'

'Go on.'

'I watched you. I was sat on top of a hill in Murmansk Oblast and I watched this giant snake of lorries wind its way to the coast. I waved to you, you know?'

'Well, I'll be damned. But what about this union thing. How did you manage that?'

'After about a year, I got to St Petersburg and managed to persuade a man to give me a job in the City Hall – hardly anyone else could read or write. I joined the union, worked hard and then last year I was invited to join the Party. I made them like me and – here I am.'

'How the Hell did you get away with it?'

'I'm a good liar, Jack. You know that.'

'You're a good survivor. It's good to see you. Really good.'

'You too, Jack. But I must get back. If Igor finds me gone, he'll come looking for me. And I'll have to start lying again.'

'You're off to London soon, aren't you?'

'Tomorrow.'

'Where are you staying?'

She dug in her bag for a piece of paper.

'It's all arranged by the London School of Economics. Here it is.'

She handed him the address.

'Good God,' said Ford. 'I don't believe it.'

It read: 1917 Club, No. 4, Gerrard Street, Soho, Central London.

'What's the matter? Is it no good?'

'I've never been inside. But it's got some pretty odd members.'

'I must go Jack. But will I see you again? In London - it might be easier for me there because Igor won't be in charge.'

'I'll be there bonny lass. The Connaught. It's a hotel in Mayfair. Everyone knows it. You'll find me there.'

'Right. I'll try. I promise, I'll try.'

She stood up to leave then changed her mind and bent down to kiss him. Jack remained sitting and felt her open mouth on his. Her passion was so intense it was desperate and her hands caressed his face with an urgent scrutiny as if she was trying to remember what life had been like before chaos came to stay.

'They stole my life Jack. You were there at the end but they stole my life. I want it back, so much.'

The tears were going to come then but she wouldn't let him see them. Irena turned and walked out of the park – eyes fixed, straight ahead. After he watched her go he looked down and saw the envelope he'd given to the barmaid. Inside was the uncut diamond.

Bella wasn't looking forward to the interrogation. She'd awoken that morning in Jessie and Arthur's spare room and it had taken a little while to recall the events of yesterday. Then the more she remembered the greater the shame – it spread like a tea stain on a table cloth. A sickly, yellowish-brown smear spoiling all the good work that the washing and ironing had done. But the guilt was only the first wave of recognition; after that came the anger. She remembered that now, too. Bill's grand announcement, another shop, another link in the chain, another year of waiting for Bella. Poor old Bella – always last in the queue. For once in her life she'd said so. She'd told him exactly how she felt: betrayed, let down by the one man who was supposed to love her. Then he'd clouted her in the face. When it had happened, the blow was so powerful, she'd felt the thud in the back of her skull before she fell. But now, when she put her hand up to her cheek, the tenderness was all at the front. She dabbed at it. The eye was sore and bruised and the skin was tight and swollen all the way down to her neck. He'd caught her a good one all right.

She got out from under the covers and sat at the side of the bed, head down, hands in her lap. She was dazed and hung over. She remembered it clearly enough but she still couldn't quite believe it. Bill Seaton had thumped his wife. In fact, he'd hit her so hard, he knocked her to the floor. She could feel it now, the rough carpet against her face – all bristly and coarse. Oh Lord! And their Tom was there too. He'd had to witness that. Poor Tom. He'd put up with a lot from his Da' – put up with a lot from life. But this? She steadied herself by putting her hands down by her sides, palms down on the bed. She breathed slowly and deeply in an effort to quell the nausea and the dizziness.

Somebody was walking about on the landing - that would be Jessie or Arthur, tending to the bairn. She remembered Tom's face as she'd walked out of the house. It was grey, shocked. She felt a need to piece together all the pieces from yesterday's jigsaw in her own mind before the inevitable questions started.

She'd walked into town and bought a bottle of gin then made her way to the allotments. She drank most of it sitting on an upturned bucket. When the gin started to take effect, she decided she was going to go back. In fact, she'd even thrown the remains of the bottle in the bin but then she'd realised that she didn't want to see Bill's face. At that moment, she determined that she didn't want to see his face ever again. Then she became angry once more. She'd walked to Lavender Avenue and looked at the houses. Through the windows she saw the inside of the rooms all spick and span with mirrors on the walls and dark wood furniture. She could smell the polish, taste the tea, feel the cushions. Not for you, Bella – you're at the back of the queue. And who put her at the back of the queue? Bill did – a bloody man. So, she did what bloody men did when they were angry, she'd walked to the Blue Bell to block it out.

She remembered becoming all confused in the Blue Bell. A man had been shouting at her, telling her she was a disgrace. Huh! She was a disgrace? But Jack came then. Bonny Jack, lovely Jack, kind and gentle Jack. Why did Jessie have to marry Arthur. Nice enough man but what a long streak of misery. Not like Jack. And Jessie herself was no Gloria Swanson, either. Plain sort of girl, really. Sharp mind, though. And sharp tongue, too. No – she could be a spiteful little madam when she set her mind to it. Principles? They don't pay bills or buy medicine or get you out of Gallowshield. As for Billy, puffed up like a bad Yorkshire pudding – all hot air and no substance. There's plenty of things you can't learn in books, me bairn. Plenty!

'Mam! Are you awake?'

That was Jessie. Arthur must have gone to work. She'd got that teacher's tone on. The tone that said, you're going to get a telling off.

Well, thought Bella, we'll just see about that.

'I'm getting dressed,' she said.

'I'll be there when I'm ready.'

Bella deliberately took her time and it was a good fifteen minutes later when she came through to the parlour.

'You've missed breakfast but I don't expect you'll be hungry.' There she sat, waving her disappointment like a flag.

'I'm fine thank you, Jessie.'

'There's fresh tea in the pot. You can help yourself.'

Bella wasn't going to turn that down even though she doubted that the restorative effects of the brew would be sufficient in this case. Even so, it was hot, wet and comforting.

She listened to the clock tick. This was normal Jessie behaviour. The silent treatment was always there at the start but once she got going, there would be no stopping her.

Eventually she spoke.

'Did you fall?'

'Sorry?'

'You have a nasty bruise on your face. Did you fall? Or did you get into a brawl in the Blue Bell?'

Bella wasn't ready to talk about that yet.

'Don't be impudent.'

'Impudent, am I? Excuse me, Mam but I don't think so. I wasn't the one who turned up here with Jack Ford, roaring drunk!'

'Jealous, are you?'

Bella was firing live ammunition and she knew it and didn't care. Last night she'd been drunk and angry, today she was just angry and for once, she didn't seem to be bothered about the consequences.

Jessie was shocked. She'd been expecting her chastened little mother to come creeping down the stairs choked with guilt and remorse. Jessie would then have annexed the moral high ground and delivered a strict, firm lesson in good behaviour. But this wasn't the schoolyard and Bella wasn't playing.

Jessie went on the attack and stood up to provide full volume.

'How dare you? In my house! In Arthur's house! You should be ashamed Mam, truly ashamed.'

Bella remained sitting. She looked straight ahead and spoke softly.

'I am ashamed.'

'Well, at least that's something – '

'I'm ashamed because of what I've allowed you to do to me.'

'Me? What are you talking -?

'You, your Dad, Billy – even our Tom. The whole lot of you.'

'Are you saying it was our fault that you went out and got drunk?'

'I am not. That was my doing and I'm not sorry for it. I'm saying that you've all done your best to make me feel worthless. You've eaten away at me for years and years with your rows and your debts; your affairs and your greed; your lies and your principles.'

She spat out each syllable of the last word as if they were so toxic she had to force them out of her system.

'I've spent a lifetime on the lot of you. Wiping your noses, soothing your bruises, clearing your messes. What a thankless task. What a waste. Ashamed, Jessie? Yes, I am. I'm bloody ashamed.'

For once in her life Jessie couldn't think of anything to say so they each sat with their spinning minds listening to the clock until Bella finished her tea. She put the cup on the saucer and stood.

'I'm still hung over. I'm going back up to lie on the bed.'

Billy called in around lunchtime.

'How was she this morning? Rough as a badger, I'll bet.'

'She's still here, Billy.'

'Still here? What about me Dad's breakfast?'

'To be honest, I think it's the last thing on her mind.'

'What?'

This was unheard of.

'There's something very wrong, Billy. I've never heard her like this.'

Jessie told him about the morning's conversation.

'What the devil's got into her?'

Billy had never been lucky – even as a boy – and true to form, as he spoke, Bella appeared at the doorway. She had her hat and coat on.

'It's not the devil, Billy. It's not an angel either. It's just me.'

'Where are you going, Mam?'

Jessie's tone was considerably more contrite than the last time she'd addressed her mother.

'Home.'

'Face the music, eh?'

'Don't be so childish, Billy. Someone will have to relieve our Tom and I don't suppose either of you two have thought about looking after your Dad. Selfish and spiteful – the whole damned lot of you.'

They were going to protest but she held up a hand like a policeman stopping traffic.

'I'll just take a look at that eye before you go, Mam. It could be nasty.' Billy advanced towards her with his doctor's voice.

'It is nasty and you'll come nowhere near it. I've told her, now I'm telling you. I'm fed up to the back teeth with the Seatons - so stay away from me.'

Breakfast at the Royal Saracen was by no means as refined a ritual as it was at The Connaught but with genuine Northern concern for the guests, it was designed to sustain until at least suppertime and, possibly, beyond. Jack decided that with the prospect of lunch with Charles Needham, it was probably wiser to give it a miss.

Needham had kindly offered to send his car and driver through to pick Jack up from his hotel and Ford, given the social status of his friend, was sat in the lobby reading his Times, fully expecting the imminent arrival of a chauffeur in full, uniformed regalia.

He therefore paid absolutely no attention to the young man in the Argyle Sweater and patched cord trousers who jammed the lady in the revolving door, tripped up the half-flight and stood panting at reception until he could get his breath back.

Ten seconds later when full vocal service could be resumed, a public school-educated baritone voice said, 'Terribly sorry. Bit breathless. Running late. Is there a Mr Ford staying with you?'

Jack heard that, all right and got to his feet just before the hotel day manager had the opportunity to put the young man in his place.

'Are you looking for me, by any chance?'

'Mr Ford?'

The stranger immediately stretched out a hand. He obviously wasn't a chauffeur – he was, undoubtedly, Charles's son.

'Julian Needham – good to meet you. My father asked me to collect you.'

'Call me Jack and thanks for the lift.'

'I haven't delivered you safely back there yet - she can be a temperamental old thing.'

All the time he was talking, he never stopped shaking and grinning.

'Are you talking about your car or your mother?'

111

'See for yourself, she's waiting outside.'

Julian displayed as much confidence driving the car as he did on first meeting – his grip on the wheel as secure as his handshake. Conversation was limited by the deep growl of the Humber Tourer, so Ford lit a cigarette as they headed through town towards the West Road and on towards Newcastle.

The familiarity of the landscape depressed him as they followed the snake of the river upstream. What unfolded was his heritage and it was like some kind of grubby Magic Lantern show. After the shipyards came the machine houses and the timber yards and then the warehouses and the storage depots. Further on were the boat builders and the rope-makers and then the heavy stuff started again: sheet metal works, armaments factories, coal staithes. Everywhere you looked, filth, grime and dirty finger nails. But even through the roar of the engine and the buffeting of the wind, Jack couldn't help but notice the lack of activity. Men were huddled at yard gates or playing pitch and toss at warehouse doors. The river traffic was absent, too. Normally, the passenger ferries would be chivvied and harassed by the skiffs and barges busting a gut to carry vital materials to the greedy manufacturers. Not today. And there was something else. Every business – large and small – had a sign on the entrance proclaiming the same doom-laden message. 'Not hiring until further notice'; 'No vacancies'; 'No hands required.'

Mr Churchill, you've got a lot to answer for, thought Jack.

They had crossed the High-Level Bridge which joined Gateshead to Newcastle when Julian signalled his intention to pull over.

'I've just got to make a delivery - won't be long.'

They'd pulled up outside a long barn of a building a few hundred yards from the quay.

Julian hopped out of the car and opened the boot. He pulled

out two hessian sacks – almost the same size as himself – and dumped them on the ground before disappearing into the building and returning with a wheel barrow.

He was emptying the carrots from the first sack into the barrow when a jolly-looking woman in her fifties appeared.

'What have you got for us today, then, Julian?'

'Carrots, parsnip and swedes in the sacks. And Dad sent one of his lambs.'

'How marvellous. And who is this?'

She gestured at Ford who raised his hat.

'I'm Jack Ford,' he said. 'A friend of the family.'

'Madeleine Phillips. Call me Maddy.'

Julian loaded all the vegetables into the barrow forming a tall pyramid, then he dragged the dead lamb onto his shoulder before depositing it on the top of the pile.

'Ready-made stew,' he said. 'Just add water. Beep beep!'

Wobbling under the weight of his burden, he steered the barrow straight through the door and into the kitchen.

'Come in and have a drink, Mr Ford. I think Julian will probably need one.'

Inside was a large kitchen with a range at one end which was going great guns under the stewardship of a circular woman with forearms the size of thighs.

'We've got pies ready, would you like one?'

'No thank you, Maddy,' said Ford, 'We're expected for lunch.'

'At the hall?'

'That's right.'

'Give them a pie each, Gertie. Dear knows when they'll be fed up there. Eh, Julian?'

She winked at the young man and Ford began to regret his breakfast decision.

They sat down at the kitchen table and Maddy poured the tea.

'You look puzzled, Mr Ford.'

'I was just wondering exactly what it is you do here.'

'We feed people.'

'Like a café.'

'Exactly like a café – only we don't charge.'

'Ah,' he said. 'You run a soup kitchen.'

'Sort of. Only we do other things as well. We call it Food For Thought. We provide hot meals in the middle of the day. And we run classes in the afternoon.'

'Cookery classes?'

'No. We teach the three 'R's.'

'To children? This is a school?'

'In a way. We teach anybody who wants to learn – adults and children alike. Illiteracy is extremely common around here, Mr Ford. Many people missed out on schooling altogether.

'When Charles bought the building, the intention was to create a kind of adult college. But we found that most of the people who wanted to come had difficulty concentrating for more than five minutes at a time. We thought that it might be because they were starving. So, we decided to feed them.'

She told it straight – completely without embellishment or emotion: here is a problem, here is a solution.

'So, this is all Charles's doing?'

'Well not all. His sister helps out a bit, too.'

'Who's his sister?'

'I am.'

The jolly-faced woman burst out laughing.

'You Needhams are a Hell of a family. I'd no idea.'

'Just wait until you get to the estate – you're in for quite a shock.'

'You might have warned me,' said Jack as he and Julian got back to the car.

'Sorry Jack but it would have spoiled the fun. Auntie Mad loves all that stuff.'

'Well bully for Auntie Mad!'

They drove through town along West Gate and out into the Northumberland countryside where the roads became narrower but much less congested. Julian decided to put the Humber through its paces.

All of a sudden, the green fields and woodland began to hurtle past them but Julian maintained his steady grin, sat back in the driver's seat and took one hand off the wheel.

After about forty minutes they turned off the road and headed down a track. After a mile or so there was a hump backed bridge (that Ford was certain would never support the weight of a vehicle) and as they motored up the bank on the other side, a large house seemed to rear up out of the farmland ahead of them.

'Home sweet home,' said Julian.

Needham's place was certainly impressive. Adlington Hall had been on this site since the Sixteenth Century – although it had been rebuilt several times. The current stone version was in the Palladian style and its angled symmetry contrasted majestically with the rolling park and woodland which hid it from view until the visitor crossed that precarious bridge. Ford guessed the house was of late Eighteenth Century design and the sheer scale and size would need constant maintenance. He noticed a gang of men re-roofing the central section as they sped through the stone arches and around the front lawn before pulling up at the main door at the side of the house.

'Made it. Thank the Lord for that.'

Even as Julian expressed his profound gratitude to the good God Almighty, great clouds of steam began to spew out through the radiator grille accompanied by a persistent hissing sound.

'She's had a leak for ages. We have to keep putting porridge oats down the radiator to bung it up.'

'Well I should let her cool down for a bit – she's had a hard day. Thanks for the ride.'

Ford walked through three reception rooms before he got to the study where he found Charles Needham going through the estate accounts.

'Good to see you, Jack. You'll be in need of a drink, no doubt. Julian has all the impatience of youth.'

'And the enthusiasm.'

'What do you make of the place then, eh? What you expected?'

In truth, it wasn't too different from Jack's imaginings – a huge great stately pile of a place with vast panelled rooms and floor to ceiling windows overlooking rambling parkland.

'More or less,' he said. 'Looks like you've been here for generations.'

'Actually, we've been here six months.'

'What?'

'It belonged to my father. We had a house nearby. It came to me when he died but he used it only in the summer.'

'Bloody Hell. It must be the largest holiday home in the country.'

'I think that's probably Balmoral.'

'But now you're Lord of the Manor.'

'I'm responsible for it, if that's what you mean – but I'm only a baronet so I don't really count. I've got big plans for this place, Jack. Really big plans. Come and look.'

He grabbed a leather drawings case from behind the curtains and rolled the papers out over the desk and began to go through each one.

'We're completely re-roofing the place. Rain's been pouring in for years and ruined a lot of the fittings. Then we're putting in central heating. Honestly, I remember the house in winter – it was like the bloody arctic.

'When that's done we're redecorating throughout and then we're going to start outside.'

He peeled off another drawing.

'These are the gardens. This lake needs to be dredged and cleaned and the walled garden needs to be landscaped with fountains and a new greenhouse for cultivation work and so forth. And then there's the farms.'

Yet another drawing was placed on top.

We're putting electricity in for all the tenants. Oh, did I say we were installing that here? Well, we are and...'

And on he went as Jack listened open mouthed at the sheer ambition of the enterprise – Project Adlington wasn't a vision, it was a dream and an expensive one at that.

When Charles had finished he ushered his friend to an armchair and refilled his glass.

'Well Jack, what do you think?'

'I don't know what to say? It's a huge undertaking.'

'Quite ambitious, you would say?'

'I would say, Charles. Who's going to do it all?'

'What do you mean?'

'Well who is going to oversee the work, manage the thing?'

'We are?'

'But you're an MP. You'll be in London most of the time.'

'I will. But there's this marvellous invention Jack – it's called a telephone and more to the point, you haven't met my wife yet, have you?'

'Electrician, is she?'

'Ha ha – no Jack. But she is the most fantastic person at getting things done. She's quite a remarkable woman.'

He met Beatrice at dinner (lunch never seemed to happen and nobody appeared to mind in the slightest). She had spent all day in the garden pulling up more root vegetables and making design sketches for the new greenhouse. The children – seven in all – had been with her from time to time but they had also helped one of the tenant farmers dig a drainage trench and cleared out an attic.

'They never stop,' said Beatrice.

'And that's exactly what they need. Children have the most incredible energy, don't you think?'

'I bet they sleep at night,' said Ford all the while thinking of the bairns in Gallowshield some of whom had the benefit of neither energy or sleep.

'We're all out like lights. But we rise early. There's so much to do. Ask them yourself.'

He didn't have to. One after another the Needham children told him of their plans for their own rooms and their patches of land, their animals and their futures. Ford had been surprised they were all allowed to sit down at the dinner table with their parents. Julian, perhaps, because he was the eldest but they were all there – right down to five-year-old Mary who had to perch on a tower of cushions in order to reach the table.

They were utterly and ridiculously charming, polite, knowledgeable and fun.

And there was no fuss at bed time either. At nine-o'clock Julian announced that he was tired.

'I'm off. Goodnight Jack, goodnight everyone.'

And they all trooped off after him.

'Goodnight Jack'; 'Goodnight Jack'; even the little one 'Goodnight Jack but will you help me get down, please?'

It was no wonder Charles Needham looked so smug with his brandy glass.

'Well Jack, I'll ask you for the second time today – what do you think?'

'I don't know what to think, Charlie. You've a lovely wife and family. You live a wonderful life in a wonderful place.'

It was his wife who'd re-appeared from upstairs who replied.

'But it's a far cry from Gallowshield? That's what you mean, isn't it?'

Lady Beatrice possessed great insight as well as great parenting skills.

'I don't think that's what Jack meant, darling' said Needham.

'Sorry,' said Ford, 'but that's exactly what Jack meant.'

'In which case, it's a fair observation and I'll do my best to answer it. Don't think for one minute that we don't all know that we are incredibly fortunate. We were born into privilege but we don't shove it up people's noses. We work hard, we think of others and we try to make things better. Remember, Jack that there is poverty in rural areas too – brutal, unrelenting poverty. Children go hungry here just as often as they do in the towns. It isn't the geography that starves them, it's the system.'

'The same system that guarantees your wealth and position,' said Jack.

'Absolutely,' said Beatrice, 'but what would you have us do, Jack? Sell up? We could do that but what would happen to all the estate workers? All the tenant farmers? All the history? This house? It all counts for something and we want to protect it but none of us believe in entitlement: not me, not Charles, not even little Mary.'

'And that's laudable,' said Jack. 'I was born poor. I was one of those starving children, I know those people like the back of my hand. I don't believe for one moment I could do what you are doing. But surely you see the risks.'

'What risks, Jack?'

'What other people see. What other people think.'

Charles nodded.

'Of course. And you're right. Bea and I talk about it often. You saw it, Jack. That's how we met. You saved me from being beaten up and that was only one of the risks. I can't hide, Jack and I positively refuse to turn my back.'

Jack was intrigued and he certainly wasn't ready to drop the subject. But that suited the Needhams down to the ground, politics was discussed at every opportunity and they were good at it. Over the next few days, Ford received a good work out for mind and body. They worked with the stockmen, the gardeners, the foresters and the gamekeepers – always together: adults, children, dogs.

'It's a simple philosophy, Jack. When they're young they love to play and do a few little jobs. As they get bigger, there is less play and more jobs. Before they know it, they love to work. It's a completely natural process. They're not forced into it – they love to be outside and doing things.'

Jack could see for himself that it worked as far as the family was concerned and it worked for the Adlington Hall staff, too. The cottages were well-maintained, wages were fair, they were free to borrow books from Charles's library.

'It's a matter of hypocrisy, you see Jack? How on earth can I stand up on my hind legs in the House of Commons of all places and spout on about welfare rights and socialism, if I don't practice what I preach?'

The theory was sound enough and the philanthropy was admirable – even though Charles would consider it to be entirely practical. The problem was, Charles Needham was practising Socialism with a safety net. It was an experiment and if it went wrong, he could reflect on the outcomes and come up with different conclusions. He had the luxury of choice. There weren't many people with sufficient resources to carry out such a project, and among his own class, Charles Needham was in a minority of one.

The next day was bright and almost cloudless, Needham decided it was the perfect day for a hike.

'Fancy it, Jack? Quick stroll up Simonside Ridge? I really feel like blowing away the cobwebs today – a good stretch of the legs will do us both good.'

Jack was kitted out with an old shirt and a pullover of Needham's and a stout pair of walking boots that Julian had outgrown. Needham had chosen a twelve-mile route.

'We don't want to overstretch ourselves, the goings not terribly good in some spots.'

Ford quickly learned that Needham could be a master of understatement. They were three miles in and just beginning to climb when Jack found himself up to his knees in mud.

'The drainage here is pretty poor. Watch you don't lose your boot.'

But there was no fear of that, Jack had been up to his neck in muck when he served in France and trudged for miles. In fact, during one single month, he'd advanced and retreated over twenty miles to the same location six times. As they moved to higher ground, the path became firmer but significantly steeper and they both began to blow a little. Eventually the land began to plateau and ahead of them was a rock face.

'It's a bit of a scramble to the top but the view will be worth it, mark my words.' He gave his backpack a solid thump.

'We'll dine closer to God, eh?'

'I'll be right behind you, you can count on it,' said Ford.

There were places where they had to go on all fours but after another forty minutes, Ford found himself at the top with a staggering view across Northumberland from the mining towns of the North Sea coast in the East; to the rugged Cheviots in the North, the luscious patchwork greens of Tynedale to the South and the forested pines that led to Cumberland in the West. They were fifteen hundred feet up and the temperature had dropped significantly. Because they were enjoying a dry spell in early Summer, all the wind managed to do was dry the sweat on their bodies. But Jack knew that this would be a very different place in Winter – unpredictable, dangerous and bloody cold.

They sat down on the bending heather with a few stern-faced, stiff-legged sheep for company and used a flat boulder as a table.

It was simple fare: sandwiches, apple tart, bottles of beer and a healthy portion of what Ford would later refer to as, 'Needham's Inquisition'.

The walk had been at Charles's suggestion. For the last four days, he'd welcomed Ford into his home, introduced him to his family, shared his plans for the estate and talked about his political objectives and ambitions. What he received in response was a quizzical look or a probing question – nothing hostile; no, nothing like that, just an uncritical cynicism. This made Needham wonder what it was that made Ford tick.

'You know Ford, out here the sheep outnumber the people by ten to one. That's because the people have all moved out – over there.'

He pointed to the coast and the sprawling, dark smudges of grey brick between the green of the land and the blue of the sea.

'They moved for money. Richer pickings.'

'I know that,' said Ford, 'I should do, my ancestors were part of it.'

'Do you think they did the right thing?'

'They did what men always do – go where the work is. Build a better life.'

'Did your ancestors find it then, Jack? This better life?'

Jack smiled at him.

'You know fine well that they didn't. They did all right at first,

I suppose. They must have done because they kept on coming. But the towns are big now – plenty of people. But in places like this there's just not enough to go around.

'So, what happens then?'

'They struggle.'

'Is that fair, do you think?' Charles threw Jack his best Inquisitor's stare.

'Fairness has got nowt to do with it, Charles. It's the way it is.'

'But not for you.'

'Not at the moment.'

'Hell, Jack – you're an enigmatic so and so.'

'I'll have to look that one up.'

'You know damn fine what it means. You're so secretive. What are you frightened of?'

Jack looked his friend in the eye and pointed at the remaining slice of apple tart.

'You see this? Imagine there are five people starving to death and there's only one piece of pie. Who gets to eat it? I'll tell you, the one who can lie and cheat and fight his way to the plate.'

'It's not that simple, Jack and you know it isn't.'

'It is the way I see it. What would you do with it?'

'If we were all starving to death?'

'Aye.'

'I'd give it to Bea and hope she got enough strength back to cook another pie because I'm damned sure I can't make one.'

Laughing, Ford cut the last slice into two with his penknife and they shared it before heading back down. The return trip was largely downhill – easier on the lungs but more treacherous for the joints. They made short work of the scramble down the crag and, once they'd passed the boggy stretch where they had to watch their footing, they strode out at a brisk rate. Needham considered what he'd learned about his friend. Ford was a conundrum. For a generous man, he gave precious little away. He looked on political theories like socialism with disdain, yet when he witnessed injustice, he could not help but act. He'd been a soldier, a warrior yet he was an individual of surprising gentility. He was a pragmatist, a loner, yet he was capable of loyalty beyond belief. Jack Ford, a man who wouldn't lift a finger but would risk his life. Needham had planned his inquisition in order to learn more about his new friend. The exercise had almost been a complete failure. Almost, because there was one thing about Jack Ford that he could be absolutely certain about. He could trust him.

They were still a mile from the Hall when Needham decided to put his faith in his judgment.

'I'm in trouble, Jack,' he said.

# CHAPTER 10

Julian had some more supplies to drop off at Auntie Maddie's on the way back to Gallowshield. It was one in the afternoon when they pulled up outside the kitchen door and Gertie, the cook, was perched on the back step with a pot of tea.

'Taking a breather?' asked Ford as he got out of the car.

'I'm fair puggled, bonny lad. Twenty-eight, we've had in the day and all the pots need doin'. I'm just having five minutes.'

Julian was filling the wheel barrow with freshly dug potatoes and even in her tired state, Gertie had her beady eye on him.

'Now just you make sure you empty them into the box young man. Last time you left the sack on the floor and I almost did myself a mischief trying to lift it.'

'Sorry Gertie.'

That lad never stopped smiling.

Ford offered Gertie a smoke and her eyes sparkled.

'Oh! Well I wouldn't normally but -.'

She wiped her hands on her pinny before drawing one from the packet.

Ford took his gold lighter from his pocket and it sparked into action. Gertie inhaled with relish.

'Is Miss Madeleine away then?' he asked.

'Why no, man. She's in the hall taking the lessons – glutton for punishment, that one.'

'Do you mind if I take a look?'

Ford made his way through the kitchen, past the tower of dirty plates and the buckets of used cutlery, to the door that lead to the hall.

He went through and stood at the back. Madeleine didn't pause for breath in her delivery but threw him a wave and a smile. They were doing a session on rhyming words and Maddie was writing them on the blackboard.

'What else can you think of? What else rhymes with "Coal". Remember – we're looking for endings of words that sound the same. Yes, Mr Whitfield?'

'Well, I was going to say 'Dole'.

She wrote it on the board.

'Very good. Thank you, Mr Whitfield. Any more?'

'Miss Madeleine, Miss Madeleine.'

A young woman tentatively put her hand up and spoke in forced whisper. There was barely enough oxygen in her breath to make herself heard. The sleeve of her dress slid back to reveal an arm that looked like twigs covered with calico.

'Come on then, Jenny – you give us one.'

How about, 'Soul?'

'Excellent.'

And up it went on the board and Jenny beamed between rib-stretching coughs.

Ford wondered how old she was. Nineteen? Twenty, maybe? It was hard to tell. The body was showing signs of long-term starvation and there was some severe breathing problem as well. Bronchitis, was it or pneumonia? Perhaps it was TB – an indiscriminate killer of those unlucky enough to be born poor.

Ford's eyes scanned the room. There were bairns without

shoes – feet dirty, blistered and cut; men without limbs – veterans of the war who'd joined up whole and come home broken; old women and men like Mr Whitfield – struggling on a pittance of a pension. Every student in the room wore clothes that were at least three sizes too big for them. And they all, at least, made the effort to try to appear interested and engaged. The Land Fit For Heroes was still some distance away.

'You've had a good turn-out – you must be pleased,' he said to Madeleine when the class took a break.

'Not really,' she said. 'We had to turn away over a hundred this morning. These are the lucky ones.'

Jack couldn't get the image of Jenny's face out of his head. She'd obviously been suffering for years and times in Gallowshield were going to get harder. With Lewis Bishop's mothballed and more yards due to follow suit, there would be many more like Jenny, more shoeless children, more misery, more hopeless poverty. When he boarded the train to London he was in no doubt why he kept on leaving the place.

The East Coast Main Line was like a tunnel between two worlds and the train was like a capsule rattling through it. You could switch off on the train and slowly re-set your mind in preparation for London life. It helped that half the stewards on board were Cockneys – the other half, Scotsmen. Ford reflected that Cockney waiting staff had that peculiar ability to offer service while maintaining just a hint of arrogance. The Scotsmen were just plain surly – the job was beneath them, they knew it and fervently believed the customers should know it, too.

He watched the hemline of the outskirts of Gallowshield drift away and he let out a deep breath. It was a relief to be on the move again – going to a place where he was largely unknown, where his past wouldn't matter and his present was whatever he wanted it to be. There were no two ways about it, Gallowshield made him feel guilty.

He dined in the restaurant car, ate steak and kidney pudding and shared a bottle of claret with a Cathedral Dean who boarded the train at Durham. London pulled people to it irresistibly - like a magnet. Whether you were successful or merely hopeful, London was where you needed to be. It wasn't that the streets were paved with gold - there was shocking poverty there too - but somehow it was spread more thinly, it was avoidable. Unlike Gallowshield and the dozens of towns like it north of Watford where it slapped you in the face and demanded your attention.

He arrived at The Connaught in time for tea which he enjoyed alone in his room. He ordered laundry service, ran himself a hot bath, lay on the bed, listened to the wireless and wondered to himself what the bloody hell he was doing there.

By the time he woke up he was hungry again but he'd missed dinner so it would be a roast beef sandwich from Room Service before he ventured out into the London night which never ceased to thrill. The deep chatter of the motor buses and the impatient beeping of the taxis, the heels on the stone steps of the underground stations, the sheer volume of people on the pavements all added to the sensation that something was happening somewhere and if you followed your nose, you might just find it. Jack knew exactly where to go but first he had to call in somewhere else, just in case. The Royal Oak had been such a disaster of a pub that, under normal circumstances, he wouldn't have even considered returning for a second visit. London had too many pleasant surprises available elsewhere. At least the pianist wasn't attempting Roses of Picardy tonight. He'd been unceremoniously dumped and replaced by a Pianola that was banging out The Sheik Of Araby. It was more rhythmic and melodic but it certainly wasn't music.

He sat quietly at a table in his dark blue lounge suit and disappeared into the shadows – observing what it was he came to see. The bar was full – well, it was near closing time in the heart of the West End – and the place was heaving with the flotsam and jetsam of human life. There were a few locals sat on stools monopolising the area immediately adjacent to the bar; small groups of theatre-goers not quite ready for their evening out to end; a couple of professional chaps in cheap suits by the door – salesmen probably – eyeing up the working girls who glanced and giggled and tried their best not to look bored out their skulls. But the majority of the clientele were visitors and sight-seers sampling some London life for the last couple of hours after supper before spending another day trudging for miles with a street map and a craned neck.

But the group of men he came to spy on were the only ones talking Russian. There were four of them huddled around a small table between the fire and the dart board drinking vodka. They were fairly loud and demonstrative by now but they had probably arrived in the early evening and talked in hushed tones until the spirit had taken effect. If Ford knew one thing about Russian men it was that they liked to drink and once they started, very little would stop them until either the money or the booze ran out. He also knew that they wouldn't put much effort into finding a particular watering hole. A good boozer for them would be the one that was nearest and the one that was open. The Royal Oak was a stone's throw from the 1917 Club and Ford's intuition had served him well yet again.

He glanced at the clock – two minutes to last orders. There was just time for one more. He ordered a whisky from the harassed looking barmaid who looked as though closing time couldn't come quickly enough. While Ford was waiting, one of the Russian men barged past him to get to the bar.

'Wodka!' he yelled at the barmaid.

'Hey steady on pal,' said Ford.

The Russian turned and stared at Ford – desperately trying to focus his gaze though the large quantities of liquor he had consumed. It was Igor Toblinski and he was very drunk. Although the stare remained concentrated and steady, the rest of his body assumed a gentle rhythmic sway.

'Wodka!' he demanded loudly.

'Wait your turn until I serve this gentleman,' said the barmaid before adding under her breath, 'Bleedin' foreigners – more trouble than they're worth.'

'Wodka!'

Igor was becoming insistent.

'It would be easier to serve him first, bonny lass, it's been at least three minutes since his last one.'

Igor swayed again and then staggered to the right crushing Ford's foot with his considerable bulk.

'How many this time?' asked the barmaid.

Igor put up four fingers then made a wild stretching gesture with his arms.

'Four doubles?'

He nodded.

Igor held on to the bar rail as she poured the drinks. His face was Bishop's purple and the sweat was dripping off him onto the marble counter top. He was breathing heavily and a peculiar gurgling sound emanated constantly from the back of his throat. Ford considered an imminent aneurysm was not unlikely.

When she returned with the drinks he flung his change on the bar and she counted it out so quickly that even Ford couldn't work out how much he'd been stung for.

Igor returned to his company listing like an Armada galleon but without spilling a drop of his precious cargo.

'I'll get yours now, sir. Whisky, wasn't it?'

'Thank you, yes, large one and something for yourself – shift's nearly over.'

'That's very decent of you, sir. Can I have a sherry?'

'You can have two.'

He stayed by the bar as the customers began to ease themselves away into the night. There were only about a dozen stragglers left – including the Russian contingent – when she started stacking the pint glasses and wiping down the bar top.

'I'll pour that sherry for myself now, if that's all right.'

'Be my guest,' said Ford. 'Tell me, the vodka drinking lot in the corner, are they regulars in here?'

'They've been around a couple of weeks, I'd say. They come in most nights about seven o'clock. Always last to go, though – drunken lot.'

'Funny bunch,' said Ford. 'They don't look like tourists and the sailors don't usually come this far up West.'

'Oh no, I don't think they're sailors. They're definitely foreign though. I can't understand a bleedin' word they say.'

Ford decided he'd gathered as much intelligence as was available.

He hadn't told her that he was coming so they both got quite a surprise. Rose Milne was pleased to see him of course, but he should have called and warned her. It was a shock, him turning up like that. For Jack the surprise laced with concern. How the Hell had she got so thin? He'd been gone only three weeks. This was ridiculous.

They were weirdly polite to each other for an hour or so while Rose did her 'Welcome To My Den Of Iniquity' routine with the punters, then Ford became impatient, took her hand and lead her out to her sentry post.

'I am glad you're back, you know. Really I am.'

'Me too,' he said. 'Can we go now?'

'No, we can't. I've got my job here.'

That wasn't the answer Ford was looking for.

'Surely you can take a night off. Lansing can cover for you this once. He disappears often enough – when the fancy takes him.'

She looked down at her shoes and felt uncomfortable. A night away from the Ham Bone Club sounded like a lifeline. It also sounded like a life-sentence. But she never asked for things. She was afraid Lansing wouldn't like it.

'It would be wrong to ask – he might have plans.'

'Bugger his plans,' said Ford. 'I'll talk to him.'

And he was gone before she could protest any further.

She just had time to light her cigarette before he reappeared carrying her coat and a broad grin.

'Turns out he was only too pleased to be of service. Your coat, Madam.'

She considered objecting on behalf of poor Lansing but Jack Ford had her firmly by the arm and steered her down the steps and out into Soho.

'Jack, I should tell you, I've got nothing in at home.'

'That's no problem,' he said. 'I know just the place. You don't mind a walk, do you?'

He took her through Piccadilly, down Bruton Street, across Berkeley Square and along Aldford Street. At first, she was stubbornly quiet. Unexpected happenings were like change of any kind – they were unsettling. But somehow the warmth of the walk and the closeness of the companion coerced her into a more relaxed frame of mind.

'How is Charlie?'

The first question signified a victory. She was meeting him on neutral ground in the shape of a mutual friend.

'He's well. A few days ago, we walked up a bloody great hill near his country house. We had a picnic on the top.'

He told her all about the hall and the family and Charlie's plans for the estate. He described Auntie Maddie and the work of Food For Thought. To top it all off he did an impersonation of Gertie, the cook, which made Rose laugh out loud.

'That's who you need,' he said. 'Gertie the cook – shall I ask Charles if I can bring her down for a few days. She'll have you fattened up in no time. Hot pots, pan haggerty, boiled mutton in broth, leek puddings – all good, home-cooked Gallowshield fare.'

'Stop! You're making me hungry. I'm not sure what any of it is but it sounds absolutely delicious.'

'And so it is bonny lass. And if there's work about, then you can afford it.'

He told her about Jenny then and all her classmates whom Gertie fed and Maddie taught. She listened with a pained look across her eyes. When he'd finished she said she didn't feel quite so hungry any more.

'The Jennies of this world are going to keep on starving whether you eat or not,' he said.

Even so, to cheer her up he told her about young Julian and the motor car that ate porridge for breakfast.

By the time they walked into Hyde Park she was snuggling into his jacket.

'Where are we going, anyway?' she asked.

'Ah well – I know this place. It's a cosy little café that stays open all night. The chef is cordon bleu. He creates superb dishes, magically blending exotic ingredients from land and sea.'

'Really? Around here?'

'Certainly, around here.'

'But we're in the middle of Hyde Park.'

'Indeed, we are Madam, and just around this corner a feast of epicurean delight awaits you.'

'Jack, are you sure?'

'Mais oui.'

They rounded the corner to the all-night coffee stall and Ford squeezed his way past the taxi-cab drivers and the Bobbies before re-emerging with two mugs, two sausages and two pickled eggs.

'There you are – what did I tell you? Fit for a Queen!'

When they got back to Kinnerton Street, Rose was almost asleep.

'You're exhausted. How on earth did you think you could work all night at that club?'

'I seem to manage all right once I'm there,' she said. 'There are ways of keeping going.'

'Ways provided by Lansing Bell, I suppose.'

'Don't be beastly about Lansing, Jack. He cares for me, you know. And when you were away, I don't know what I would have done without him.'

'Got some sleep for a start.'

She decided not to take her sleeping powders from the box in her bedside cabinet that night. She didn't like the way he looked at her when she poured them. Instead she used her spare box in the bathroom. If Jack had seen her he would have made a row and there was no sense in worrying him. The water in the glass began to fizz and pop. Funny that, he was a worrier and she would never have put a man like that down as an old fuss-pot. People were really odd, weren't they? Still, he'd come back to her and that meant a lot. Usually the men in her life just disappeared into thin air. If only he'd stop worrying about her, everything would be fine. Rose threw down the salty mixture – in another few minutes she'd be calm and then there would be blackness.

# CHAPTER 11

Keeping up the silent treatment had been far easier than Bella had thought it would be. It had been a bit strange for the first few days but after that she discovered she was actually getting pleasure from it. And it was a private pleasure which made it all the more deliciously mischievous. She looked at her face in the mirror before adding some more of the powder she'd bought at the chemist's. What a price? But the girl had said make-up would be the best thing for covering up the bruises. The swelling had gone down but the discolouration was still there – the angry reds and blues had been replaced by sickly-looking greens, yellows and browns. The black eye didn't hurt though, it was just a bit tender to the touch – but she wasn't letting on about that. Not to anyone.

Bill had tried of course – in his own way. But making apologies was never going to be his strong point. Too much pride.

The day she'd come back from Jessie's he'd looked up at her from that wheelchair and said he hadn't meant to hurt her – hadn't meant to knock her down. Hadn't meant it? He'd been knocking her down for years and it would have to stop. But she didn't say that to him. She only thought it. She hadn't said anything at all. That made him angry again but she knew he

135

was angry only at himself. Bella simply wouldn't react. Instead she'd hung up her hat and coat, put the kettle on and made him a corned beef and tomato sandwich.

'Anybody in?'

It was Tom. Apparently, he was the only member of the family she could bear to have near her. She loved them all, of course. But Tom was her first-born and the one who, gender aside, was most like his Mam. Odd that – for all the brains of the other two, it was Tom she felt closest to. Big, strong and steady. Kind, humble and gentle. Yet he was the poor bugger who'd been sent to prison for thievin' and brought shame on the family. Well that was according to Bill but Bella had seen through that eventually. How could stealing from rich folk to feed your dying wife be shameful? Utter nonsense. You do what you have to do – there's no shame in that.

'In here, pet.'

But it was Tom's wife, Dolly, who came in first.

'Mam!'

Dolly ran over to her and gave a great big cuddle.

'Hello, Dolly love – I wasn't expectin' to see you.'

Tom got his apology in. He was good at them.

'Sorry Mam but she made us tell her. She knew something was wrong and I wasn't going to lie.'

His mother held her daughter-in-law's face in both hands and smiled at her while she spoke to Tom.

'What are you apologising to me for? I never told you to keep it a secret.'

'No, you didn't. But Da said no-one was to know. But I didn't think it was right to shut Dolly out like that.'

'Certainly not. She's as much family as anybody else. Aren't you, pet?'

'I should hope so, too,' said Dolly. 'Does it hurt? Sit down – I'll have a good look.'

She looked closely at the mark and wiped a long, blonde curl away from her face. She was a bonny girl – lovely soft red lips, thick hair down to her shoulders and a smile that could warm a draughty room on a Winter's night.

Dolly clenched her teeth together and breathed in between them, furrowing her brow.

'Ee my word, he's caught you a right whack.'

'Yes. Yes, he did.' Bella remembered the thud at the back of her skull.

'He didn't mean it, Mam.'

'Oh, he meant it all right, Tom. You were there. You saw him. It was no accident. He swung his fist and clouted us to the floor. Of course, he meant it.'

'Well perhaps for that second he did. But he shouldn't have done it. And he regrets it now, you know.'

'I see. That's what it is. You've come to see if I'll make peace.'

'Well no but Jessie said -'

But she wouldn't let him finish.

'Jessie! What in God's name does she know about it? She was the one who thought I'd got this in a fist fight at the Blue Bell.'

'Well, you know you do like a drink, Mam.'

'Can you blame us? Putting up with this lot for thirty-five years? Would drive anyone to bloody drink.'

Dolly shot a glance at her husband which made it plain as speech that he was making things worse.

She adopted her most soothing tone and put her arms around Bella's shoulders.

'Nobody's blaming you now, Mam. You're all right and that's the main thing. I've been that worried. I thought I'd done something wrong when Tom was trying to keep me away.'

'You Dolly? Why no. You'll be wondering what sort of lunatic family you've married into.'

'All families have their ups and downs you know – look at me and Jack. We fought like cat and dog when we were married.'

'Oh aye? And did Jack ever belt you?'

Dolly looked at Tom and then back at Bella.

'No Mam. He didn't.'

'There then – we'll say no more about it.'

Dolly hadn't quite finished. She owed it to Tom to say something else.

'But he used to slice us in half that tongue of his. And words can be just as hurtful.'

But Bella had heard what she needed to hear. She wasn't interested in anything else.

Cissy Kelly was sat on her hunkers against the side wall of Seaton's shop. Her family had come over from Ireland sixty years earlier during the potato famine. They'd arrived in Britain with tens of thousands more to find work in the mines and on the roads and on the railways. More than a few had turned up in Gallowshield. The work wasn't as plentiful these days and with three boys, three girls and one on the way, Cissy's mother had been delighted when Dolly had offered the child board, lodgings and ten bob a week to work as a cleaner and learn how to be a shop assistant. And Cissy had matched up pretty well once she'd been de-loused and scrubbed to within an inch of her life. She wasn't great with figures and she had trouble writing the price tickets but the customers liked her. She was charming and funny and a good worker, too.

When Dolly and Tom came walking up the bank towards the Cobbett Street shop, they were more than a little surprised to find Cissy sobbing outside.

'Whatever's the matter, Cissy?' In a second Dolly was down

by her side, arm around her, cuddling.

But Cissy wouldn't look up, she kept her head down and her hands over her face and whatever noises she made between sobs were completely unintelligible.

Dolly tried again and even a third time but Cissy's breathing had gone into spasm and what with all the tears and the snots it was just impossible to get to the bottom of the trouble.

Dolly dragged her up on her feet. In full, open view, she looked as though Dolly should have saved herself the trouble of all the hot baths in front of the fire. Cissy attracted grime like a magnet. The soot from the wall had ground into her dress, her hands were black from the pavement and there were two rivers of silt running down from her eyes - most of which had been smeared across her cheeks as far as her ears.

'Right, young lady, here. Blow hard. Then count to ten.'

Cissy took the handkerchief and did exactly as she was told.

Tom and Dolly looked at each other and pulled a face at the unpleasantness of the noise.

'Have you counted to ten yet?'

Cissy nodded.

'Right. Take a deep breath and hold it.'

Cissy did.

When she got almost to bursting point and her little eyes darted from side to side in mounting alarm, Dolly decided to let her off the hook.

'Breathe out then.'

The breath came out in a great whoosh and Cissy doubled over again until normality was restored.

'Right,' said Dolly. 'I'll ask again. Whatever's the matter? Why aren't you minding the shop?'

Cissy's face started to crumple again but she thought better of it when Dolly brandished a firm forefinger and wagged it up and down.

'There's no need for more waterworks. Whatever it is, we'll sort it out.'

Cissy swallowed hard and did her best.

'It's Mr Seaton, Mrs Seaton.'

'Me Da?' said Tom.

'Is he all right?'

'Oh aye – he's all right.'

'Well what about him?' Dolly was getting impatient now.

'He's sacked us.'

'Sacked you? What for?'

'Thievin. But I haven't taken nowt. Honest.'

Dolly bent down to Cissy's level, gently got hold of her chin and turned the girl's head towards her own.

'Have you stolen anything from the shop, Cissy.'

'No Mrs, I haven't. I like being here, you know I do.'

Dolly looked at Tom.

'Your Dad must have made a mistake. I don't think she's done anything wrong.'

'Take her back to her Mam's for a bit. Try to get her cleaned up. I'll talk to him.'

Dolly did what we she could with the one corner of the hankie that was still clean. Tom went inside to find his father.

'Oh. It's you.'

Bill was at the far end of the counter, spectacles on and with a ledger on his lap.

'How did you get on with your Mam?'

'Never mind that. First things first – what's been going on with Cissy Kelly?'

'How do you know about that?'

'Me and Dolly found her around the corner when we got back. Terrible state she was in, breakin' her heart and her just a bit lass – fourteen-year-old!'

'I sacked her. I had no choice.'

Bill was dismissive and looked back at his figures. He didn't want to talk about Cissy Kelly.

'So I hear.'

'She's a thief. Has to be.'

'Oh, has to be does she? Did you see her take something?'

'No, I didn't but I didn't have to. Figures don't lie.'

'What figures?'

'These figures, Tom.' Bill brandished the ledger.

'Look, see here. This shop had never taken less than a hundred and forty pound a week. Right? Well there's been a steady drop over the last three weeks. Not much at first but this last week it took just over the hundred. What do you have to say about that?'

Tom went over to look at his father's neat, careful hand. The figures were formed so precisely it was if the very numbers on the page were priceless treasures.

'I say Cissy Kelly wouldn't know what forty pound looks like. She's never seen that much money in her life.'

'She's a thief Tom. She's probably squirrelling it away to that family of hers. The father's a shifty looking bugger – all those scars.'

'He's a road digger, Da. Those scars are tar burns from an accident.'

'Face facts man – it's theft. It can't be Dolly so it must be the lassie.'

Typical Bill. If it wasn't black it must be white. He'd always been a hard man – strict. He worked like Hell through the week, enjoyed the match and a few beers on a Saturday, and then there was hymn-singing at chapel on a Sunday. Bill Seaton had always been a taciturn type of man but he'd always managed to enjoy a laugh and a joke and a bit sing-song when he got the chance.

But since the accident there'd been a profound change. And it wasn't just his temper either – when a man's in constant pain you can expect him to be on a short fuse. Bill had turned into a proper miser. All he ever thought about was money. He didn't even bother with Chapel any more. He'd found a new God.

'Have you done a stock take?'

'How can I do a bloody stock take when I'm stuck in this damned thing, you idiot.' He banged on the arms of his wheelchair in frustration.

'I'm an idiot now, am I?'

'Push us home.'

'No Da. Not until you apologise.'

'What have I got to apologise for you impudent young devil?'

'That's your problem isn't it, you never know when you're in the wrong. Worse than that, you don't even know when you're hurting people.'

That played right into Bill's sweet spot.

'Hurting people? You don't know the meaning of the word. Look at me.'

Infuriated that Tom looked away, Bill took a deep breath and raised himself from his chair.

'Look at me!'

Tom waited until the echoes from his yells had receded. Then he said.

'I can see, you Da. You should be grateful. By rights you should have died in that rock fall. I was one of the ones who dug you out – remember? Sometimes I wonder why I bothered.'

It was only after four o'clock that Warrior Street Elementary reminded Arthur Ashton of his own school days. When the children were there and lessons were in full swing, the headmaster was viewed as a stranger – an alien authority who was to be reluctantly obeyed while at the same time suspected. Arthur was well aware that his position generated those feelings and they weren't restricted to the pupils. His staff were capable enough on the whole but they were never comfortable with him as their leader. For years Arthur had wondered what he could do to mould them, inspire them, create an energetic, dynamic team of educators that would devote themselves to the intellectual and physical improvement of their charges. In the end, he ran out of energy and meekly accepted what he was – an outsider. The only teacher who had ever come close to measuring up to his own exacting standards was Miss Seaton. She was the only one who had ever managed to lift the veil of drudgery that fell over every classroom. God knew it was hard. There was little or no help from most of the parents, resources were pitiful, pupils were often sick and malnourished. But Miss Seaton somehow managed to generate at least a spark of enthusiasm for learning – a miraculous feat, indeed. But then, much to the detriment of Warrior Street Elementary, and much to his own surprise, she had agreed to marry him. Shortly afterwards, the impending arrival of little Arthur meant that the new Mrs Ashton could no longer teach in the school and enthusiasm for learning was put away in the classroom cupboard behind the broken cricket stumps and the un-used rugby ball. When the school was full, the building was a foreign land to Arthur – he didn't even understand the language, most of the time. But when it was empty, he felt at ease. Perhaps it was the smell – that nostalgic mixture of chalk dust, mop heads and disinfectant. That and the sounds of the heavy wooden doors closing and reverberating down the corridors, their brass fittings clicking reassuringly into place. A school without children could be anywhere – even in Kent, where he grew up.

The young Ashton had thoroughly enjoyed his school days.

He loved the lessons, the games, the order, the rules – he even learned to love the puddings. His parents had told him exactly what it would be like and it was exactly as they had described. And as he worked his way through the well-trodden path of conjugations and declensions, he could feel himself gradually growing into adulthood, slowly evolving into a responsible and worthwhile person ready to take up whatever position of importance lay in store. That had been his station in life and he had accepted it unquestioningly and embraced it happily. And everyone he knew then had done the same: Tibbs had gone into banking, Fletcher was successful in commerce and Jenkins was at the Foreign Office. He had a letter from Jenkins just last week, postmarked Rangoon. Many of the others had died in the War, of course. They'd joined up straight from university. But none of them were his particular friends. Not like Tibbs, Fletcher and Jenkins.

Ashton walked into each classroom as he made his way through the building – the echo of footsteps made him feel as if he wasn't alone in the place. He closed the odd desk lid, straightened the odd map on the wall, replaced the odd blackboard rubber on its little shelf exactly in line with the modesty panel of the teacher's desk.

'Been working late again, Mr Ashton?'

Arthur smiled at the caretaker.

'You can lock up now, Mr Dunkley. It's all quiet.'

He strode out into the playground before stopping once more.

'Oh, and Mr Dunkley – the cupboard door in 3b has loose hinges. Will you see to it please? Thank you.'

Ashton closed the iron gate at the bottom of the yard and set off for home, his recollections had unsettled him. By the time he entered his house he had identified the feeling – it was guilt. He had been neglectful of his duty.

'Have you had a good day, Arthur?'

Jessie was going through the usual motions after receiving the ritualistic kiss on the forehead.

'Jessie, I have had an epiphany moment.'

He looked quite agitated and Jessie felt compelled to probe more deeply.

'Really? And all I've done today is washing and ironing. Tell me more.'

Arthur proceeded to apologise to his wife. He'd let her down badly and was ashamed. Despite Jessie's protestations that she had noticed nothing of the sort, he went on to explain that he had allowed himself to become too passive, to let the world slip by unchecked.

'In other words,' said Jessie, 'You don't feel like you've been enough of a boss.'

'Of course, I understand that you would always see it in those rather industrial terms,' he said. 'But I prefer to think of it as leadership. I have been given all the necessary skills, training and social conditioning. I have been lucky enough to receive every advantage on offer in this modern world and I regret to say that I have been wasting my time when I should have been far more vigorous.'

Jessie was now having an epiphany of her own. What on earth had happened to her husband?

'Really, Arthur? And are you talking about your professional life? Or our domestic circumstances?'

But Arthur was looking serious.

'I mean in everything. Obviously, what happens at school is my responsibility and the home is, to a large extent, your domain.'

'I see – the home is my domain.'

'Yes of course. But I feel there is so much I should be doing with the wider family.'

145

Jessie could hardly believe that she was having the conversation.

'The wider family? You must mean my wider family because what's left of yours is in Kent and we never see them.'

Arthur was unflinching.

'Yes. That's exactly what I do mean.'

Jessie was so flabbergasted she asked the wrong question.

'What exactly is wrong with my family that you feel the sudden need to lead them out of the wilderness.'

'Where would you like me to start?'

'Anywhere you like.'

And he did. First there was Tom, so desperate to find a cure for the woman he loved that he had turned to a life of crime. Then to add misery to his misfortune he took up with another man's wife and lured her away from her home.

'A terrible wrong, Jessie.'

Then there was Billy, a bright, talented young man who had excelled academically, no doubt about that. But he had allowed himself to get into debt at the expense of others – those nearest and dearest to him. His politics were dangerously Left Wing and he showed no signs of knuckling down to a responsible position. Furthermore, he was, instead, wasting his time working with people who would never be able to pay him properly for his services.

'Providing for them so freely, will only entrap the poor in their misery, I'm sure you see that.'

It was Mam and Dad's turn next.

'Since his accident your father has become an angry man. He has shown a flair for business and that's good. But he has become obsessed by it. He struck your mother, Jessie. He knocked her down. And he did that dreadful thing when his shops were doing well. Times are harder now and there is less money to spend. This will affect him even more severely than before.

As for your poor mother, I don't where to start.'

Even though she was stunned by the onslaught, Jessie managed to speak.

'Well for goodness sake, don't stop now.'

'Very well. After the fracas with your father she turned up here drunk as a lord. We had company here, Jessie – guests. Granted they weren't my sort of company – but they were still visitors to our home. I know that there is violence in some families and that is to some degree understandable when people don't know any better. But when we married I thought the Seatons were a fine, upstanding, hard-working, decent family. As things have turned out, I was wrong and I have done nothing to help. I truly am very sorry.'

Jessie was reeling now. Her husband had returned home and, like a surgeon, meticulously diagnosed everything that was wrong with everybody she loved.

'You missed someone out?'

'Who?'

'Me.'

'Jessie there is nothing wrong with you that some appropriate adjustment to your family circumstances couldn't cure.'

She had no idea what that meant.

'Well you've been through the faults of my nearest and dearest – what do you intend to do about it?'

Arthur stroked his forehead, deep in thought.

'I think I should begin with your father. He is the head of the family so if I can achieve some progress with him, perhaps the others will simply fall into line.'

Of course, thought Jessie, because that's exactly what Seatons do.

'When will this take place? If you are going to have a heart to heart with Dad, I think it's best that I'm not there.'

147

'He's coming over tonight with the shop accounts. No time like the present, I will begin at once. It's time he got to know the real Arthur Ashton.'

Good idea, thought Jessie. Then you will meet the real Bill Seaton and may God have mercy on your soul.

Billy could barely contain his joy.

'Your Arthur?'

Jessie was beginning to wish she hadn't told her bother.

'Yes, my Arthur. What's wrong with that?'

'Well come on sis, you have to admit it – it does have disaster written all over it.'

'Well I thought so too, at first. Then I thought he's got a point. Everything he said was true.'

'I don't think it matters one jot whether it's true or not – the minute your Arthur starts reading the Riot Act to Bill Seaton there'll be Hell to pay.'

'Well it can't get much worse, can it? Mam's sent you, me and Dad to Coventry and Dad's blowing his top every five minutes. Dear knows what it's like in the house when they're on their own.'

'Rather peaceful, I should think. Might make a nice change after all these years.'

He went to the bar and got himself another pint and a port and lemon for his sister.

'I might need another sub from you later. The prices in here are outrageous!'

Jessie wasn't impressed. She hadn't let on about Arthur's critique on the rest of the family.

'Drink less. It's cheaper,' she said.

Jessie dug in her hand-bag and pulled out the paper she had taken from Needham's coat.

'I want to talk to you about this.'

Billy's eyebrows immediately headed skyward.

'Have you still got that paper? What did you bring it here for?'

'I want to talk about it.'

Billy looked around but they were the only ones in the snug.

'I'm not sure a pub is a suitable place for this discussion. Why haven't you got rid of it?'

'How?'

'Burn it, sis. Destroy it. It's dangerous.'

'I'm not at all convinced it should be destroyed. Did you see the list?'

'What list?'

'The list of people they say they are going to keep under surveillance.'

Billy was starting to babble in his anxiety.

'I saw that there was a list but I didn't go through all the names.'

'Mikhail Bukanin's on that list.'

'Bukanin?'

'Yes. The same Bukanin who's coming here to speak: the man we're all going to listen to. Don't you see Billy, the Government is going to send someone to spy on him – spy on all of us, probably. That can't be right. They want to bring back internment as well. Lock people up. Whatever happened to free speech?'

'I don't know, Jessie. I'm no expert in this sort of thing but I do know that the Government – whoever it is – tends to win in this sort of battle.'

'Ramshackle Mac didn't win, did he? With that scandal over the Zinoviev letter.'

'Ramshackle Mac was hopeless but even if he'd been brilliant he would have been hung out to dry by the Press. Look sis, this is not our fight. We're not revolutionaries! Just burn the damned thing.'

'Sorry Billy but I'm not ready to do that – not yet.'

'Well for God's sake stop waving it about and put it away. It's not the latest edition of Titbits.'

She put it back in her handbag.

They walked home through the park.

'I'm not sure they'll be finished yet you know, Billy. It's still quite early.'

But Jessie needn't have concerned herself, as they turned into the avenue they saw Bill parked on the pavement outside Jessie's front gate wearing a face carved out of granite.

'Something tells me there'll be no more business conducted tonight,' said Billy.

'Come on, he'll be freezing stuck in that chair.'

They ran over to him.

'You two took your bloody time.'

Billy put the back of his hand against his father's cheek to check his temperature.

'We didn't know you were going to be out in the cold, did we?'

'What happened, Dad. How did you get out here? Where's Arthur?'

Her father glared at her.

'Your man's inside. And I'm out here because I pushed mesel' out. I wouldn't spend another minute in that house.'

'But why Dad, why?'

'I'll tell you why. I spent an hour listening to that man while he was lacin' into me. Angry. Greedy. Violent. An hour! And I never said a word, mark you – not one word. I just kept on agreeing with him and saying I was sorry.'

'So, what's the problem?'

'When he'd quite finished leatherin' me, I asked politely if he could see his way to lending us a few quid to cover the lease on the new shop until things pick up.'

'Oh dear,' said Jessie.

'You know what he said? To me?' Bill paused to take in more breath.

'He said it would do me good if I learned to cut my cloth. Did you hear that? Cut me cloth? I'll cut his bloody throat! Billy - push me home.'

Billy raised his hands in a helpless shrug and turned to push his father back to Coventry.

Jessie went inside to find Arthur listening to the wireless – a glass of sherry was perched on a side table next to his chair.

'Did you enjoy your evening?'

'Never mind my evening. We came back to find Dad sat outside in the cold. He could catch his death, Arthur.'

But her husband remained totally calm.

'I didn't throw him out, you know. It was his choice. In fact, it was his command – all I did was open the door for him.'

'Honestly Arthur, if that's your idea of a heart to heart, then you are terribly mistaken.'

He looked at her with barely disguised smugness.

'A heart to heart was your phrase, Jessie. I always intended to tell your father some home truths. It turns out he'd rather not face up to the truth, that's all.'

But Jessie saw more than that. She saw in Arthur the capacity to bully an older man - a crippled man. And, worse still, be self-righteous about it.

'But he's my father.'

'Yes, he is, but I don't see what difference that makes. He needed to be taught a lesson.'

'And you needed to be the teacher?'

He slowly and deliberately lifted the glass and took a gentle sip of his drink.

'I felt it my duty, yes.'

Arthur had always been a rather cold, stiff, formal individual but she had never known him to be vindictive. Jessie had always been sure that Arthur Ashton was a decent man underneath that awkwardness, a gentle man.

'He asked for money, too.'

'So I heard,' she said. 'And you wouldn't help him.'

'For his own good, Jessie. Surely you see that.'

'Explain?'

'That was all he wanted. He listened to everything that I said and simply nodded his agreement. There was no sincerity there at all, it was written all over his face. Then he asked me for financial assistance. I turned him down flat. This might come as a surprise to you and your family, Jessie, but I am not a fool.'

She listened to his account of the exchange with her father. It was exactly the same as Bill had described it himself.

'No Arthur. You're not a fool. I never thought you were, but I also never thought you could be a complete bastard.'

She stood behind his chair and put her hands on his shoulders.

'Jack Ford doesn't have a monopoly, you know.'

'No,' she said, 'Not any more, he doesn't.'

# CHAPTER 12

'When you told me you'd lost the document, you never said what it was about.'

'I can't tell you exactly, Jack. It was handed to me on strictly Privy Council terms – private and confidential, you understand.'

Mr Henderson spoke then.

'I think, if Mr Ford is going to be able to help us, we have to trust him, Charles. Perhaps you could outline the nature of the contents without revealing any of the confidential details.'

For the first time since they'd met, Ford could see that Needham was anxious.

He sought further reassurance.

'And that would be all right with you?'

Henderson's chin made circular chewing motions as he considered his response.

'None of this, Charles, is all right with me. But given the circumstances, I don't think we have a lot of choice.'

Ford had been asked to meet Charles Needham in the Central Lobby of the Palace of Westminster. His name was put on the list at reception and he was told that, when asked, he was to say that the purpose of the meeting was to discuss Government policy on road haulage.

Charles arrived to meet his friend from the direction of the Commons.

'It's all a bit tricky, Jack. I can only talk to you about this in the presence of the Chief Whip.'

Jack had been about to make a joke but one look at Needham's face told him that this was not the time.

When they arrived at meeting room 12b, Henderson was already inside.

'Good of you to come, Mr Ford. This is a delicate matter. What we say in this room must stay in this room. Do you understand.'

'I know what a secret is, Mr Henderson,' Said Ford, 'But as far as understanding goes, I don't have a clue what you're talking about.'

Henderson, a short, plump avuncular-looking man with an obvious capacity to turn nasty, nodded to Needham indicating that he should get on with it.

'Jack, you remember I told you I was in a spot of bother.'

'Yes. It was when we went for our walk up Simonside. You said you'd mislaid an important paper.'

'That's right. But at the time, I thought that it was probably in the London house or here, in the office.'

'You can't find it, can you?'

'I've hunted high and low. Eventually I had to tell the Chief Whip.'

He explained that the document was a briefing memo from the Cabinet Office detailing current Anglo-Soviet relations. It expressed the Conservative Government's concern about Russian espionage activity in India and Afghanistan and undercover efforts to stir up anti-Imperial feeling.

'The Bolsheviks aren't going to stop at Russia, Jack. It seems that they are trying to spread revolutionary fervour throughout the world – even here, at home. The Government is floating some rather radical proposals to prevent this from happening.'

I bet they are, thought Ford.

Needham continued.

'There is evidence that they do it through infiltration. They identify possible supporters in Trade Unions, the Left Wing of the Labour Party and through certain members of the Armed Forces. The Tories have decided it's time to start fighting back.'

'And how do they intend to do that?' asked Ford.

'Some of those proposals are extreme, to say the least: arrest without charge, internment, forced deportation of foreign nationals.'

Jack understood.

'What we had during the war?'

'That's right. The document also lists a large number of Russian citizens who are to be kept under surveillance when they are here in the United Kingdom.'

'It sounds like pretty heavy stuff.'

Needham looked as though he was carrying the weight of the world on his shoulders.

'The thing is, Mr Ford,' said Henderson. 'This document itself is just the Government's way of flying a kite. They draft a paper laying out some quite extreme solutions to a few problems. They are aware that they have little chance of getting them all passed into law. But this system allows them privately to take the temperature of senior members of the House – the Privy Councillors. It's a way of testing how far they can go.'

'Ask for tuppence, take a penny,' said Ford.

'I'm sorry?' said Henderson.

'Old negotiating ploy from my time in the Fitters Union,' said Ford. 'We were trying to up the hourly rate so we asked for tuppence, hoping they might settle for a penny an hour extra.'

'Exactly that,' said Henderson.

Needham stood up now and stared out of the window and across the London skyline.

'But if that document got into the hands of the Press or worse, the Russians themselves, it would cause us no end of embarrassment. We would be accused of either deliberately sabotaging the Government by making their plans known, or of helping them oppress our fellow Socialists. The Leader writers would have a field day.'

'It's not my job that I'm worried about, Jack. I think you know me well enough to believe that. It's the entire Labour movement. That forged letter from the Russian Foreign Secretary, Zinoviev, helped to bring down our first Labour Government. Another blow like that could be the end of us.'

Jack could see the seriousness of the situation but he was still confused.

'I understand your predicament, gentlemen – but what on earth has all this got to do with me?'

'Fair question,' said Henderson.

'When Charles first told me about this, er, mishap – we re-traced every meeting, every journey, every step he had taken between receiving the document and subsequently realising it had gone missing. Since then he has searched every location. We think it may have been lost or stolen during his visit to Gallowshield. He addressed a meeting there organised by the Labour Party and attended by many trade unionists.'

'Yes, he did,' said Jack. 'At the Memorial Hall. I was there.'

'You'll have read in the Press, Mr Ford, that the Tories believe that all Labour members and trade union supporters are bed-fellows of the Russian Communists.'

Jack smiled but Henderson wasn't finished.

'That is a lie and a smear. But...' There Henderson paused for effect.

'But there are a significant number of communist supporters and a few genuine agitators. Mischief makers, Mr Ford, who feel betrayed by the modern Labour Party and would go as far as to wound their own side to achieve their aims.'

'Et tu Brute,' said Ford.

'Quite.'

'Can you help us, Jack? Can you help me?' Needham was pleading now.

Ford shrugged. He honestly didn't know. There were a lot of people in the hall that night – Matt's free beer had seen to that. He knew almost every one of them and the majority wouldn't be able to spell 'Briefing Memo' never mind do any damage with it. That wasn't true of all of them, mind. A few of them were downright dangerous.

'We've contacted the hall and nothing was handed in,' said Charles.

'How do you even know you were in Gallowshield when you lost it?' asked Ford.

'On my last day in the House before recess, I received a letter from my brother. I put it in the inside pocket of my coat. On my way through Central Lobby, a messenger handed me the document. I put it in the inside pocket of my coat and made a mental note to put it in the safe when I got to Adlington. I next wore that coat to the meeting at Gallowshield. A week later when I checked the safe, I found the letter from my brother.'

'And no briefing memo.'

'That's right. I'd put the wrong envelope in the safe.'

'I can make a few calls – just low key - asking if anybody's heard anything.'

'Are you sure you can trust these people, Mr Ford? You were a union man, you know these hardliners.'

'I was Mr Henderson and I do. There's only one feller I can

really trust. He still lives and works up there. If Matt Headley knows anything, he'll tell me. He was my corporal during the war and he succeeded me at the Fitters Union. He's a full-time official.'

Henderson was writing Matt's name down. Jack had the feeling that if Matt turned out not to be quite so trustworthy, Henderson would get a sudden urge to seek retribution.

'I appreciate it,' said Needham. 'I remember Matt – he seemed a good sort. And thanks for coming in.'

'Don't mention it. First time in the Houses of Parliament as a matter of fact.'

'Is that so, Ford? You look and sound as though you were made for the place,' Henderson had reverted to cuddly Chief Whip.

'Come along, we'll have a quick one in the Stranger's Bar before you go. Outside of these meeting rooms it's the only other place where any real business gets done.'

Jack walked back to Kinnerton Street though St James's and up Constitution Hill. He liked to go on foot in London, it allowed him the time to fully appreciate the self-importance of the place and its people. Gallowshield just wasn't like that. Even during the good times, it couldn't quite manage to shake off the shame of the bad times. He saw a nanny and her two charges: a baby in a pram and a toddler pounding relentlessly at the shiny knob on his spinning top. Even the children had it – that sense of ownership, that feeling that the world belonged to them. It wasn't merely a question of money either, the poorer ones had it, too – like the young lad there next to Eros, the shoe-shine boy. Even he had an obvious gleam in his eye. It was the glimmer of hope; the whiff of possibility - even though you had nowt – the gut feeling that good times were just around the corner. Gallowshield was never like that. Gallowshield was the kind of town where good things had only happened in the past and that perspective gave the present a sickly hue. All the future held was fear.

The memories of his hometown led him to recalling that night at the Memorial Hall when Charles Needham had delivered his speech to the faithful. There was a good chance that somebody there that night had not been as faithful as they should. He went through the faces in his mind's eye – all the usual suspects, like a rogues' gallery. Needham's coat had been hung up in the office which was next to the toilets. Once the bar was open and the speeches had started, anyone could have slipped in there unnoticed – all eyes had been on the platform. Ford's preferred option for Chief Rogue was Les Mallow but even Jack had to admit that he couldn't see Les rifling through another man's coat pockets on the off-chance he might dig up some dirt. Anyway, if Les had got his hands on it, the document would have been all over the front page of the Daily Mirror faster than you could say World Exclusive. None of the other members of the group gathered by the bar that night were serious candidates, either. He knew each of them well and Ford didn't believe for a moment that either Billy, Matt or Jessie would ever dream of doing such a thing.

No, it had to be one of the many others in the hall that night – and, God knew, there were plenty to choose from. But was anybody desperate enough or fanatical enough for this? Ford still had his doubts. He'd think about it over lunch. He was wondering whether he could persuade Rose to get ready and join him as he ran up the stairs to her flat and let himself in with key she'd given him.

'Rose, I'm back – are you up?'

He looked into the bedroom. The covers were thrown back and there was no sign of her. The kitchen was empty and there

159

was no note on the little table.

'Rose!'

Still no reply. He stood and listened. He could hear water running.

Ford tried the bathroom door but it was locked. When he stepped back, he stumbled as his shoe slid on the surface of the hall carpet. He glanced down – the carpet was soaking wet and water was seeping out from underneath the bathroom door.

'Rose – are you in there?'

He banged on a door panel and rattled the handle but still there was no response.

Suddenly, Ford's mind conjured up images of Rose Milne floating dead in the water; of bleeding soldiers drowning in mud; women screaming, men crying. His imagination was a kaleidoscope of those fears locked in his memory. But even as these images featured scarily in his thoughts, Ford's actions were swift and purposeful.

He barged the door with his shoulder but it was heavy and well-made and he couldn't get nearly enough purchase in the narrow hall to shift it and still the water was spilling out onto the carpet. Ford ran into the lounge and picked up two small drinks tables and positioned them in front of the wall opposite the bathroom door. Standing between them and raising himself up on his palms, Ford could get enough swing to aim two-footed kicks at the door panel nearest the lock.

After four kicks, Ford was sweating and his shoulders and arms were aching with the exertion. After the next kick, there was a crack and he could clearly see a split in the wood. At the following kick, the panel gave way and Ford fell to the floor – cracking his head on one of the tables.

He was still seeing stars as he dragged himself to his feet, put his hand through the hole in the panel and unbolted the door.

The bathroom was full of steam and he struggled to make his way to the tap end to turn them off. He opened a window and could just about make out the figure in the water. And the water was pastel pink.

Jack grabbed Rose under the armpits. She was a dead weight and he struggled to stay on his feet as his leather shoes held no traction on the soaking floor tiles. He gathered himself for an enormous effort and finally managed to get her head and upper body over the side of the bath and gravity did the rest. With the momentum generated, the body slid out of the bath across the floor and Ford found himself sat back in the hallway once more, with a wet and unresponsive Rose Milne on his lap. Her head lolled forward onto her chest and blood continued to pour from her nose down the rest of her body and onto the sodden floor.

Ford was panting heavily now and it took him a moment to straighten her out, kneel beside her and see if she was breathing. He thought he could feel something on the back of his hand and he turned her onto her side. As he did so, the blood that had collected in her throat, slipped out in an ugly crimson slick. It must have dislodged something because a gurgling sound came from deep inside her and little bubbles of blood and mucus appeared between her lips. Then she began to cough and spit the sticky red goo from the side of her mouth.

But still she wasn't awake and no amount of cheek slapping would revive her. Ford grabbed a pillow and blanket from the bedroom, propped her up and covered her, then ran to the phone box at the end of the street to call a doctor.

'She told me she's been suffering from a nervous disposition for some time. I understand melancholia has been diagnosed.'

The doctor looked about fifteen years old and Ford found it difficult to take him seriously. Then he remembered Billy Seaton, another young man who looked no older than a teenage youth but still, he was a fully qualified and perfectly competent practitioner. Ford didn't take Seaton seriously, either.

'Yes. I think it began some years ago after her mother died.'

'Are you her husband?'

Ford shook his head.

'I'm a friend.'

'Is there a close relative I can talk to?'

The doctor clearly was unsure of Ford's status with regard to his patient.

Ford wanted to shove his status up his backside.

'Listen doctor, I'm a very close friend. She has no other blood relatives that I know of. So if you don't mind, tell me how she is?'

The words were polite enough but the manner in which they were delivered were at best insistent and at worst threatening. The young man was in no way prepared to refuse Ford's request.

'No harm in telling you what she told me, I suppose.'

Rose had been having trouble sleeping – not unusual in people who regularly work during the night - so she'd taken some sleeping powders when she'd got home. She slept for a few hours but when she went to take her bath, the medication was obviously still active in her system. The warm bathwater had made her drowsy again and she must have nodded off before turning the taps off.

'Oh really,' said Ford – not believing a word of it.

'What about all the blood?'

'Ah!' said the young doctor as if to say, I wondered about that, too.

'The blood had me baffled at first. But turns out it was only a nose bleed. Perfectly common in children and young adults – especially women.'

'A nose bleed? Caused by what?'

162

'We don't always know the cause, Mr Ford. But in this case, it's irrelevant because the nose has stopped bleeding. And all her vital signs are good. Heart and lungs are operating normally, blood pressure is a little low but steady, body temperature is fine.'

He offered a smug smile but Ford wasn't even close to being satisfied.

'I came home to find her unconscious in the bath with blood pouring from her face. Are you saying there is nothing to worry about?'

But the doctor wore the confidence of youth with an easy condescension.

'I'm saying that your arrival was extremely timely. If Miss Milne had slid down the bath and under the water, we might possibly have been dealing with something far more serious. As it is, we have a young lady with a nose bleed who fell asleep in the bath. Don't concern yourself about the appearance of the blood. When you've seen as much of it as I have, you soon learn that a little goes a long way.'

'Does it really?' Ford couldn't be bothered even to add sufficient sarcasm to his tone.

'Oh yes, Mr Ford – you'd be surprised. I'm fairly satisfied that Miss Milne is not really ill at all – just a little run down. Of course, the nose bleed won't have helped so she should take it easy for a few days and rest as much as possible. I've also recommended a change to her sleeping medication – which is a little old fashioned now.

'We now have a faster acting barbiturate - it's called Neonal and it should stop any delayed reaction like the one Miss Milne experienced today.'

'More medication?'

'It's the inevitable progress of science, Mr Ford. There are wonderful new drugs coming on to the market every month –

each more potent and efficacious than the last.'

'Well thank you, doctor. Send your bill to this address and I'll get around to it.'

As the front door closed behind the man, Ford was already pouring himself a drink. He was exhausted and he was angry.

There was a tap on the front door.

'Anyone at home? Rose, darling? Are you decent?'

The jovial tones of Lansing Bell served only to add to Ford's discontent.

He poked his head out of the kitchen and gestured to Bell to enter.

'Come through to the kitchen. Rose is in bed. She isn't well.'

'Whatever is the matter? She was in fine form, last night. Absolutely tip top!'

'Really? Well according to the doctor, she fell asleep in the bath and suffered a nose bleed.'

'Oh.' Bell didn't like Ford. He was rather frightening. Not being sure exactly what to say, he tried some middle ground.

'That doesn't sound too bad, does it? I'm sure she'll be right as rain after a little rest.'

'Like I said – that's what the doctor thinks. It's not what I think.'

'And what's that?' Bell had the strangest feeling that jack's opinion was not going to be particularly pleasant. He poured himself a drink but his hand was already shaking.

'I think you fill her so full of chemicals that she doesn't know whether she's coming or going. One minute she's euphoric, the next she's suicidal. When I arrived here this morning she wasn't asleep in the bath, she was unconscious. If I hadn't managed to break down the door, she could have died. Do you understand?'

Lansing looked out into the hall and what was left of the door with the panel kicked out.

He took a large swig of his drink and tried to remain calm.

'I try to help Rose. Ask her yourself. What I give her, you could have bought from any pharmacy before the war. It's just a tonic, a pick-me-up. That's all.'

That much was true and Ford knew it. He'd known officers take coca in the trenches – either in liquid or powdered form. And once the Yanks joined in 1917, it became commonplace – there was even a wine made from it.

'Even so. I want you to stop. Give her a chance to get everything out of her system.'

Lansing started to panic then.

'Stop? But how will she cope without the little lifts? She'll never manage to work? It's what keeps her going. What about the Ham Bone?'

Ford raised his voice.

'I don't care about the Ham Bone, Lansing. I care about Rose.'

'No Jack. I don't think you do.'

It was Rose's voice and she appeared at the kitchen door in a clean silk robe to cover a clean pair of silk pyjamas.

'Darling!' Lansing went over to kiss her cheek.

'You look fine. See Jack, all that worrying for nothing. She is good as new. What did I tell you?'

Ford looked at her. She was standing all right. Her face was made up and her hair was brushed. But there was an empty look about her, her cheeks were sunken and her eyes were glassy – pupils the size of golf balls.

'I am fine. It's sweet of you to worry about me Jack, but I won't have you controlling me. I don't need that.'

As she spoke, her nose began to drip. Not blood this time.

'I don't want to control you, bonny lass. I just want you to be well. Say the word and I'll bugger off.'

She sniffed.

'We all need something Jack. Look at you, you drink like a fish. I need my medicine. I'm grateful for what you've done but I think you'd better go now.'

Ford walked towards her, took the door key from his pocket and placed it in her hand.

'Just so you know,' he said, 'This is why they all leave.'

He felt whole enough as he walked vaguely in the direction of The Connaught. His suit was still a bit damp from the bathroom incident but he was in no hurry. There was still a bit of adrenalin buzz: first from the rescue, then from the conversation with the doctor, Lansing had added a dash more and finally, Rose, herself, had put the tin lid on it. To make matters worse, he'd left without finishing his drink.

'Look at you, you drink like a fish.'

He heard her words again as he slipped into a pub.

Yes, he thought. I do drink like a fish.

The pub was deserted – only fifteen minutes before closing time. But Ford liked it that way. He took his glass deep inside, away from the doors and windows into the shadowy places where conversations with himself were always re-assuring and the spirit always reviving. All pubs had them. He considered for a moment and concluded that he felt quite at ease with himself. Rose had been a thoroughly enjoyable interlude but an interlude nevertheless. She could never have been a long-term investment. She had taught him some things and he had done the same. It was a fair exchange and it was better to have parted on those terms. Ford congratulated himself on being able to push Rose just hard enough for her to believe that she had contrived the ending. He liked her well enough and watching her misunderstand her own pain made him uncomfortable. He knew perfectly well that she was on thin ice but there was little point in rescuing people who didn't want to be saved – he didn't have the patience or the goodness for that. Anyway, it only caused resentment in the end. Far better to cut the ties before they became significant and then have the freedom to work alone. Ford was a hunter, a predator – he wasn't designed to carry passengers.

# CHAPTER 13

When the clouds parted, the moonlight cast a blue wash over the yard. There was a cat somewhere over yonder. Maybe it was Mrs Poskett's tabby. That cat had always been a charmless beast – even when it was a kitten. Bella took a drag on the cigarette she'd stored in her pinny pocket and looked up at the moon. It was big tonight, close enough to appear as if it was just out of reach. Bella offered herself the consolation of a sardonic grunt. That was the story of her entire life: just out of reach. Her eyes were getting used to the gloom now and familiar things began to emerge from the shadows: the old bogey that Bill had built for Tom (wheel-less now), old pit boots with their soles hanging off in a pathetic, permanent smile, chains and lengths of old wood, broken poss sticks and rusting tools collecting webs and dust in the lean-to by the house. Lots of stuff – worthless stuff – tossed into the yard because no-one could be bothered to get rid of it altogether. And, you never knew, there might be a day when something might come in handy. It never did.

Bella spat a stray strand of tobacco out from between her teeth and then studiously brushed it off her knee and onto the ground. It could be worse, she thought, at least it's not raining tonight. It was cold, though – too cold to be out in her nightie. She pulled her coat further around her shoulders and pressed herself further into its lining, trying to avoid the coarse woollen outer which scratched annoyingly at her face. She reached down and slid a hand inside her shoe. Her feet were freezing and she hadn't even noticed. (Bella hadn't even thought to put her socks on – well that was her own damned fault.) She stamped her feet up and down to get the circulation going and gave thanks for the sheltered spot by the shed door which she'd chosen specially to position the crackett. With the shed on one side and the wall at her back, there was protection from the wind. You needed that – even in late summer. There was always wind in Gallowshield poking and biting at you, driving you mad. And you could hear it much more clearly at night, making the trees creak and the rooves rattle. She wondered why that was: why night-time sounded so different from the day. And suddenly she knew, it wasn't that night-time sounded different, it was because the day sounded different. Something was always there through the day that was missing after dark. She was so pleased with herself, she actually said it out loud.

'The seagulls have gone to bed.'

Their constant clatter had rendered them almost inaudible for every day of her life. Moaning, warning, greeting, gossiping, bickering – it was an incessant accompaniment to life on the north-east coast. But when it went away, the world sounded different. Tonight, in the shadows and the inky stillness, it was as if Bella was somewhere else, far away – the web-covered remnants in the yard mere mementoes of a time gone by. She rubbed her hands together, the skin dry and rough like crepe paper.

Then there was the sound of flushing and a familiar announcement.

'Bella! I'm done.'

Three little words that meant her time had definitely not gone by. She was here and this was now and Bill was ready to be lifted off the netty.

They had the manoeuvrings off to a fine art. He twisted himself around ninety degrees while she pushed the wheelchair in and swung it sideways. One side bar was dropped and he had sufficient strength left in his arms to lever himself up and over for the six inches necessary to shift his body from one throne to the next.

In order to propel him up the yard, Bella needed to have her arms fully outstretched and to lean forward with all her weight and push from her hips and her knees. It wasn't far but she was blowing hard by the time she tilted him over the step of the back door and into the scullery.

She knew the drill so well now, she pushed him on three feet then turned him and backed up to the three steps that led into the kitchen. She dropped her hands and Bill's weight slid back. Pull, step and heave, pull, step and heave, pull, step and heave. Bella always took a breather at the top of those steps. She perched on the fat arm of the old sofa, tiny beads of sweat tingled on her forehead and her aching arms felt light, like feathers blowing in the wind. Even though she performed the task half a dozen times a day, the sheer exertion of shifting her husband's weight almost vertically always left her drained.

'Look at you, Bella' said Bill. 'You're bloody knackered!'

She glared at him as if to say, of course I'm bloody knackered and it's you who has made me this way. But still she didn't speak.

She got up to re-join the struggle with the wheelchair but Bill raised his hand to stop her.

'All right. You won't speak to me and I can't say I blame you. That's the way you want it and I understand.'

She paused for a moment. This ritual of Bill's nightly visits down the yard had been going on for weeks in complete silence.

'Will you listen to me if I speak?'

She pushed him to the table and lit the lamps.

'There's bottles in the cupboard. Fetch two glasses an' all.'

Bella hadn't had a drink since the disastrous day that had ended in Hell but there was gin and there was whisky - apparently there were going to be words, too. Well, it was about time.

Bill spoke and Bella listened. Eventually, she asked a question and he spoke some more. As they talked the sun came up and after more talking, Bill had to be pushed down the yard again. In the end, they reached an agreement. They were too tired to do anything else.

Jack didn't want to tell Matt about Needham's troubles on the telephone – it was too risky – and the tale was too long and complicated for a telegram, so he decided to put it all down in a letter. When the envelope dropped on the door mat in Lavender Avenue, Sarah viewed it with suspicion. By the time Matt came down to breakfast, it was resting against the tea pot.

'Somebody's got nice stationery.'

Matt put his glasses on to look at the handwriting.

'It's from Jack. That'll be posh hotel stationery, knowing him. I wonder what he wants? Never was one for letter-writing.'

He put it back against the tea pot.

'Well it must be important, it's marked private and confidential. Aren't you going to open it?'

He could see she was desperate to know what it said but being married to Sarah didn't offer Matt the opportunity for many little victories. In the strategic conflict of his marriage, he knew for certain he would never be able to win the war and that he would undoubtedly come second in almost every battle. But this was a skirmish and here was a chance to frustrate the enemy.

He couldn't resist it.

'I'll look at it in the office, pet. I know you don't like me reading at the table.'

She shuffled her bottom in her seat, arched her back and crossed her arms.

'Not when it's newspapers, no. But this is different. It's a letter.'

But Matt was unmoved and apparently concentrating on buttering his toast with unnecessarily measured strokes.

'I can see what it is, pet. I'm sure it can wait until I'm at work.'

Sarah was steaming. But there was nothing she could do. Matt had said so himself, Jack was not a regular correspondent, so whatever was in that letter must be important. She tried one last attempt.

'If you read it now you've just got time to write back. I can pop it in the post box on my way to Ethel's. I've got a stamp.'

But Matt was in a rich vein of form this morning.

'No need. We've got one of those new franking machines in the office and the postman collects our mail every afternoon at four o'clock – never misses.'

To add insult to injury, Matt peppered Sarah's clean tablecloth with toast crumbs as he spoke.

Defeated, she rose from the table to put on her hat and coat and delivered her final salvo.

'Seeing as I'm surplus to requirements, I might as well go and catch my bus. I've a lot to do today. And I want you home in good time tonight, Matt Headley. That garden shed needs a coat of creosote before Autumn sets in. So, don't go disappearing off to the Blue Bell on the way home.'

Dear God, thought Matt, she must be miffed about that letter if she's dredged up the garden shed. That's just spiteful.

He'd already decided to save Jack's letter until later in the day. There was always a point when he needed something to take his mind off the misery that filled his mornings. It had been like this for weeks now, a constant queue of members at his door all making applications for the hardship fund. They never came alone either. If he was lucky they just brought the wife, but sometimes they felt it necessary to have the entire family in tow just to prove that little Tommy definitely had impetigo and that Mildred's cough was developing into galloping pneumonia. Sometimes he thought that the union office was turning more and more like Billy Seaton's surgery every day.

The sad thing was that the hardship fund was so low that it, too, was suffering from malnutrition. Work on the river was at a standstill and hardly any skilled men were in work. Most of his members were on quarter subs because they were unemployed and the rest were so far in arrears that they wouldn't qualify for any help even if assistance was available.

All Matt could do with the most urgent cases was point them in the direction of his friend's makeshift surgery but the situation facing Dr Billy Seaton was even more grave.

The free clinic which he ran with the help of a local Church of England priest, was housed in a disused warehouse. In the years immediately following the war, there was plenty of work along the Tyne but that didn't stop killer diseases like tuberculosis and influenza carving great chunks out of the local population. The flu epidemic had just started to ease when Billy agreed to volunteer there after qualification. But it was more than amply replaced by the diseases of poverty and poor hygiene the moment the local economy began to fail. TB and pneumonia were commonplace, as were scarlet fever, rubella, diabetes and polio. Gallowshield was on its knees yet again.

Mina Tubbs, his secretary, came in with Matt's tea.

'Sir Horatio's office has been on the telephone, Mr Headley. He wants to know if you'd be good enough to meet him this evening for drinks.'

Despite his best efforts, Matt had been unable to secure a meeting with Manners since the Yard gates were locked up tight.

'Lewis Bishops gone into the bar business, has it?'

'No Mr Headley, the message was that you were to meet him in the lounge bar of the Royal Saracen Hotel at half past six.'

'I see. Ring her back and tell her I'll be there.'

The mere mention of the name 'Manners' made Matt think of Jack and that in turn reminded him of his friend's letter.

'Hold the queue for twenty minutes, can you Miss Tubbs? Just while I get my tea.'

As soon as she'd left the office he opened the letter and sat back in the chair to read. When he'd finished he read it again and then a third time, to make sure he'd absolutely understood.

He scribbled a note on his pad.

It said: 'Miss Tubbs, please send a telegram to Mr J Ford c/o The Connaught Hotel, Mayfair, London. The message is as follows: Heard nothing this end. Will keep eyes peeled. Matt.'

Then he followed Jack's instructions. He tore the letter into sixteen pieces, put them in the metal waste paper bin and put a match to them.

'Good evening, Councillor Headley.' The concierge knew Matt well, enough – a sure sign of the distance Matt had come since the war. A regular at the Royal Saracen? Ten years ago, even the thought of that would have been laughable. But not now. Riding shotgun for Jack Ford had had its advantages and Matt had risen from the dole queue to full time assistant when Jack was regional Secretary of the Fitters' Union. Then when Jack had left, he'd inherited the top job and that's when he'd struck gold in the shapely form of Sarah Lytton. She'd been the one who'd encouraged him to run for the council and subsequently persuaded the Lady Mayoress to bully her husband into proposing

Matt for the Policy and Resources Committee.

'I'll never get on that,' he'd said. 'You've got to be elected three times to make P and R. You're wasting your time, Sarah.'

But he hadn't counted on Sarah's innate ruthlessness and the fact that the Lady Mayoress had gone to school with his wife.

'I had no idea the old school tie held so much sway in Gallowshield,' he'd said when he heard the news of his appointment.

'It doesn't,' she'd said. 'But Mrs Atkinson is keen on chapel and she doesn't like it known that her parents were living over the brush when she was born.'

The P and R Committee was heavy on paperwork – but Sarah had helped him with that, too – and Matt had soon learned that it wasn't the 'Policy' bit that made the committee important, it was the 'Resources'. Every job that the council was asked to do, every penny it was asked to spend went through P and R and that made its members powerful people. And it was generally believed that that power could be influenced by things like dinner dances at the Royal Saracen Hotel.

But whatever power was wielded by council, it cowered under the shadow of the mighty Lewis Bishops and the man at its helm was waiting for him.

'Good of you to come, Headley. What will you have?'

Matt desperately wanted a pint.

'I'll take a whisky and soda, Sir Horatio – thank you.'

Manners was on him in a flash.

'Ford's not here, you know. You can have a pint of beer if you'd like one.'

'No, no. Whisky's my drink, these days.'

Ten seconds in to the conversation and the old goat already had Matt on the back foot.

But the advantage of whisky was that it was fast acting –

especially when you weren't used to it and Matt soon got up the courage to get straight to the point. They both knew that times were hard and men were workless. There was no point in painting pictures.

'Why did you ask to see me? Has there been a change?'

It had been only a faint hope and Matt wasn't at all surprised when Sir Hory slowly shook his head.

'No change. Lewis Bishops will stay closed until trading conditions improve – and that doesn't look like being any time soon, I'm afraid.'

'I see. So, what's this then? A catch-up for old times' sake?'

'Not exactly, no.'

Manners looked at his old adversary. The problem was that Headley wasn't Ford. With Ford this would have been so easy. Outline the deal, discuss the terms, decide the rake-off, proceed accordingly. But Headley was different. He was careful, cautious. He knew he lacked brain power so he wanted to check things, seek reassurance, cover himself.

'Can I trust you, Mr Headley?'

Matt took another swig.

'You can trust me to be honest.'

'That's not exactly what I asked.'

'I know.'

Matt was playing his hand well and Manners was impressed. The potential deal he wanted to make wasn't worth all that much but it was all that he could drum up in the present climate. And for Manners, a life without business was like a crystal glass without Scotch – an empty vessel.

'We need to keep this private at the moment, Headley, because nothing is signed. Nothing will be signed unless I have your agreement that I can proceed without union interference.'

Matt was suddenly very interested indeed.

'Jobs?'

Manners nodded.

'Some. Not many. No what you're used to. Maybe a hundred, hundred and fifty.'

'On the Tyne?'

'For the most part.'

'At Lewis Bishops?'

Rather than try to explain the situation by responding to Matt's questions one at a time, Manners decided to give a fuller description of his idea.

'There is a very slim chance that I might be able to put together a deal whereby a new company rents some space from Lewis Bishop to do some prefabrication work.'

'What's that?'

Manners explained that due to a shortage of highly skilled labour, companies abroad were finding it difficult to complete orders for small vessels with high specifications. He had come up with a proposal to build parts of those vessels on the Tyne and have those components shipped abroad for final assembly.

Headley listened carefully.

'So we wouldn't be building the whole thing?'

'That's right,' said Manners, 'final assembly would take place elsewhere.'

'We wouldn't be shipbuilders though, would we? We'd be making bits.'

Manners could see the idea had come as something of a shock.

'We'd be making the best bits,' he said. 'Let's have some more drinks.'

During the next half-hour, the yard chairman gave the union man a harsh lesson in economics. Britain might make some of the best ships in the world – although, sentimentality aside, that was open to argument – but that was irrelevant when they were too expensive.

'No-one can afford to buy them, Mr Headley.'

'But during the war, we couldn't build them fast enough.'

'That was because the German navy kept blowing them up.'

But now the war was over, world trade was flat and sterling was over-valued – British ships were simply too expensive.

Matt wished Jack was there, or Sarah. They were so much better at this.

'But the lads have all taken pay cuts. We agreed them – you and I.'

'Yes, we did, Mr Headley. But that was never going to be enough – not in the longer term. That's why the yard had to be moth-balled. The only way I can find to get a few of your members back to work is by doing the work our competitors can't do – the precision work.'

'And why can't other countries do that?'

'Because they haven't got enough skilled men.'

'Why not?'

'Because they were all killed fighting for Kaiser Bill.'

Manners had very gently led Matt to the clifftop. Now he'd just given him a push over the edge.

'You want us to build this stuff for the Germans?'

'Lower your voice, old chap. We don't want the world and his wife to know, just yet. '

'But the Germans? Are you out of your mind? Surely there's some other way?'

Manners spelt it out. The Germans weren't the final customers but German workers would undertake the assembly of the ships.

'The German economy is in an even worse state than ours. They're undercutting everybody just to keep some sort of a wage in people's pockets. They've got riveters and painters and joiners and unskilled men coming out of their ears. What they haven't got is enough engineers. That's where you come in. We use the machine shop at Lewis Bishop and ship the components out through the quay. What do you say?'

'I say why don't the board of Lewis Bishop want to do it?'

Manners lost nothing by telling the truth.

'Some of them don't like the Germans and flatly refused to do business with them. I said let bygones be bygones. In the end, we reached a compromise. The new company could do the work and rent the premises and equipment from Lewis Bishop who would be the landlord. I ask again, what do you say?'

Matt didn't know what to say. He needed time to think, to consult. He had never heard of such a thing before. Build bits? Where was the satisfaction in that? For some it would lie in a full belly and a warm, dry house: tabs to smoke and beer to drink.

'I'll need time.'

'You can have some. But don't take too long. This is the only game in town Headley and I don't want to miss out. The Germans won't wait forever.'

'I know that. But there's a lot to consider.'

He ran his hand through what remained of his hair.

'We fought a war, Sir Horatio. People died – thousands and thousands of them. And now you're asking me to recommend to my members that they forget all about it?'

Manners understood the problem perfectly well but he was only interested in whether Matt would support him in a solution.

'I think you'll agree, Mr Headley, that I didn't have to come to you. I could have placed an advert in the paper and had a thousand applicants the following day.'

'Huh! You'd have been blacklegged and you know it.'

'Yes, I would and that would have been an inconvenience – no more than that. But far better for me to concentrate on trying to land this deal with the Union on my side. Don't you agree?

Wars come and go, Mr Headley, but business is business. Ring the office when you've decided, I'll be waiting for your answer.'

Jack was baffled. How could he have got it so wrong? After much deliberation on his part, he'd decided that he had never come across a woman who didn't enjoy taking tea at Claridges. When Irena had finally got in touch, he'd suggested meeting there. The setting was elegant, the service was impeccable, every detail was just so - from the floral displays to the position of the teaspoon on the saucer. But despite the Herculean effort taken to provide every customer with complete satisfaction, his companion was contorting her body most peculiarly to unsuccessfully try to hide the fact that she was in tears.

'We don't have to stay here if you don't like it. We can easily go somewhere else.'

She took his hankie and tried to do a repair job on her face.

'It's not the place, Jack. This is a beautiful place.'

'Well, what then?'

'Don't you know?'

He was genuinely stuck but entered into the spirit by having a stab at it.

'Would you rather have had champagne?'

That made her laugh.

'Jack! For a clever man, you're a bloody fool.'

'I can't be that foolish – I got a smile out of you.'

After a few more carefully positioned wipes and a bloody good blow, Irena Kuznetsova explained herself. It wasn't that she didn't like Claridges: on the contrary, she loved Claridges. In fact, she belonged in Claridges. But once she went back to Russia, the chances of her ever being able to take tea in Claridges again were virtually zero.

Jack listened patiently while she shared feelings she had willed herself to keep hidden for eight years – feelings that she'd wrapped up tightly under the cover of coarse woollen coats and stout work boots. It wasn't only the luxuries of life that Irena couldn't afford. She couldn't afford the feelings either. Her ability to bury them deep inside had kept her alive but once they were out, she was vulnerable.

'You know Jack, they think they rule the world with their equality and their citizenship and their pompous preaching. But how greedily they hang on to what was never theirs. People are cruel and mean and protect only themselves. Class is irrelevant – privilege is privilege.'

The crisply starched waitress brought the lacquered wooden cake stand and rattled off the names of the delicate patisseries like she was rattling off the list of runners and riders at the 4.30 at Wincanton.

Irena chose a sticky rum baba oozing with sweet spirit and puffed out with cream.

Her eyes flashed at the first fork full.

'Just like the cakes they make in the Ukraine – only better,' she said.

'That'll be the rum.'

Slowly, the elegance of the surroundings and the sheer decadence of the Teatime Selection revived her and reminded her that the best of anything was there be appreciated and not endured.

'You've got a short memory,' said Ford.

'I have an excellent memory.'

'Then you should remember where you were a year ago, then compare that to where you are today. That should teach you not to worry too much about tomorrow.'

'That sounds like one of your silly mottoes.'

'It is one of my silly mottoes – but it's also true. In the war, we never thought much about tomorrow. It could be fatal. We were all scared to death of death.'

'I'm scared now, Jack. Even here, with you. Drinking tea and eating cakes in this wonderful hotel. I'm terrified. I have to get away from them.'

She paused then and looked at him straight in the eyes.

'I have to ask you something. Will you help me?'

Jack wasn't surprised. He knew full well when he'd met her in the park that she would be looking for a way out. The new Soviet Socialist Republic wasn't designed for Countess Irena Olga Goliksyn and Irena Kuznetsova would encounter very few opportunities to make a run for it. As soon as he made contact with her, as soon as she found out that he had money, as soon as she knew he wanted to see her in London, her mind had been racing.

She stared at him, waiting for a response. Her hands were clasped neatly on her lap and her back was straight, her head tilted upward and her eyes unwavering.

Russian Countesses weren't good at begging – they were more used to demanding things.

'I tried to get you away from trouble before. It was a miserable failure.'

'Yes, it was,' she said. 'In a way, perhaps you owe it to me to make a better job of it this time.'

Ford reached in his pocket for cigarettes and lit one.

'Let's say I could help you. What would it involve?'

'I don't know. I have no proper identity. I want to be far away – America, maybe. I would need some money – not too much. I've learned how to survive on little.'

Ford looked at her closely. With the right clothes and connections, Irena still had plenty of resources at her disposal.

She could make it all right.

'What's to stop you disappearing right now? We could leave here, go back to my hotel and you could be on a trans-Atlantic passage next week.'

'I have no papers. They wouldn't let me leave this country. Anyway, if I get away from them, I have to be me – the real me. Countess Goliksyn.'

Ford's mind was working overtime now. That would take time. There were plenty of Russian emigres in London but they would need to find someone to vouch for her, then there'd be the forms, the bureaucracy. Asylum wouldn't be easy.

'I'll need to talk to somebody. See if it's possible.'

'Who is this somebody?'

'A friend of mine, a politician. Perhaps he could help us.'

'I haven't got long, Jack. We are leaving for Gallowshield soon. That's our last stop in Britain before we return to Russia. I might not get another chance.'

'I'll talk to him tonight. Can we meet again tomorrow?'

'I will try but they watch the women like hawks. There are only three of us in the delegation and the men prefer it if we remain at the 1917 Club unless there is an event. We can go sight-seeing or look around the shops in the afternoons but that is all.'

'Is Igor Toblinsky still around?'

'That man is a pig. His greedy little eyes follow me all the time.'

Ford laughed.

'Sounds to me like Igor's got good taste.'

It was five o'clock and Irena had to head back to the 1917 Club.

'There is no speaking engagement tonight and I need to be in time for the evening meal. What about tomorrow?'

'Can you meet me here? Same time?'

'Yes. You stay here, Jack. I'll walk out by myself. Don't forget to talk to your friend.'

She leaned forward to kiss him and marched briskly out of the lounge.

He called the starched waitress and settled his bill while wondering whether Charles Needham's range of influence extended to providing safe passage for former members of the Russian aristocracy.

He walked through reception and out into the street. A few seconds later, a short, stout bearded figure in a thick tweed suit stepped on to the crowded pavement behind him.

# CHAPTER 14

'Oh, it's you.'

Bill couldn't hide the disappointment in his voice when Jessie pushed the pram into the kitchen.

'Like that, is it? I thought you'd be happy to see your grandson. That's why I pushed him all the way from our house.'

'Of course, we want to see him.' Bella had already reached inside, wormed her experienced fingers under the warm bundle before launching him into the air.'

'Careful Mam, he's not long been fed.'

'Wheesht yersel'. He's happy to be out of that pram – aren't you me little Arthur?'

The mere sound of the name set Bill off.

'Let's hope he's better-behaved than his father.'

'Aye well. I've come about that an' all.'

Jessie hadn't been able to settle knowing that her father had fallen out with her husband. Bridges would have to be built.

'Have you indeed? Come to apologise?'

Jessie was trying desperately hard not react. She sat on the chair beside him and put a hand on his.

'No Dad. Not exactly apologise but at least try to explain.'

Bill snatched his hand away.

'I don't see what there is to explain. I was there in the room with him – you were in the pub with our Billy.'

'True – but Arthur's told me all about it.'

'I bet he has an' all. One side of the story.'

Jessie had made a strategic error. In her desperation to put things right, she hadn't allowed enough time for the dust to settle. And she hadn't bargained on something else, either. Her mother and father had kissed and made up. She was outmanoeuvred and outgunned.

And now it was Bella's turn to throw a grenade of her own.

'Fancy, leaving your poor father out on the pavement. It's a damned disgrace.'

'It was Dad's idea to leave the house. All Arthur did was grant him his wish.'

Bill couldn't deny that but he could retaliate with the truth.

'I may not have much but I do have my pride. I went to that man to ask a favour – a family favour. He turned me down flat and started lecturing me about profligacy. If he knew the life me and your mother have had to bring up three bairns on a pitman's wage – if I'd had me legs I'd have flattened the bugger.'

Bill was in full flow and Jessie could feel herself glowing red.

'I see. And violence would have helped the situation, would it?'

'And there's something else you need to learn my girl,' said Bella.

'Oh aye? And what's that, Mam? I already know how to drink!'

Bella wanted to slap her daughter for that but because she was holding the baby she took a deep breath and lowered her voice.

'You need to learn that families stick together.'

'Stick together? Don't make me laugh – you and Dad haven't spoken to each other for weeks.'

Bella placed the baby safely back in the pram before approaching.

'We always stick together against the world outside. We might fight like cat and dog behind closed doors but when the chips are down we help each other out. Or didn't you teach that at that school of yours?'

This was an onslaught on a scale that Jessie hadn't imagined. She hadn't seen them so united in anger since Tom admitted to thieving.

'But surely you'll admit that Arthur took a stance for the right reasons.'

Bill wasn't in a mood to admit anything.

'What reasons? That I'm a bad investment?'

Jessie crouched down beside his chair.

'No Dad – it wasn't personal. It was the principle of the thing.'

'Oh, you and your bloody principles. Turn your back on your own family, what kind of a principle is that?'

She had no answer. She looked around her and all she could see was hostility. Even her childhood home had become enemy territory.

'What's to be done then? Do you want me to talk to Arthur again and see if I can change his mind?'

'You'll do nothing of the sort,' said Bella.

'We'll get through this – just like we've got through everything else. Without your help.'

Jessie knew from bitter experience that when Bill was in this mood, nothing would shift him. She did her best to save face by trying to change the subject but her mother and father were so entrenched in their animosity that all she received in return for her efforts were monosyllabic grunts. Bella didn't even offer her a cup of tea.

Jessie left defeated and desolate. The love of her parents had always been the solid rock of constancy in her life – a powerful force that comforted and cajoled and catapulted her into adulthood. She'd always believed it to be the most powerful force in the world. She'd just learned that there was something even more powerful – their love for each other. Despite the fights and the silences, the insults and the anger – even the punch in the face – their love was brutally profound. And if Jessie Ashton lived to be a thousand years old, she would never possess anything like it.

She pushed the pram down Palmerston Street and turned right up the bank towards the coast. As soon as you turned your face in the direction of the sea, the wind ran to meet you. But it was one of those clear, bright days in early September when there was only a suggestion of the bitter cold to come in the months ahead. The steady motion of the pram had rocked little Arthur off to sleep and his canvas cocoon and soft woollen blankets provided ample protection from the evening gusts.

She put her hand on the blankets. Her Mam must have knitted them years before – yellow and white lambs-wool squares, held together by the tiniest of stitches. She'd made them for Tom, then Jessie had them and finally, Billy. Bella had created a barricade against the elements for a generation of Seatons. And now, there was another one feeling the benefit.

Yellow was an odd colour choice for a boy, thought Jessie, imagining her big brother, Tom, as a baby. But of course! Mam would have been hoping for more. Perhaps she was even hoping for a girl in which case blue or pink would have been wasteful.

Over the hill and down the other side was the bandstand and from there she took the cliff-top path to the little row of benches that overlooked the sea. There was no-one else around – it was past tea-time and the pubs were open. The wind was stronger on the tops. It whipped across the sea straight from Scandinavia and there was nothing in between to check its progress. She touched the baby's cheek again. No, with the pram hood up against the sea he was still warm as toast and utterly oblivious to the world outside. Jessie tucked him in even tighter – gently making sure that there was plenty of cover over his chest and neck. She remembered the feel of that blanket under her chin – delicately soft but with flimsy hairs that tickled your nose. She almost convinced herself that she remembered what it felt like to look at miserable old Gallowshield passing by as she travelled backwards in her four-wheeled carriage: giant, grinning faces peering down at her, the sympathetic tones of her Mam's voice when she stopped to chat, the rhythmic 'dum-dum,' 'dum-dum' of the tyres as they passed over the paving slabs. The recollection of all those details transported her back to a time when Jessie Seaton had felt utterly safe. That came as quite a shock but she knew it was true. As a baby, she'd felt completely secure – secure enough to simply exist and be totally satisfied with that.

Jessie couldn't quite recall when that state of affairs had changed – she was fairly sure it wasn't a sudden transformation – but she could remember things being very different very quickly. Even before she started school she was worrying, anxious. The feeling that starts deep in your tummy, like dozens of butterflies flapping about – not a pain exactly, but an unpleasant sensation, a sickly feeling, a dread.

What if Dad starts shouting? What if Mam gets cross? What if Tom gets hurt? What if I lose my shoe? What if nobody likes me? What if Billy doesn't qualify? What if I fail?

That feeling had stayed with her ever since. In fact, she was feeling it now. She felt a need to hold her son so Jessie picked him up out of the pram and began to cuddle him. He stirred for a second, then, reassured by the support and scent of his mother, dropped straight back off to sleep.

Jessie leaned forward from the waist, pulling her baby closer to her for protection. That scene at her Mam's house had been awful. Both of them setting about her like she was the enemy. It wasn't her fault that she'd had to marry Arthur. Yes, had to marry him. Who else would have taken her on after Jack? Jessie was all too well aware that she was no bathing beauty, no special catch for a young man. There was Les, of course. She knew he adored her. But what sort of life would she have had with him? A pacifist revolutionary who was so high and mighty in his Socialism that no yard foreman wanted to employ him. Oh no. Politics were one thing but practicality was another. She could never have, would never have considered a future with Les Mallow. Arthur, on the other hand, had been a Godsend – a more devoted husband and father than Jack would ever have been. Her mother had been right about one thing though – family comes first. But Jessie didn't belong to the Seaton family – not anymore. Arthur had been right too, when he'd decided not to give Dad that money and when he'd tried to explain himself properly, he was shouted down and castigated.

What was it exactly that her Mam had said? Families stick together.

'Arthur,' she said to the child, 'Your Mam is going to make you a promise. I'm going to stop worrying about other people and what they think of me. For better or worse, there's you, me and your Dad. The rest of the world can go to Hell.'

She strode off down the path, past the bandstand towards home. There was just one thing she had to do before she got there.

'The bloody Germans? You're kidding?'

As a general rule, Matt Headley didn't trust his wife to keep secrets. Her innate curiosity meant that in order to receive information, she had to trade. He had learned during his short marriage that petty misdemeanours, illnesses, debts owed, indiscretions and any form of accidental mishaps were all tradeable commodities as far as she was concerned. But Matt was by nature a private sort of bloke who didn't go in for gossip of any kind, so he pretty soon began to keep whatever tittle tattle he came across, to himself.

This was different though. Matt had tried to keep mum about his conversation with Manners but he desperately needed to tell somebody and he knew that, whenever anything really important was concerned, he could trust Sarah.

'What are you going to do?'

'I don't know, pet. Most of the lads fought in the war and all of them will have friends or family killed or wounded. Those that gets jobs would be in favour.'

'Obviously,' said Sarah, 'Beggars can't be choosers. But the rest of them are going to hit the roof.'

Matt nodded and ran his hands through his hair.

'That's right. And they won't forget it neither. So, when it comes to re-electing their local official you can bet your life it won't be me.'

'What about telling Manners you won't give official backing?'

'Aye – I thought of that. The problem is that head office wouldn't sanction it. Trade with Germany is perfectly legal. Manners has got me over a barrel and I don't think he even knows it. Dammit Sarah. What am I going to do?'

Sarah sighed and went over the ground.

'Let's see if I've got this right. Lewis Bishop have locked the yard because there's no work and eight hundred of your members are on the dole.'

'Aye. That's right.'

'Manners wants to start a new company to build parts for a ship that's being assembled in Germany. But that company will only employ one hundred or so.'

Matt was becoming impatient and irritated.

'We know all this.'

'Hang on a minute man. I'm thinking.' She waved a dismissive hand in his direction.

'That would mean that seven hundred blokes would still be without work, picketing the lock-out at Lewis Bishop's while the hundred crossed the line to graft for the new firm.'

'What do you think I've been telling you for the last hour? If this order was for any other customer, the lads without work would just have to lump it. But because it's for the Germans they'll feel within their rights to go berserk. They've all been out of work for weeks – they're almost ready to set fire to the Town Hall and start a bloody revolution as things stand now!'

Sarah threw her husband one of her looks – the look that said prepare yourself because I'm going to tell you to do something you don't want to do.

'You can't solve this on your own Matt.'

'I know that, pet. That's why I'm talking to you.'

She tutted. He hated it when she tutted because it made him feel like an impudent bairn.

'I can't help you either, Matt. But the good news is that we both know a man who can.'

Matt was stunned.

'Jack? You mean Jack?'

'I mean Jack Ford.'

'But he's nowt to do with shipbuilding now. And even if he was, not even the great Jack Ford could get us out of this mess.'

Sarah knew she'd dented her husband's pride but she truly couldn't think of a better way.

'Listen Matt – this is serious. You could lose your job here and I could lose this lovely house and I'm not having that. Maybe Jack can help and maybe he can't. You won't know until you ask him.'

'You always thought he was a better man than me.'

'Now don't you sulk Matt Headley. We've been through all this before. You're a better husband, better union man, better human being than Jack will ever be, God bless him. But when it comes to dirty dealing and conniving, Jack's the best there is.'

'Aye,' Matt said, nodding solemnly, 'That's true.'

She placed a hand on his across the kitchen table.

'Forget about all this business for tonight, Matt. Go to the Bluebell and have a couple of pints with the lads. There's a steak and onion pie for your supper. Come home and get a good night's sleep.'

He looked lovingly at his wife.

'You're right Sarah. No sense brooding.'

'I'm so glad you agree, Matt, because you'll be up sharp and getting on a train to London first thing in the morning.'

'What?'

'You heard me. He's staying at The Connaught. And mind....'

She wagged a finger in his face.

'You behave yourself down there – none of your funny business just because you're with your Army pal.'

'It's our only chance, Bella. We don't have a choice.'

Bella grabbed her glass and took a swift gulp of gin.

'But Bill. I don't think I can do it. I'm frightened.'

The scrape of footsteps in the yard halted the debate.

'Anyone in?'

Bill answered.

'Come away through Tom, lad. Me and your Mam's in here.'

Tom came in through the scullery and up the three steps into the kitchen. He stopped in the doorway and pushed his cap back on his head.

'Whey, there's a sight for sore eyes. Wait 'til I tell Dolly.'

His mother and father were sat together at the table, glasses in hand.

'Now mind, none of your cheek.'

'No cheek, Da. I'm just pleased to see my Mam and Dad enjoying each other's company without knocking seven bells out of one another.'

'That's forgotten,' said Bella. 'And we'll thank you if you let bygones be bygones.'

'Consider it water under the bridge. I'm delighted – didn't feel right, you two scrapping - for more than a day or two, anyway.'

'Howay and grab a glass and a seat son. There's a favour we have to ask.'

'You mean there's more? I thought that the urgent news was that had peace had broken out. What now? Do you want me to sign the Treaty of Versailles?'

Impatient as ever, Bill wanted to get on with it.

'No. This is business. It's important.'

'There you are Tom,' said Bella, 'You see? Everything's back to normal.'

'Obviously. What's up?'

'Well it's this son – you have to take your Mam down to London.'

Tom looked at his father, then he looked at his glass. He looked at his father again, but there was no hint of a smile. Da' wasn't joking. He took a swig.

'London? Why?'

'Three reasons: one, because I can't go in the is damned chair; two, because your Mam can't go on her own and three, because we're asking you to.'

Bill put his cards on the table. The shops had started to lose money as soon as Lewis Bishop decided to mothball the yard.

And that happened just a few days after Bill had signed the lease on the new shop in Trevelyan Street.

'And will they not let you off the lease?'

Bill shook his head.

'Will they buggery. Jowett's will allow me to sub-let if I can find anyone daft enough to take it on – otherwise I'm stuck with it or they'll sue us for five years' rent.'

Tom whistled.

'So, you've got money troubles?'

Billed sighed.

'I overstretched. You were right about that new shop, lad. But I was greedy - me eyes were bigger than me belly.'

'What's your plan then?'

Bill looked at his wife to make it clear he was accurately explaining the deal they had both agreed.

'We borrow the money to buy ourselves out of Trevelyan Street and then we re-stock the other shops with essentials – bread, vegetables, mutton, cheap tabs. If we can borrow the money to get out of the lease, we'll get by.'

'Are things that bad, then?'

'There'll be no new houses, that's for sure,' said Bella, 'And every week that goes by, your Da's paying rent on a shop that's nigh on derelict.'

Tom wasn't the brightest but he knew how to add up.

'What about the repayments? What the bank will charge in interest will be higher than the rent?'

It was Bella's turn to look to her husband for re-assurance while she explained.

'I'll be asking Jack for it. That's why you have to take me to London. I was thinking he'd maybe give us good terms.'

That name again. Jack Ford – saint and sinner all in one.

'The poor bugger. Jessie's got his heart, I've got his wife and you two want his money. I bet he can't wait to see the back of us Seatons.'

The note said it plainly enough. There was a late vote on the Slum Clearance Bill – he'd be delighted to see Jack but there was a three-line whip and he would have to stay within range of the Division Bell. Meet in Central Lobby at 9pm.

Ford had an early supper in his room before leaving the hotel. It was a filthy night – torrential rain that fell like wet soot and low cloud and fog made visibility difficult - finding a cab was impossible.

Brolly up, Jack tried to avoid the road side of the pavement where the puddles had gathered to overflowing and the passing traffic sent it spewing into the air. The good news was that the pavements themselves were more or less deserted when the weather was as foul as this.

He ploughed on through Green Park and through Palace Gate. He had half an hour to kill before he met Charles, so he popped into the Shepherd Inn on Wilfred Street for a large scotch and a dry-off by the fire. The pub was quiet, one or two stalwarts had braved the elements but there was no need to elbow his way to the bar. There was time for one more and at quarter to nine he pulled his collar up, his hat down and steadied himself for the last leg of his journey.

He certainly didn't hear them coming – the howling gale saw to that – but Ford had taken just a few steps along the street when he was attacked by four men who came at him from behind.

He was grabbed by the shoulder and spun around only to meet a large fist coming the other way. That was followed by another and another and then he was on the ground and he knew what would follow. He remembered the rain falling down his cheek and the gritty chill of the hard pavement against his side as the kicking started. Somehow, between blows, he managed to curl up into a ball to protect his organs but that served only to force the attentions of his attackers on to his head and back. One of them shouted and the kicking stopped. The leader bent over Jack.

'Stay away from Russian women.'

Then Ford felt the man's spittle run down his face and the kicking began again. The pain was overtaken by a growing sensation of nausea that started low down in his gut and clawed its way up. Ford felt his body begin to shake violently but still the assault went on. Then he saw himself falling through the air, down, down, spinning, turning. He tried to grapple his way back but his strength was gone.

Just as Ford lost consciousness, somewhere he heard a faint whistle and the clatter of boots running and sliding into the distance.

When his eyes finally opened it was at the end of such a deep sleep it took Jack a full minute to comprehend that there was a very persistent nurse determined to ask him questions.

'Are you feeling better, Mr Ford?' Are you? Do you know where you are?'

As soon as he tried to move, the pain from his broken ribs stabbed savagely at him and when he tried to speak, the cuts and swellings on his face had the same effect.

His mind was sufficiently alert for him to know what he wanted to say, but he couldn't co-ordinate his thoughts and movements to speak.

'You'll be very sore, Mr Ford. You've been the victim of a vicious attack.'

Ford managed to raise both eyebrows as to say 'Really?'

'You're a bit of a joker, aren't you Mr Ford? At least you haven't lost your sense of humour.'

She checked his pulse and fussed around his bedding.

'I'm Nurse Chivers. I'm Day Shift.'

He was trying to get his bearings. The fog in his head had lifted sufficiently for him to see that he was in a hospital and that the nurse was now sat on a chair next to his bed. There were another two beds in the room but they were empty. The sun was shining through the windows. It was daytime.

A sudden feeling of sickness welled up inside him and he turned his head away from her.

'It's ten in the morning. You've been asleep for quite a while.'

Ten o'clock in the morning? That didn't sound quite right.

He tried to move his legs to get out of the bed but even the thought of movement made him feel dizzy.

'Please don't even consider it. You have concussion on top of everything else. And you're on morphine. That makes you wobbly on your pins. But it keeps the worst of the pain at bay.'

Ford wondered why on earth she sounded so cheerful.

He felt strongly that he should be somewhere else, but the reason why was only slowly beginning to form in his memory.

She lifted a glass to his lips.

'Try to sip at this. We need to keep your fluids up – you had quite a night.'

Did I? Right, Nurse Chivers, I'll do a deal with you - I'll tell you my bit if you tell me yours.

'You were brought in by ambulance at nine thirty last night with multiple injuries.'

What sort of injuries? He could see her face now. Young and pretty, desperately trying to be older and wiser. Her black hair was just peeping out under the white folded head square.

'They are written down on this sheet here.'

Good girl, Nurse Chivers. Let's have it then.

She went to the board above his bed and took out his patient record.

'Let's have a look, according to your diagnosis you have got concussion, severe bruising and swelling around the eyes and cheekbones, a nasty cut on your lip, four broken ribs and...'

A partridge in a pear tree, Nurse Chivers?

'And contusion of the kidney.'

Ah, thought Ford, that would explain it.

'I'm sure you're in a lot of pain.'

I feel like I've just gone ten rounds with Jack Dempsey.

'The policeman said there was a gang of them but they ran off. You were lucky he was around.'

Yeah. I'm a really lucky feller.

The tide of sickness was ebbing a little and the nurse's account had prodded his memory into action. He remembered the pub on Wilfred Street. He'd never been in there before. Why was he there? Needham. Yes! He was going to the House to meet Needham to tell him about the Countess. It was raining – pouring down – and the wind was howling. He remembered being swung around and the first fist that came thundering into his face. Then he remembered the warning.

'Stay away from Russian women.'

He heard the voice in his head but he couldn't identify a face. It had been pitch black and he was on the ground. Rain and blood all over his eyes. He remembered trying to focus but he couldn't see. After that there was just pain and blackness.

'I need to go.'

He heard the sound of his own voice. Well, that was something. He could speak.

Nurse Chivers found it hilarious.

'Go? Go where?'

Ford didn't have the energy to explain any further so all he said was, 'Home.'

'But haven't you heard what I have just said? Bed rest for you.

I have to run along now

but I'll just give you some more of this before I go.

He was putty in her hands as she cradled his head and poured the medicine down his throat.

'I'll look in in a little while.'

Three hours later, Charles Needham put his head around the door.

'So, this is where you're hiding.'

Ford opened his eyes. As far as he was concerned, Nurse Chivers had only just left.

'Good God, man. You look bloody awful.'

That made Jack smile and the sudden movement of his lips made him yelp which made his ribs respond with an agonising jolt.

Needham hurried to his bedside.

'Take it easy old friend. You've had a right going over but the doctor says there's nothing major. You just need to lie low for a bit until you feel better.'

Ford took a deep breath.

'Close the door, Charles. I need to talk.'

Ford found that the only way he could speak was to take shallow breaths and keep the sentences short and whispered. That way he could keep the electric shocks emanating from his ribcage to a minimum.

'Have to get out of here. Woman in danger.'

The words were few but the look in Ford's eyes told Needham all he needed to know about the seriousness of the situation.

'First you have to tell me what's going on,' he said.

It took Ford twenty minutes but by taking his time and pausing to control the pain, he managed to explain about Countess Goliksyn.

'Meeting her at half three. Claridges.'

Ford pointed at Needham and nodded his head.

'Yes of course I'll go. But given what's happened to you, I doubt if she'll be able to keep the appointment. But you're right. We have to try.'

Ford smiled.

'Can you help?'

'She sounds an amazing woman, your Countess.'

'Amazing,' said Ford. 'But they'll kill her.'

'I know. I've read the reports – absolutely brutal.'

Needham explained the procedure. It was becoming increasingly difficult to allow Russian emigres into the country unless they were wealthy and extremely well connected. But the Countess was already here under an assumed name. What she needed to do was to seek political asylum.

'How?' Asked Ford.

'The rules say she can stay if she can prove her life would be in danger if she returned to Russia.'

'How do we prove that?'

'I think you just did,' said Needham looking at Ford's battered face.

'If she turns up at Claridges, I'll take her straight to our place – Beatrice will look after her. She'll be quite safe.'

Ford put out an arm and grabbed his friend's wrist.

'And what if she doesn't turn up?'

'Then old chap, we'll have to think again, won't we?'

The next day the hospital doctor wanted to keep Jack in the ward but he was finally persuaded to relent. What swung it was the fact that he was staying at The Connaught. Comfortable rooms, good nutrition and a doctor on call if needed.

'You'll need to hire a nurse, too, to make sure you don't stiffen up when those ribs start to heal. She'll also protect you against yourself, Mr Ford. You have to take it very easy indeed for a few days. Broken ribs like yours could easily puncture a lung and you could end up with pneumonia. We don't want that, do we?'

No, we bloody don't, thought Ford and, anyway, he was too tired to argue.

Nurse Chivers accompanied him in the ambulance and he was awake enough to do a deal with her: cash in hand to come in and see him first thing in the morning and an hour or two when she'd finished her shift in the hospital.

She tried desperately hard not to look impressed as she pushed his wheelchair down the ambulance ramp and across the pavement into the foyer of The Connaught Hotel. She was obviously looking after a very important patient in a very important place and that made her feel very important indeed.

A voice boomed from one of the armchairs hidden behind the pillars around the oak reception desk.

'Jack! By lad, you look as if you're in bad fettle.'

Jack managed to turn his lolling head to his right. He was obviously hallucinating because he was immediately transported back to Gallowshield. Clear as day, he could see the familiar, chubby figure of Matt Headley walking towards him with a concerned look on his face.

The explanations started before they even got as far as the lift. But by the time they got into the suite, Nurse Chivers had formulated a plan which caught Matt completely off his guard.

'What do you mean, you can't stay to look after him? I thought you said you were best friends.'

'Well we are but –'

Nurse Chivers was in no mood for 'buts' and Matt Headley was rapidly being forced into retreat.

'Mr Ford has been seriously injured. He was attacked in the street, Mr Headley. And in case you haven't noticed he is in no condition to look after himself.'

Ford was, by now, happily tucked up in his bed. His bed-gown had been swapped for his silk pyjamas and, despite the pain, he wore a satisfied grin on his face as he watched his best marrer being put in his place by the young woman. The man who resisted the full might of the German Army was being beaten to a pulp by a twenty-year-old.

And she hadn't finished with him yet.

'Mr Ford and I have agreed that I'll pop in before and after my shift to see to his medication. But somebody is going to have to look after his routine needs and I don't see anyone else in this room.'

Matt appeared to be looking frantically around in the vain hope that Florence Nightingale might pop out of the wardrobe.

'But you don't understand Miss. I've got to get back to Gallowshield. I only came down here to ask Jack for some advice.'

That was a major tactical error.

'I see. It's all right for you to come down here to ask for Mr Ford's help – but when he's the one in need, you're quite happy to walk away. Is that it?'

Matt threw in the towel.

No, that wasn't it. He would send Sarah a telegram and explain. He was sure she would understand, given the circumstances.

Jack was equally sure she'd hit the roof and immediately assume Matt was lying about Ford being ill just so he could spend a few nights on the town with his mate.

'I'm glad to hear it. It won't be for long. A young, fit man like Mr Ford should be back on his feet in a week or two.' Nurse Chivers didn't intend it, but that observation only served to make matters worse.

'Two weeks down here? I can't do that – it's two bob a pint!'

Nurse Chivers tutted loudly as she put on her coat and handed

203

Matt the medicine.

'He'll need another two teaspoons of this at ten o'clock and make sure he doesn't roll over on to his side while he's asleep. I'll be back at half past seven in the morning.' Her departure was so sudden Matt was left standing with his mouth open when the door closed behind her.

There was a tap at the door and Charles Needham entered. With the mental agility of an experienced politician it took him less than ten seconds to place Matt Headley's face, remember his name and politely shake his hand. He walked over to the bedside.

'I went to Claridges, Jack. She was no show, I'm afraid.'

Jack clenched his fist and shook his head in disappointment.

'A couple of foreign-looking men came in at four o'clock. They could easily have been Russians. Perhaps they were looking for you. I waited until they left then I came straight here.'

Ford was still finding it difficult to speak because every movement sent a sharp pain shooting across his torso.

'Thanks for trying, Charles.'

'What do you want to do now?'

What could he do? In this state, he was worse than useless. He was going to let the Countess down yet again.

So much for the great Jack Ford.

'I need to think,' he said.

# CHAPTER 15

'Tom – sit down there and don't move. You might break something.'

Tom was tired, the bus from the station had been packed and he'd had to stand all the way from King's Cross. He was only too happy to oblige his mother.

Bella walked up to the oak desk and addressed the young man with the polished hair, the immaculate nails and the tight, green tunic.

'We have come to see Mr Ford.'

'Is he a guest at the hotel, Madam?'

'Of course, he's a guest. You've not got him here against his will, have you?'

The young man looked up from his leather-bound lists and saw a woman who reminded him instantly of his grandmother.

'Er..no Madam – I don't think so.'

An older, stern-faced gentleman in a black jacket leaned across and whispered something to his junior colleague before turning away.

'Do you have an appointment?' The young man was flicking through the guest register and obviously praying that she did.

'No,' said Bella. 'Mr Ford is a friend of ours. A good friend.

We've come down on the train all the way from Gallowshield to see him. We are at the right place, aren't we?'

The clerk suddenly looked relieved as he found the name he'd been searching for. He looked over his shoulder to check that his supervisor wasn't listening.

'Oh yes. He's in the Grosvenor Suite on the Third Floor. His keys aren't on the rack so he must be in his room. Do you want a concierge to show you the way?'

'A what?'

'Somebody to take you.'

'Oh no, son. I've got our Tom.'

She looked over to her son and gave a 'get over here' gesture with her hand.

Tom came lumbering up behind his mother and towered over both her and the oak reception desk.

'Tom Seaton, pleased to meet you,' said Tom, in his best Sunday voice and his old tweed suit that was at least two sizes too small.

He proffered a giant paw at the clerk and the shake was gingerly reciprocated.

'We'll manage perfectly well, thank you,' said Bella.

The clerk watched them as they made their way to the lift. He was still sweating when the doors closed and they disappeared.

Matt was pacing the floor when there was a knock on the door. He'd been pacing since seven o'clock that morning. He was feeling guilty while Jack slept – guilty about leaving Sarah, guilty about wanting to leave Jack, guilty about having spent the night on a hotel sofa. It oozed out of every pore.

Should he answer the door? He found himself gnawing at his thumbnail.

The knock came again.

'Come in,' he said.

When the door opened, the three of them just stood there looking at each other for about twenty seconds.

Eventually, Tom ventured a question.

'Matt?'

'Good Lord,' said Matt. 'Tom, Mrs Seaton – come in, come in, shut the door. What on earth? Jack never said-, well I'll be buggered. Why are you? Er, never mind. Howay in, then!'

Bella looked straight past Matt's blustering welcome and saw Jack in the bed.

'Oh no, Jack! What's happened?'

Even while she was speaking she was unbuttoning her coat, removing her hat and advancing towards the patient – all at the same time.

She was at his bedside before Matt could even answer the question.

'He was beaten up, Mrs Seaton. Some Russian fellers. Night before last.'

'Oh Jack, you daft beggar.' She put a hand on his forehead.

'He's far too hot. Get that window open. Tom!'

Tom jumped to it and Matt just stood – guilty again.

'I have been looking after him, you know? I had to stay with him all last night.'

Bella looked around at the exquisite appointment of the Grosvenor Suite with its en suite facilities, beautiful furnishings and impeccable décor.

'Pity for you,' she said.

'He doesn't look too clever, mind. He's had a proper hiding.'

'I think we can see that for ourselves, Tom Seaton. Right Matt Headley, I want to know everything.'

As far as Bella was concerned, she was now in charge. Men could fool around with their politics and their deals and their sport and their mates. But when it came to the bairns, the old and the sick –men knew nowt and were not to be trusted.

She grilled Matt for five minutes until she was completely satisfied that Jack was not in imminent danger of dying.

'Even so, I'd rather our Billy was here.'

'Honestly Mrs Seaton, he's got access to the best doctors money can buy. All he can do is lie still until he starts to heal up. And anyway, the nurse is coming in again tonight after she's finished her shift.'

'What shift?' For one horribly bizarre moment, Bella thought the nurse might work down the pit.

'Her shift at the hospital,' explained Matt.

'We need tea,' said Bella. 'Can this fancy hotel make tea?'

'I suppose so,' said Matt, 'But they brought coffee up with the breakfast this morning.'

'Organise some tea for us all, Mr Headley and I'll make a list.'

'A list? What for?'

'For all the things we're going to need.' She looked at him as if he was stupid. Men? As old as they were, sometimes their brains were brand new.

Within half an hour Matt and Tom were despatched on a shopping mission. Lord knew where they would find pearl barley, leeks and a ham shank in Central London – but they'd have to try.

'If you can't find a proper grocer's, ask someone – and not a rich someone, a proper someone.'

That was her final instruction when they walked out of the door but even so, Bella wasn't feeling exactly confident in their ability to deliver.

She was alone with Jack, now and he was showing signs of waking. She drew the desk chair up next to his bed.

When Jack finally stirred, there she was looking down at him. Her eyes like two shiny blackcurrants and the smile as comfortingly familiar as ever.

'Did Matt send for reinforcements?'

'No, he didn't, bonny lad. Me and Tom just happened to be coming down anyway.'

'You and Tom? Come up to London often, do you?'

'We were coming to see you, you daft beggar. We had no idea of the state you'd got yourself into.'

He smiled at her. He'd always felt closest to Bella. Although he liked the whole family and had genuinely fallen in love with Jessie, it was Bella who really knew and understood him. What surprised him was that despite all that knowledge and understanding, she loved him for what he was. She wouldn't want to change a thing.

'Me?' he said, 'Why? Do you need something?'

'You can forget all about that now. We'll wait until you're better then we can talk about it.'

But Jack insisted. He might not be able to move but he could listen and whatever the problem was, it must be serious if it had forced Bella out of Gallowshield and into the big bad city – even if she did have Tom to ride shotgun.

'See that cupboard over there? It's a bar.'

The black eyes twinkled even more brightly.

'Pour yourself a drink and tell me all about it.'

As soon as the gin hit the lips, out it all came. Slowly at first but after a few minutes it was as if the two of them were sat by the kitchen fire in her Gallowshield terraced house – chewing the fat, like they always did.

She told him about Jessie being all high and mighty, and Arthur giving Bill the cold shoulder. She explained how she'd sent the whole family to Coventry because none of them had stuck up for her, except Tom.

'You'd best pour yourself another,' said Jack. 'I still don't know why you've come to see me and the lads will be back soon.'

'It's the shops, Jack. Bill says he's got one of these,' she handed him a piece of paper.

Jack looked at Bill's firm hand on the sheet. He'd written it down for her so she wouldn't forget.

'Liquidity crisis,' said Jack.

'Aye – that's it. It's not good, is it?'

Jack shook his head.

'It's not good and it sends a lot of businesses under. What happened?'

'Have a look at these while we talk.'

She went over to her handbag and handed Jack the accounts.

She told him about the shop in Trevelyan Street and how the day after Bill had signed the lease, Lewis Bishop's had closed its doors.

'The lawyers won't let him off the lease, Jack. We could scrape by on the other two shops selling cheap stuff but we can't afford to spend the money to get Trevelyan Street fixed up properly. We can't afford to stock it either.'

She was ashamed and looked away.

'But the rent is killing us Jack. Bill said it would take all our savings. We need to get out of that building.'

Jack wriggled in the bed and his face gave away the fact that it hurt like Hell.

'There, I've set you back. I shouldn't have let on.'

'No,' said Jack. 'I want to be propped further up on these pillows.'

Bella got behind him and reached her arms under his armpits and yanked.

'Better?'

'Mrs Seaton, you've got a grip like a riveter – get us some more of that medicine.'

He looked at the figures Bill had sent through. The shops had both been profitable until the shutdowns. Margins were good, labour costs were low and Bill certainly knew how to keep a firm hand on the purse strings. True, that was when there was paid work about, but even during bad times people still needed to eat, wash, mend clothes and do laundry. And it wasn't as though everyone in the town was unemployed. The pits were still open and the council would have to keep going somehow. If anyone could make corner shops work under those conditions, it would be Bill. He'd been taken off guard by the closures. He'd overstretched and the shops he already ran were holding too much expensive stock.

Eventually, he looked up from the papers and said, 'Mrs Seaton, I'm not going to help you get out of Trevelyan Street. It would be wrong.'

Bella looked crestfallen.

'Oh. Oh well, I understand, Jack. We just thought –'

'Hang on a minute. I didn't say I wouldn't help you. Of course, I'll help, but Bill is trying to do the wrong thing?'

'How do you mean?'

'If things are as bad as you say, then commercial property in Gallowshield is going to be cheap. He shouldn't get out of Trevelyan Street – he should buy it. He should buy Cobbett Street an' all while he's at it.'

'Don't talk daft man. I've just told you, he's spending all our money on rent.'

'Aye and you've told me it's killing the shops. Pass me my jacket.'

He took his cheque book out of the inside pocket and wrote out a cheque.

'Send this to Bill and tell him to get this deal done. The sooner he stops forking out for rent, the better.'

'But Jack – this cheque is for eight hundred pounds?'

'I know what it's for and you're good for it. Tell him to get both shops for no more than seven hundred and fifty. With the rest, he can do up Trevelyan Street and buy you a new Winter coat. Mind – I want to see that coat with me own eyes. No coat – no deal.'

She reached out to hug him but Ford backed off.

'Have a care, bonny lass. I'm an invalid, you know.'

She kissed him on the forehead instead.

By the time Nurse Chivers arrived for her evening visit, the Grosvenor Suite of The Connaught Hotel had been made fit for purpose. A portable bed had been placed in the sitting room for Mrs Seaton, Matt and Tom had booked into a small guesthouse on the Bayswater Road and Jack's bedroom had been cleaned and aired to a standard that Bella considered satisfactory.

'They have staff to do this sort of thing, you know?' Ford had told her.

'I don't care if they've got the Archangel Gabriel red-leading the front step. I don't know it's clean unless I've done it myself.'

There was no arguing with Bella when she was in that mood and since the lads had trudged all the way to Covent Garden Market for the cleaning materials, she might as well put the scrubbing brushes to good use.

'And how's the patient?'

Chivers breezed in like a cheerful Spaniel – bright-eyed and eager to please.

'I'm knackered,' explained Ford.

'You seem to have a lot more support all of a sudden. I was worried about leaving Mr Headley on his own. I though he was going to burst a blood vessel under the strain. How's the pain been?'

Ford had to admit that the pain was still there whenever he

moved.

She took his blood pressure – normal.

'Are you managing to eat all right?'

'He picks at his food. Not enough to keep a bird alive,' said Bella.

'I had soup at lunchtime,' protested Ford.

'Soup? You can't call that soup. It was like dirty dish water.'

'It was consommé, Mrs Seaton – it's supposed to look like that.'

Nurse Chivers was enjoying the exchange but insisted that the more he could eat, the faster he would recover.

'Actually,' said Bella. 'That's something you could help me with, bonny lass.'

Nurse Chivers looked at her. She wasn't certain that nurses should be referred to as bonny lasses but she couldn't possibly bring herself to argue with such a capable woman.

'What's that?'

Bella held up a string bag full of groceries.

'I've got all the ingredients for a nutritious broth – just the thing for Ja-, Mr Ford. But I've got nothing to cook it on. I wondered if you'd come with me down to the kitchen to talk to the chef. If it came from you it might sound official – what with your uniform and everything.'

She threw Chivers a conspiratorial wink.

'Hold on a minute,' said Ford. 'Are you seriously going to ask the head chef at The Connaught Hotel if you can put a pan of broth on in his kitchen? You must be off your rocker.'

'It sounds a perfectly sensible idea to me, Mr Ford.' said Nurse Chivers. 'Let's go, Mrs Seaton. It has to be worth a try at least.'

Although given the chance, Ford would always prefer the company of women to men, the constant fussing over his well-being was becoming tiresome. He was glad to sit with Tom and Matt if only for a few minutes.

'Tom get us a drink bonny lad. It's all in the cupboard. Whiskies all round, eh? And Matt – we haven't had a chance to talk since you got here. What was it you thought I might be able help you with?'

'Well it's, er, a bit confidential like.'

'Hey,' said Tom. 'Don't mind me, I'll just go out for a walk or something.'

'No, you will not,' said Jack. 'Matt, I trust Tom Seaton like I trusted you in the trenches. Him and me did time together, remember? Howay lad – I'm a captive audience. What's the problem?'

Matt spilled the beans about his meeting with Sir Horatio and the offer of work for the best of the skilled fitters.

'I see,' said Ford. 'So the problem is the other six hundred and fifty men who'll miss out?'

'That's not so much the difficulty, Jack. People will have their noses put out of joint of course, but there would still be work on the river and that's a good thing. No, the problem is the contracting company – the firm that's assembling the ship.'

'Oh aye?' Ford was interested now. 'And who is that?'

'It's German.'

Matt's timing as always, was impeccable. Just as Ford was holding his glass to his lips, Matt dropped that bombshell. Ford spluttered into his whisky and spread it all over his clean bedclothes. Then he started to laugh and the pain wracked through his body until he convulsed himself almost into a ball. Then the laugh came again and the process continued until he was in rapturous agony and tears were streaming down his face. Joy and pain in equal measure.

Matt sat on the bed and stared at his friend. His face blank with shock.

Eventually, when Ford's mirth had subsided sufficiently for him to try to take another sip of his whisky, Matt asked him what he thought was so funny.

'Not funny, Matt. Ironic – that's all. Horatio Manners - whose son was a hero killed by a whiz-bang - doing business with the very people who killed him. Would you credit that?'

'To be honest, Jack I found the whole thing very difficult to believe. But I'm not bothered about the morals of Sir Horatio Manners, am I? I'm bothered about how this news is going to go down with my members. I'm serious, Jack. This could finish me – either way.'

Jack thought about it. His old friend was quite right. If he looked to be supporting the deal, the people who fought in the war or lost close relatives in it would be strongly opposed. And more than likely, Matt would get the blame. On the other hand, how could he oppose any sort of deal that would any jobs back to the Tyne. Matt was in a tough spot.

'Is Sarah worried, Matt?'

'Worried enough to send me down here to talk to you, Jack.'

'Aye marrer. That means it's serious. Do you know who has placed the order with the Germans? Because let's face it – I can't think of anyone who has any money.'

'Sorry, Jack - either Manners didn't know or he wouldn't tell me.'

'Then that is what we have to find out.'

'Why?'

'Because he who pays the piper, generally calls the tune, bonny lad. That's why. Now you two, gives us a hand to get to the netty before the womenfolk get back. That bedpan's embarrassing.'

Nurse Chivers came back to say goodbye. She'd left Bella downstairs in the kitchen chopping leeks to go into her restorative broth.

'The chef can't take his eyes off her. He can't understand a word she says but I think he's fallen in love.'

'If she's in a kitchen,' said Ford, 'She'll be happy enough.'

'Is that whisky in that glass?' She had on her strict voice again.

'It's medicinal,' said Ford.

'Says who?'

'Says me. If I don't get enough of it, other people get sick of me.'

'You're an incorrigible reprobate. Good night.'

Jack grunted a farewell as the door closed. He was on the mend all right. His body was still broken and agonisingly sore, but his mind was regaining its agility. Countess Irena was top of his agenda but he was powerless to go out and find her. But Matt and Tom were here now. Perhaps they could do some of the hard yards for him.

He called them over to his bedside.

'There's something I need you do to for me.'

Ford outlined his plan. It was risky but if they did what he told them, it wouldn't be dangerous.

They listened carefully and when he'd finished, it was Matt who resisted.

'I can't do that, man! I'm an elected councillor.'

Jack raised his eyebrows.

'Oh, I didn't realise it was against the rules for a councillor to help a mate out when he was in need.'

'It's not. But you're asking us to break the law, Jack. That would be wrong.'

Jack still kept his voice soft and gentle.

'Wrong. Yes, it would. I see that now. Just forget I said anything.'

'Aye, right,' said Matt, relieved.

216

But Jack hadn't finished.

'And I'll forget how to pull the strings necessary to find out who's asked the Germans to build them a ship. And then I'll forget how to solve the problem you've found yourself in, Matt.'

Matt was horrified.

'But that's blackmail!'

'No, it's not, Matt. It's favours for friends. That's what mates do for one another, isn't it? Will you do it, then?'

'Of course, he'll do it,' said Tom. 'I wouldn't care but I'm the one who is taking all the risks.'

Bella came in then with a steaming bowl on a tray.

'Ee, are you lads still here? And I've only brought up enough soup for Jack. I thought you'd have been away to the pub by now.'

'It's OK Mam – we're just going. Goodnight Jack.'

'Goodnight lads. And good hunting.'

It was eight o'clock by the time Matt and Tom walked into the Royal Oak. Jack had been right about one thing, it wasn't much of a pub. The service was slow, the chairs were hard and the beer was bad. But they hadn't come here to enjoy themselves.

'That's them by the dart board – just where Jack said they'd be,' said Matt.

There were six of them huddled together deep in conversation – all drinking vodka and taking it in turns to get onto their feet to recharge the glasses.

'It gets dark around nine o'clock,' said Tom. 'We'll slip out then.'

'Now don't take any chances, Tom. You aren't going there to steal anything. This is just like a recce – that's all. So no heroics.'

'Heroics? Me? No fear for steady men, Matt. I may not know much but I did learn how to break into places. Getting inside will be easy enough – I just need to make sure I can get out quick if I have to.'

They took their time over their pints and wandered out into the night just after nine. Matt stationed himself as look-out on the corner by the back alley where Charles Needham had been attacked. Tom walked straight past him and down the back-lane behind the 1917 Club. The back door into the yard was locked shut so he looked up the lane, left and right, before reaching up to the top of the wall and pulling himself up and over.

Tom looked down to check his landing place before releasing his grip on the wall. He softened his drop by bending his knees immediately on impact with the ground and before doing anything else, he unlocked the back gate in order to speed his getaway.

He could feel the throb of the blood pulsing through his skull underneath his cloth cap. He might be an experienced burglar, but that didn't mean he enjoyed his work. He'd made a lot of money from thievin' but that had bought meat, fresh milk and eggs for his dying wife. He would do it again like a shot if Dolly needed him to, but he had always hated stealing. It made him feel cheap, dirty - dirtier than he'd ever felt when he worked down the pit hacking at coal seams for a living.

Staying close to the wall, he worked his way up the yard. There was hardly any moonlight but there was just enough spill coming from the buildings round about. As he got closer to the club itself, a lamp on the kitchen window sill was sufficient to guide him to the back door. He tried it. Locked. Tom bent down and lit a match to check. Peering through the keyhole he could plainly make out the end of the key. It was secured from the inside. He couldn't force it – Jack had warned him that there could be women inside the building: at least, two, hopefully, three.

He stepped back again and looked up. His gaze followed the line of the drain pipe. There were three floors. As far as he could tell, the first-floor windows were all tight shut. Perhaps the guests on the attic floor were more keen on fresh air. He knew the trick here was not to panic. If he rushed anything, the chances were that he would make a mistake and revert back to his usual clumsy self. In his head, Tom gave himself a severe talking to. He was doing this for Jack – the man who had just lent his parents more money than Tom had ever seen in his life. This was a first instalment on the repayments, it was the least he could do. Anyway, what was the worst that could happen? Matt Headley was on sentry duty and he would see the Russian men coming back in plenty of time for Tom to get away. Proper old soldier was Matt – experienced, too. Tom had worked with him when they'd gone sheep stealing together in Northumberland. That had been another of Jack Ford's schemes and it worked well until Tom had dropped a bucket. The noise had alerted the local bobby who'd been snooping around. Jack had had to belt the poor bugger before he could raise the alarm. They'd got away with it that time, they would get away with it now.

Tom grabbed the drainpipe and went up, hand over hand. He took a breather at the first floor by resting his boot on the protruding sill. He was sweating and panting under his thick wool coat but he had nothing else that was black – so it would have to do. He could see the guttering now just above his head. He pulled on it as best he could and it appeared to be secure. He levered himself up on to the lower roof.

After another short rest, he edged himself along to the middle of the building on his backside in a sitting position with his feet dangling over the edge. He was now in front of one of the attic windows. Tom nearly slipped as he reached around with his right hand over his left shoulder to check the latch. The twisting motion had forced his weight round and he had to hold on tight to the guttering to stop himself crashing to the yard below. His heart was pounding like the massed drums of the Royal and

Sutherland Highlanders, now.

He took half a dozen deep breaths and positioned himself further back against the roof slates. Maybe that would hold him steadier as he tried the latch once more. He didn't have to pull at the frame – his finger slipped straight in between the frame and the pane - the window opened on its hinges. The latch was broken. It was child's play then to anchor his weight on the sturdy frame and swing his body around until he was crouched on the inside sill – like a watching vulture perched on a branch. The only danger now was that somebody might be asleep inside. He eased aside the curtain and, with the same hand, managed to lift up the nets. He couldn't see much in the shadowy greyness but, more importantly, he couldn't hear anything either. The room was empty.

Tom lowered himself to the floor and closed the window. He wouldn't be coming back this way so he wanted to leave it as he found it. Feeling his way around the room he quickly established that it was shared by two men – presumably two of the fellers in the Royal Oak – and from the smell of it they enjoyed a smoke and a drink. He found the door handle and turned it as gently as he could. He felt the give as the latch slipped back out of the lock, he opened it as slowly as possible but the door moved easily without creaking and, after a moment, he was out into the upper hall.

The building was definitely occupied, he could hear music – a gramophone – coming from two floors down. Confident that the scratchy sound of the singer would disguise any noises he might make, Tom checked the three other rooms on the attic landing. Two further bedrooms were also inhabited by males and the additional door led to a large, deep storage cupboard which had been shelved out for bedding, books and bits of old junk.

Downstairs, the music stopped and the sound of women's

voices drifted faintly up the stair well. He stood inside the cupboard with his back against the wall until another record began to play. Tom lit a match then to see what else was on the shelves: old oil lamps, some rags, a cracked china dog, two brass candlesticks and a pile of old newspapers. Lying on the newspapers was a scrap of paper with some writing on it, he bent down to read it but the match had burned down and was scorching his thumb. Tom blew out the match and was plunged back into darkness. He put the scrap of paper in his pocket.

He closed the cupboard door and descended the stairs to the first floor. He was careful to keep his weight to the wall side of each step so that his bulk was supported without the wood creaking. There was more light here, stretching out from the ground floor lamps. Tom could easily make out a large bathroom and four further rooms. The one at the front of the building was obviously Bukanin's. Only one man slept in the large double bedroom with the bay windows over-looking the street. But Tom had to admit that the occupant was a neat and tidy feller. Two suits hung neatly in the wardrobe and shoes were polished and lined up for inspection beneath. There were books by his bedside, too, and three large pipes as well as a leather pouch brim full of cherry-scented baccy. Underneath the bed were four wooden crates containing bottles of beer. One of the crates already had a few missing so Tom didn't see the harm in helping himself to a sample. All right for some, he thought as he conjured with the idea that, despite the workers' revolution, in Russia - just like everywhere else - some were more equal than others.

The next room was obviously for the women. There were three single beds – all made and ready for bedtime. But then Tom saw something odd. Two bedside cabinets had personal possessions on them. One had an alarm clock, a scent bottle and a notepad. The other had a hankie, a watch and a half empty glass of water.

The third cabinet was completely bare. He checked the clothes. There were dresses and skirts and shoes to fit two women – one larger than the other. To make sure, he checked the chest of drawers. There it was again: two sets of undergarments in separate drawers. Tom had never known a lass want to get her underwear mixed up with another woman's – no matter how close the friendship.

The sound of the record swelled slightly and he heard the voices again. Then there were feet on the stairs. Tom stood behind the door with his back to the wall and waited. A gnawing feeling began to swell in his stomach and it was accompanied by the dread that came from the shame of what he was doing. He heard the bathroom door open and close. He was fairly sure he had all the information that Jack had asked for. He decided to grab the opportunity to make a break for it.

He moved as quickly but as lightly as he could out of the door, down the hallway and past the bathroom. He turned to take the next flight of stairs to the ground floor. He could see the door to the sitting room was ajar and the music was still playing. With a bit of luck, he could sneak past, down the passage, into the kitchen and out through the back yard. He started to hurry as he made it to the kitchen. As he entered, he almost barged straight into a slight, young woman coming the other way.

She immediately gasped and took a step back. They stood staring at one another for a few seconds and Tom wished he'd blacked his face. She took a deep breath and spoke.

'Did you get what you wanted?'

The Russian accent was thick but Tom understood what she was saying plainly enough.

'I haven't taken anything,' he said.

'Then wait.'

The young woman turned and walked over to the kitchen

bench. She picked up a knife and began to hack away at some bread.

'Take this,' she said, and handed him half the loaf.

Tom couldn't think of anything to say and he was desperate to get out of there, so he took it, smiled, eased past her, unlocked the door and rushed out into the yard.

'Thanks,' he yelled over his shoulder as he pulled open the back gate before pelting up the back lane.

Matt saw as his friend emerge out of the alley at full speed and instinctively started running himself.

The two of them ran straight down Gerard Street dodging the punters, the touts and the girls who were looking for business.

'What have you got under your coat?' asked a breathless Matt. 'Jack said you weren't to steal anything.'

'I didn't, man. The wifey gave us half a loaf on me way out.'

The next day, Jack sat and listened intently as Tom told his tale. He was looking and feeling a lot more like himself although mobility was still a problem – every movement, every touch seemed to find its way to his ribs which screamed their disapproval at every available opportunity. But at least Jack was out of bed and into a dressing gown. He could walk to the bathroom if he had assistance and without it, he could manage to make it to the drinks cabinet.

'You're sure, then, Tom.'

'Aye. The lads are bunking in together on the very top but Bukanin has a room of his own at the front over-looking the street.'

'Anything of interest in there?'

'Not really. His clothes are hanging up in the wardrobe and his pipe collection and books are on the bedside table.'

'No vices, then.'

'He likes a drink, but they all do. I found four crates of these under the bed.'

He tossed Jack a bottle of beer he'd pocketed from Bukanin's room.

'Souvenir for you.'

'Thanks - so what about the girls?

'Their room is on the same floor as Bukanin's. Two sets of clothes, two sets of shoes, two sets of personal stuff and three beds.'

'Maybe she had a room somewhere on the ground floor,' said Matt.

'I didn't get the chance to poke about but all I could see was a kitchen, a sitting room and a bloody great meeting room right at the front. There may have been a cellar but I didn't have time to go snooping around. The two women were both on the ground floor listening to music, when one of them came upstairs – that's when I ran for it.'

Jack smiled.

'And bumped right into your daily bread.'

'Don't laugh, Jack. But I was petrified. She just stood there – staring at me. Then when she went for the knife I really believed I was done for. But then she started slicing the the loaf and said, "take this."'

He looked almost wistful.

'She had really kind eyes.'

'She must have thought you'd broken in looking for food. Mind you, you don't look that hungry to me.'

Tom suddenly remembered the upstairs cupboard.

'Oh aye, there was this an' all.'

He dug into his pocket and pulled out the scrap of paper he had found on the pile of old newspapers.

'It just says "I'll be in the Park over the way." Probably got nothing to do with this at all.'

He handed the note to Jack.

'It has everything to do with this, bonny lad. Do you want to know why?'

'Go on, then,' said Matt.

'I wrote this note. And I gave it to the Countess in Gallowshield.'

'Get away,' said Tom.

'It's true. Look Matt – you recognise my handwriting. It was the morning after I walked your Mam back to Jessie's, Tom. I found out that Irena was staying at the Balancing Eel. She was with another Russian feller, Igor Toblinski. So I went round there and handed that note to the barmaid. Ten minutes later, she came out of the pub to meet me in the Marine Park. Now we know for sure. My guess is they locked her in that cupboard, Tom, until they could move her to somewhere safer. Somewhere I couldn't get to her.'

'It's possible,' said Tom. 'But like you said, if she's been moved, she could be anywhere. We've got no chance of finding her never mind getting her out.'

# CHAPTER 16

Matt and Tom headed back north but Bella wouldn't hear of leaving Jack just yet.

'I'll know when I'm not needed,' she said, 'but until then, Jack Ford – you'll do as you're told.'

Well, if she was going to insist on looking after him, he may as well have a little fun and broaden Bella's horizons into the bargain.

'I need to get a message to Charles Needham,' he said.

'That MP feller?'

'That MP feller. Can you take it for me?'

If Jack needed to send a message to a Member of Parliament, it must be important.

'Where does he live?' she asked.

'Well,' said Jack, 'He lives in Park Lane but this message needs to get to his office.'

'Where's that?'

'What do you mean "where's that?" – he's an MP, Mrs Seaton. His office is in the House of Commons.'

There wasn't much that could stop Bella Seaton in her tracks but she looked as though she'd been hit by the Flying Scotsman.

'It's in Westminster,' added Jack, helpfully.

'Oh, but, but I can't.'

He looked at her and tried to hide his own smile.

'Why not?'

She started stammering.

'Well I mean, I couldn't. Not there. It's too...er, well, you know?'

It had taken an enormous act of will and desperation for Bella to summon up the courage to talk to the receptionist at The Connaught. The thought of entering Parliament and asking for the Right Honourable Charles Needham was giving her palpitations.

But Ford was determined. If a woman like Mrs Seaton - born and bred in Gallowshield; who had worked hard all her life; brought up three children and scrimped enough to send one of them to university – if a woman like that came to London and looked after a sick friend but didn't get the opportunity to see some of the sights, then something was far wrong.

'Can't one of the porters do it?'

'No – they only run messages around and about the hotel. Anyway, this message is confidential. Wouldn't trust it to just anybody. I'd take it myself if I could.'

Ford knew fine well he could easily have sent Needham a telegram and he'd have been round like a shot, but this way was much more fun – and Jack needed to be entertained.

'But I don't know how to get there.'

'Here,' said Jack, 'Take a taxi – the porter will get one of those for you – to the Palace of Westminster. I've written it all down for you. Then when you see Charles, give him this envelope.'

'All right, Jack. I'll do it. But I'm not happy about it.'

'I'm very grateful, Mrs Seaton.'

When she returned with Charles three hours later, Bella Seaton was in a state of utter euphoria.

'Ee Jack – that was the most wonderful thing that's ever happened to me.'

'What? Better than meeting Bill?'

'What? You're joking, aren't you? When I met Bill, I could have had a dozen like him. But Parliament? That was a very special place.'

Ford winked at Needham.

'Did you get lost?'

She was offended at that.

'I most certainly did not. Why?'

'Well you only went to drop off a message. You've been gone for ages.'

Needham couldn't stand it and immediately let Bella off the hook.

'We went for tea, didn't we, Mrs Seaton.'

'Yes, we did.' And she added, 'On the terrace.'

'Did you indeed? Well that's more than I've ever done.'

'And then we went to Annie's bar for a quick one and then we had a walk along the river before tearing ourselves away to come to see you.'

'Well,' said Jack, 'You shouldn't have hurried back on my account.'

'I thought you said it was urgent,' said Bella.

'It is. But I love it when you have a good time.'

'I've never seen anything as grand as that in all my born days,' she said. 'Mind you, some of them windows need a good leatherin'.'

'Did you have any luck with that information I asked for?' said Ford.

Needham sat down with him at the desk.

'I did, Jack. I had a word with a pal of mine in the Foreign Office and he reckoned there were only two places they might have taken her. The Russian Embassy in Kensington Palace Gardens – which he thinks is unlikely – or Arcos?'

'What on earth is Arcos?'

Needham explained that Arcos was short for the All Russian Co-operative Society.

'It's a trade organisation that buys and sells things on behalf of the Soviet Government. It could be anything from machinery to mackintoshes.'

'Ships?' asked Ford.

Needham nodded.

'Certainly – Arcos deals with all their trade in the United Kingdom. They spent over a million pounds with us last year. And it was through them that the trade union delegation was invited to stay at the 1917 Club – both organisations sprang from the Co-operative Movement.'

'I see,' said Ford. 'So, would anyone connected with the 1917 Club here, have information about Countess Irena?'

'I would doubt that very much, Jack. The Russians keep their dirty laundry well and truly private if they can get away with it. Fraternal Socialism is all very well when you share the same general aims and objectives, but kidnapping and murder are quite different. The Russians know that that sort of thing doesn't go down well here. Especially when a woman is involved. That's why they've moved her. If she'd have been discovered locked up in Gerard Street, there would have been one hell of a stink.'

Bella no longer waited to be asked - it was past six o'clock. She brought over glasses and a bottle of Scotch.

'That poor lass,' she said. 'And you think she's been locked up all this time? You have to tell the police, Jack.'

'Wouldn't do any good,' said Needham. 'If she'd have been in the 1917 Club there wouldn't have been a problem – the police could demand entry if they had reasonable suspicion. But if she's in the embassy, the police have no jurisdiction whatsoever. If she's in the Arcos building we'd need concrete evidence. Barging in there would have huge consequences for Anglo-Russian relations. It's just too risky and the Government wouldn't wear it.'

Jack handed Needham a full glass.

'Cheers,' said Needham. 'The Russians are brilliant at this stuff. They know fine well that Western Governments want to trade with them freely, so we are desperate to establish diplomatic links. But the Russians do sometimes use those links for their own ends.'

'How?' Bella asked.

'Funding other Communist parties like the one here in Britain, encouraging activists to spy for them, infiltrating trade unions – that sort of thing. Essentially, they want to spread revolution across the world. And they aren't too keen on the Nation State.'

'Aye,' said Ford. 'And they don't like it if you get in their way, either.'

'They do not. Especially if you're a Russian aristocrat.'

Ford remembered the bloody war in Murmansk after the revolution when the white Russian army was routed. Some of the atrocities he'd witnessed in Northern Russia were as bad as anything he'd seen on the Western Front.

'They won't do anything to her while she's in Britain, will they?'

'Not unless they have to. Assuming she's still alive, they'll try to get her out of the country and back to Russia. That way she can stand trial and they can make an example of her.'

'What will happen to the lass?'

Needham shrugged.

'She'll be imprisoned somewhere like Siberia where conditions are appalling or she'll be executed as an Imperialist spy – an enemy of the people.'

'And if we're going to stop it, we're going to have to do it ourselves.'

Needham corrected him.

'I'm afraid you can't include me in that, Jack – much as I'd like to help. I've gone as far as I dare. That document I told you about is still missing – chances are I just lost it and it's disappeared forever – but I can't take any risks.'

Jack turned to his friend.

'Chief Whip been blowing in your ear again, eh?'

'He most certainly has, Jack. I'm to have as little to do with our Russian friends as humanly possible.'

'Even when a young lass is at stake?'

The priorities of politicians left Bella completely baffled.

'Don't worry Mrs Seaton. She has Jack on her side. All is not lost, yet.'

'But he's been in the wars himself,' said Bella.

'Far too many bloody wars,' said Jack.

'And you're not the only one, Jack.'

'Oh, aye? Somebody else at the end of their tether, are they?'

Charles had his serious face on again.

'A good friend of ours. Rose Milne.'

'Good God. What now?'

'She collapsed at the Ham Bone Club. Lansing Bell found her at the bottom of the steps at four in the morning. The members just assumed she was drunk. God knows how long they'd been stepping over her on their way home.'

'Where is she now, hospital?'

'She's back at home, Jack – resting. I only found out today.'

'Well what are we hanging around here for?' said Jack. 'Let's go.'

'But you can't walk.'

'You'll give us a push, won't you, Charlie? And Bella, give us that pan of broth, I'll carry it on my knee.'

The Gallowshield North Constituency Labour Party Executive didn't gather all that often when there was no election looming, but, in accordance with the Articles of Association, Les Mallow had called a Special Meeting to discuss 'a matter of the utmost gravity.'

'You're going out again?' said Sarah. 'You've just come back from London.'

'Don't I know it,' said Matt. 'It's bloody Les, isn't it? 'A matter of the utmost gravity' - pompous bugger.'

'Well try not to be late Matt Headley. There's no matters of grave importance to be found down the Blue Bell.'

There were seven members of the executive - Les Mallow, Jessie Seaton, Billy Seaton, Matt Headley, Malcolm Poskett, Jackie Rimmer and Charlie Haliday – and they met in the draughty hall of St Mary's Church which was conveniently positioned not two hundred yards from the Blue Bell.

Les had had a busy day. Having satisfied himself that he was well within his rights according to the rubric, he'd personally written and delivered all the invitations to the meeting, drafted the agenda, booked the hall and still found time to arrive early in order to heat the water for the tea urn.

There was only one item up for discussion, the forthcoming visit of Russian Trade Union delegation leader, Mikhail Bukanin.

Old Charlie Haliday, a tiny man with an incredible capacity for beer and a remarkably detailed memory of the outbreak of the Crimean War, was in the Chair and invited Les - who had so unexpectedly called this meeting at short notice on domino night – to explain himself.

Les Mallow was not about to be destabilised by such low-level sarcasm. He was far too stoic for that.

'As I said in my note inviting members to the meeting, this is a sensitive matter and it concerns some confidential information which has come into my hands.'

Jessie Seaton began to squirm in her seat. She tried desperately hard not to glow red but she could feel her temperature rising. She surreptitiously tried to blow cool air down the collar of her blouse and turned her shoulder away from her brother so she could not see the look of horror on his face.

Les continued.

'It concerns a secret paper, passed between senior Ministers of the Government and elected Members of Parliament representing this Party.'

At this point, Matt stopped thinking about beer and started to pay Les his undivided attention.

But Les was in the unfortunate position of not being able to say anything in any detail.

'This is so serious that if I share the information, I may commit a criminal offence. And then, Brothers and Sisters, if you heard the information and therefore had knowledge of it, then you, too, could be committing a criminal offence.'

Old Charlie was becoming confused.

'Excuse me Les. Are you saying that you know summat but you can't say what it is?'

'Yes,' said Les.

'Well what are we sitting here discussing it for?'

'Because I don't want to act alone,' said Les.

'Well keep your gob shut,' said Charlie.

'I can't,' said Les.

'That's true,' said Matt.

That brought a giggle from Charlie, Billy and Jackie Rimmer.

Jessie felt like a coward. She should help Les, after all, she had posted the unexploded bomb through his letter box. But it was Billy who came to the rescue.

'Mr Chairman, if Brother Mallow can't say exactly what information he has, can he at least inform us about its general nature?'

Relieved at receiving the necessary prompt, Les flung himself at the opportunity and outlined the position in exactly way he had rehearsed numerous times in front of the mirror.

'The document I have in my possession describes how suspicious the Establishment is of our Socialist Brothers and Sisters in Russia. It accuses them of stirring up revolutionary fervour – even here in Britain. Furthermore, it proposes a series of draconian measures which could be taken against those who associate with our international Socialist brethren.'

And he hadn't finished.

'I'm sure none of us is surprised at such a policy coming from the Tories. But what if this information has been kept secret by Members of our own Labour Party, Brothers and Sisters? That would be a betrayal. And I believe that this Constituency Party should propose a Conference motion to have any MPs with such knowledge, expelled from our Party.'

He'd said his piece and, in the end, he'd delivered it well. Les let out a huge gasp as he sat down as if he'd just been relieved of an enormous weight.

'Is that a proposal, Brother Mallow?'

Les nodded and Charlie asked if anyone would like to speak to the motion.

Matt stayed silent – he was thinking. Les had shown some of his hand. Even if he won the vote tonight, a proposed conference motion would first have to be voted on and agreed by all card-carrying Members in Gallowshield and then it would have to go into the ballot at National Executive level before it even saw the light of day at Conference. Bukanin could be drawing his old age pension by the time that happened. But Les was up to something. Matt could smell it. But why was he wasting his energy on a piddling constituency party meeting? Then the penny dropped.

What Les was doing was stirring up trouble. He was cleverly letting it be known that he was a man on the inside and, therefore, a man of power. And then Matt knew what Mallow's next move would be. He would hand that document to Bukanin – probably just before he made his keynote speech at the Gallowshield rally. Then Les would be riding on a crest of a wave just two weeks before Matt would be seeking re-election as Regional Secretary of the Fitters Union.

'I'll second Brother Mallow's proposal.'

That was Billy Seaton again – stepping into the breach again so his sister wouldn't have to do the dirty work.

Damn, Les Mallow.

Matt was forced to speak.

'Is this where we've come to, Mr Chairman? A place where senior Members of the Party can be placed under suspicion and scrutinised by hearsay? I'm sorry, Brother Mallow but all we have is your word that there is any evidence against these Labour Members of Parliament – whoever they may be.'

'I know that,' said Les, looking around at all the faces around the table. 'I'm asking you all to trust me.'

The vote was carried with four votes in favour, two against and one abstention and the meeting was closed. Old Charlie Haliday was desperate to get to the pub and Matt Headley was desperate to talk to Jack. Les Mallow had conducted that meeting like he was Sir Henry Wood at the Proms. He knew exactly who he could carry along with him and who would fall by the wayside. He knew he'd win and he'd done it without firing one round of live ammunition.

It took Charles Needham less than fifteen minutes to push Jack's wheelchair from The Connaught Hotel to Rose's Knightsbridge flat. It took Jack Ford thirty-five minutes to climb the three flights of stairs that would take him to the front door. He took them one step at a time and he leaned against the wall all the way up. But he was determined to see her.

'They said the key would be under the plant pot,' said Needham as he disturbed the aspidistra on the window sill.

'Rose! Rose! It's Charles and Jack, come to call.'

There was no answer so they made their way inside.

'Bedroom's through there,' said Ford, nodding at the far door.

Charles knocked and Jack followed behind, holding on to whatever would support his weight as he passed.

Rose was lying in bed stretched out luxuriously on numerous pillows. Her head was back and her eyes were staring at the ceiling.

'Hello darling. Didn't you hear us come in?'

Charles strode towards her. She was muttering something.

'Rose? Can you hear me?' The muttering continued but she didn't seem to be registering Charles at all.

The area around her nose was red and sore and little bubbles of spittle were gathering at the corners of her mouth. As far as Jack could see, she hadn't eaten a square meal in weeks – she was skin and bone and her complexion had a dull, grey sheen to it like last week's wash-day water.

'Can you make out what she's trying to say, Jack?'

Jack pushed himself to the bedside and bent down to listen.

She was speaking very faintly, but he heard it plainly enough.

'I had a little bird,

Its name was Enza,

I opened a window
And in flew Enza.'

'I can hear her all right, Charles but she's out of it. High as a kite.'

'What do you mean? She can't be.'

Charles came forward then and gently slapped her cheek but she just kept repeating her little rhyme – over and over.

'What do you think, Jack?'

'I think she is completely pie-eyed.'

'Drunk?'

'She's intoxicated certainly. But I don't think it's the drink.'

'That's it,' said Charles. 'Tomorrow, I'm taking her back to Adlington Hall with me. London is going to kill her.'

Charles was pushing Jack through hotel reception when the concierge stopped them to pass on the message to phone Matt at the Royal Saracen in Gallowshield. The news of Les Mallow getting up to his old tricks came as no great surprise to Jack.

He told Charles all about it over a nightcap.

'It's fallen into enemy hands, Charles, I'm afraid. Mallow will use it for his own ends without a doubt. He was after that Regional Secretary's job when I had it. He'll give the document to Bukanin for sure.'

'Any advice?'

'Prepare for the worst – hope for the best. We know who's got the document and we know what they intend to do with it. That's two steps further forward than we were yesterday.'

'Are you always this optimistic, Jack?'

'Me? Optimistic? Get away to Hell, man. All I'm saying is we've got some time. Perhaps we can get our retaliation in first. Now remind me, when does Bukanin travel to Tyneside?'

'His keynote speech is at the Gallowshield rally on Saturday night. My guess is that the delegation will leave London on Friday.'

'And this Arcos organisation. Where are they based?'

'They've got storage properties all over the place but their headquarters is here in London – Moorgate.'

Moorgate was on the edge of The City and just a mile or so away from the river. Ford wondered whether his influential friend had any contacts in the London Port Authority.

'I know the Chairman as a matter of fact, bit of a Tory but he knows his cricket.'

'Can you get in touch with him tomorrow? I want to know how many Russian ships are departing from London before Saturday.'

'I'm not sure, Jack. I wasn't joking about the Chief Whip. He made my position very clear. The Party wants me to steer well clear of anything to do with the Russians.'

'That's all right. Just ask him for the full list of ships and I'll work the Russia bit out all by myself.'

'I'll see what I can do, Jack. But you be careful – these are vindictive, ruthless people and you can't take them on single handed – especially at the moment. You're a poorly boy.'

'Don't I know it.'


Matt wasn't in Sarah's bad books for very long. He hadn't been to the Blue Bell at all, he'd had to go to the Royal Saracen to telephone Jack.

'Something happened at that meeting, didn't it?'

'It did,' he said and sighed as he sat down at the table.

'Les Mallow, by any chance?'

He had to admit it, her instincts were generally as sharp as her tongue.

'Is it bad, Matt?'

Matt explained what had happened. He tried to skip over the

part where he suspected that Mallow was doing all this to steal his job but that was useless. Sarah was way ahead of him.

Her eyes narrowed and she scrunched up her fingers into talons.

'Oh I could scratch him until he bleeds. Les 'too-good-to-live' Mallow. No wonder he's got no wife. He's as much charisma as a wilted cabbage, that man. What did Jack say?'

'He said he'd be in touch. Tomorrow.'

'Well he'd best get a move on, Matt. Pretty soon this town'll be crawling with Les Mallow's communist mates. We'll all be drinking vodka by Sunday night unless you and your best marrer get cracking.'

Matt was up sharp for work the next day – he didn't even wait for the alarm. His mind had been racing all night and even Sarah had tossed and turned. They were just sitting down to breakfast when there was a knock on the door.

'The front door – at this time of the morning? What can be wrong now?'

Sarah was always ready to ask the questions but she wasn't in too much of a hurry to find out the answer. She looked at Matt until he went to open the door.

'Telegram for Mr Headley.'

Matt signed for it and brought it inside.

'Jack?'

'Let's have a look.'

He sliced the envelope with the knife that had been buttering his toast and spread a huge smear of grease across the contents.

Sarah looked at the floor – too livid to speak.

Never much of a scholar, Matt was trying to digest Jack's message and he was obviously finding it difficult because he was silently mouthing every word – such was his level of concentration.

He looked at his wife in exasperation.

'You'll never guess what, Sarah.'

'Go on.'

'He wants me to go to Germany.'

If Matt had been puzzled by the telegram, that was nothing compared to his amazement at his wife's reaction. Quick as a flash she dropped the tea towel and was headed for the stairs.

'You'll need clean clothes packed.'

He yelled up after her.

'Are you not going to ask why he wants me to drop everything here and go to Germany?'

'Well I'm guessing it's to do with that ship.'

Maybe it was, but for the life of him, Matt couldn't understand how.

He looked at the telegram again.

Matt, go Germany stop Gallowshield Ferry to Holland stop Train to Bremen stop Tell lads to do what I tell them stop Send message when arrive stop Jack

It had been a bad night and daytime was shaping up even worse.

'Will you need your best suit?'

'How the Hell do I know? I have to slip out a message while you're packing, Sarah. I'll be back in half an hour.'

Sarah was in the middle of telling him not to go on any account when she heard the back-door slam. She sat on the bed holding a clean white shirt for Matt. She brought it up to her face and inhaled it. It was fresh and crisp and smelled of Lux. That was the smell of her husband, when he was sober. A man who went to work in a fresh, clean, crisply ironed shirt. That had always been her dream, her driving force. When she'd washed and cleaned for others in their posh houses, she'd fooled herself with the thought that a house like that would be hers one day. And now she had the house and the kind-hearted, gentle man to go with it. No – he wasn't the smartest, but he was willing and with her help there was no telling how far they might go together. But now there was trouble on the way and they might lose the lot because of that jealous bastard Les Mallow. Well Sarah Headley wasn't going back to poverty. Not for anyone.

She said it out loud, 'Come on Jack - you're all that's standing between me and the gallows. Because if we lose everything, I'll swing for that bugger.'

She'd have to pick out another shirt for her man going away. That one was damp.

# CHAPTER 17

Much as he loved Bella, Jack had to admit to an overwhelming sense of relief when she'd finally agreed to go home to Gallowshield. It was Nurse Chivers who'd swung it – God, bless her.

'This wheel-chair is needed back at the hospital so I'll send our driver for it. I've brought you a walking stick instead. You should be fine with that, if you take it steady.'

The mere mention of the chair reminded Bella that she had a man at home who would always need to be on wheels. Jack was on the mend – the nurse had said so – and she ought to be back in Gallowshield at Bill's side.

'Thanks for everything you've done, bonny lad. And don't forget about that hot pot. It's all ready for you in the kitchen and I've told Gaston to put it on a low peep about six tonight.'

Gaston was the Sous Chef who'd thought he'd come to The Connaught to train under the critical eye of acclaimed head chef, Louis Varel. Instead, he'd found himself heating up left-over hot pot for Bella Seaton.

Solitude gave Ford time to think as he pored over the London Port Authority's log of shipping movements for the next seven days.

The Thames made the Tyne look like a much-neglected backwater with dozens of arrivals and departures each day. But there was precious little flying the new hammer and sickle flag of the United Soviet Socialist Republic. There was one, however, due to leave at dawn on Friday from St Katherine's Dock. The SS Krasnayar was described as a cargo ship of 3500 tons carrying machine tools and engine parts to Primorsk, in Northern Russia.

St Katherine's dock was just over a mile from The Arcos offices on Moorgate. Ford went through the copious lists one more time but inevitably came to the same conclusion. If he was Bukanin and he wanted to get Irena out of the country and back home to Russia, the Krasnaya was the obvious choice.

Ford figured that to reduce the risk of being discovered in the act of enforced repatriation, they would try to get Irena on board under cover of darkness and, if she was likely to make a last-ditch effort to make a run for it, they would probably try to get her on board just before embarkation.

He did the sums in his head. There'd be the crew, say, twenty-five; plus, an escort from Arcos – probably another three or four. That was twenty-nine men - almost two platoons' worth. And there he was – an ex-soldier, on his own and not exactly fighting fit. It was time to work out how to shorten the odds.

He decided to recce the site and took a cab to the dock to save his ribs from the jostling they would inevitably receive if he ventured out on foot.

The docks were busy, too, though and he took his time limping his way carefully down to the water's edge.

The language of the river was always delightfully different. Ship workers – whether builders, repairers or dockers – invented their own ways of communicating. It was like a shorthand recognised only within the trade. And when it was yelled at the top of the voice, in that Cockney way with swallowed word-endings, it was virtually unintelligible – at least to Ford. There was another intriguing element to the dockers' lingo – a sign language to direct the crane driver perched high in his cab far removed from the scurrying activity on the ground. But Ford didn't need an interpreter, he could see for himself exactly what was happening as the cranes delicately hefted huge, bulging nets full of barrels and wooden crates out of the open belly of the generous and docile ship.

The only road running directly on to the quay ran to about a hundred yards from the dock side where it was blocked off by cast iron bollards. The only way for a vehicle to get all the way to the ship would be through one of the giant warehouses where wagons stood now, their drivers waiting impatiently for their turn to be loaded.

Ford lit a cigarette and sat on one of the bollards. The sun was bright but there was a cool, Autumn breeze drifting in from the river. If he closed his eyes he could be back in Gallowshield. The gulls had followed the ship upstream and were noisily squabbling among themselves for any scrap of discarded edibles they could scavenge from their surroundings.

And besides their discontented squawking, there was the background hubbub of physical labour mixed with mechanical grind as chains tautened, engines chuffed and steel doors slammed.

He had to admit to himself that he derived a certain satisfaction at being able to watch other men work – especially if that work was genuinely hard graft. These fellers were part of a trade union, of course, but even so they were hired by the day – 'Standing On The Stones' they called it. A man would turn up at the dock gates at six in the morning and provided he was picked by the foreman, he would be reasonably paid for his day's toil. But there were days – even for the good workers – when there was no work and he would have to go home empty handed.

Jack could see that the men worked in gangs attached to each crane. Each gang appeared to have a leader and the leader was the man who was giving the hand signals to the crane driver. At mid-day the leader of the gang working nearest to him, shouted 'Muggo!' and all the workers immediately downed tools to take a tea break. This was his chance.

Jack got up and carefully eased his body upright before gingerly attempting to negotiate the slippery cobbles – stick in hand. He called to the man.

'You fellers taking a break now?'

'Who wants to know?'

Ford was all too well aware that the dockers protected their working practices fiercely. Any suggestion of a time and motion study would be seen as threatening and would be aggressively discouraged.

'Just making conversation my friend. I'm a union man myself. Fitters Union, Gallowshield Branch, paid up member since I served my time. What are you? The foreman? The boss? What do they call you?'

'I'm Top Man, if that's what you want to know. Call me Finn.'

Jack shook his hand.

'My name's Ford, Jack Ford. Can I buy you a drink, Finn?'

Finn looked Ford up and down. His clothes didn't suggest that he was a shipyard worker but the yellowing bruises around his eyes and the walking stick offered the potential of an interesting story. And Finn enjoyed a good tale.

'All right. I can give you twenty minutes. The Wharf Inn is just here.'

Finn was a short, squat, no-nonsense kind of feller whose father remembered the great London Dockers strike of 1889. Finn listened intently to Jack's proposition. He asked some questions too and wanted names. Jack provided the answers and they appeared to be the right ones because Finn held out an enormous, greasy hand to clinch the deal.

'The Krasnayar will have to leave port by five thirty that morning at the latest. I can give you safe passage until then but after that, you're on your own. There'll be nothing more I can do.'

Jack handed over the envelope. The deal had cost him a hundred quid – fifty for the dockers, fifty for the bobbies. But if the plan worked, it would be money well spent.

Ford stopped at the Telegraph Office on his way back to the hotel. Matt would be half way across the North Sea by now and would dock in Amsterdam within a few hours.

Jack addressed the telegram to Herr Franz Lohmann, Production Director AG Weser, Shipbuilders, of Bremen, Germany. It was four years since Jack had done Herr Lohmann a massive favour over the re-fitting of The Majesty. It was time to ask for it to be reciprocated.

Back in his hotel room, Jack began to ponder whether it would be enough. He knew he'd done all that he could, but people had short memories – especially people in business.

Lohmann had been desperate after the war. Reparations had forced German ship owners to hand over the pride of their fleets to Allied nations in compensation for loss of vessels through German U-boat attack. The Majesty – built in Bremen by AG Weser and then called the Berliner – was a liner and it had been handed over to Cunard who in turn, had passed it on to Lewis Bishop for a complete re-fit. Ford's fitters had work coming out of their ears in 1921 while the Merchant Fleet was being replaced but German shipbuilders had been starving to death. Ford remembered the letter he had received from Lohmann begging for any work that could be put their way. In the end, Ford had persuaded Manners to transfer the engine re-build to the Bremen

Yard. Manners hadn't cared a tuppeny damn – not at the price the Germans were offering to do the work. Even so, they'd had to ship the job to Weser's through a company in Sweden to cover their tracks. No-one knew – not even Matt and he had been Ford's deputy at the time. Would Lohmann do the decent thing now the boot was on the other foot? Matt Headley was travelling almost a thousand miles to find out.

Bill had never been so happy to see his wife – not because her trip had been so resoundingly successful, although it had. He'd missed her terribly and it had taken him completely by surprise. At first, he hadn't known exactly what was wrong, he'd thought he was going down with a cold. It was when Tom had come home without his mother that he'd understood. Where was Bella? His disappointment was obvious – even to himself. Dolly had looked after him well, of course – grand lass was Dolly – but it just wasn't the same without Bella. She and Bill hadn't been parted in thirty-five years of marriage and because she'd always been there, Bill simply hadn't realised that she was as much a part of him as his legs had been. And God knew how much he missed them.

'You did well, pet. You did damned well. Jack's a canny lad and all that but since he finished with our Jessie, well....I wasn't sure he'd help us. He wasn't obligated.'

But Bella knew Jack better than her husband.

'He didn't think twice Bill. And him on his sick bed an' all.'

'He'd had a right hammerin' then?'

'He did that. Ribs smashed in, black eyes. He had to have a nurse, even in the hotel.'

'Aye,' said Bill. 'I'll bet. Even when he's on the bottom he can find some pretty lass to go running about for him. He's Jack the Lad all right.'

And then: 'Bring that tin box over from the sideboard, I want to show you something. And get us both a drink while you're at it. I feel like celebrating.'

The lockable tin box was a regular feature of most working-class homes. It stored the legal fundamentals, the documents recording the rites of passage of both life and death: birth certificates, Christening certificate, marriage certificate, rent book, national insurance card, Billy's Graduation Certificate and the two latest additions - the deeds to two properties.

'If we keep going like this we'll have to get another box, Bill.'

Her eyes twinkled as she opened the envelopes and pulled out the thick parchment papers drawn up by Jowett and Co. Solicitors.

'So, Jack was right then? There was no problem with the price or anything?'

'You know what, Bella? They were nice as nine pence. As soon as they knew I was going to make a cash offer to purchase those two buildings, they had that little lassie bring in the tea and biscuits. We chatted for half an hour then settled on the price, three hundred and fifty pounds apiece plus their costs.'

'And how much were they?'

Bill spat out the figures in disgust.

'Fifty pounds, can you believe it? They said it was to cover their fees and disbursements – whatever they are.'

Bella was thinking. It had worked out exactly as Jack had said it would - seven hundred and fifty pound the pair.

'Ee Bill, how are we going to pay Jack back all that money?'

Cautious as ever, Bill had done the sums as soon as he had received the cheque. He laid his hand on hers.

'We can pay him back at least a hundred a year. That's about a pound a week per shop which is less than the rent would have been. And if we can pay it off any sharper, so much the better.

Jack was right Bella – renting's for fools. When we're done, those shops will give us a nice little pension.'

'All thanks to Jack Ford.'

Billy walked in.

'What is? What's thanks to Jack Ford?'

Bella started to fold the papers and stuff them back in the envelopes.

'It's business, Billy Seaton,' said his father, 'Nowt for you to bother yourself about.'

But Billy had come in on the end of the conversation and he wasn't ready to let it lie.

'Keeping secrets, now are we? I heard Jack Ford's name mentioned. That's never a good sign.'

One look at Bill's face was enough to tell Bella that his blood pressure was about to burst through the top of his head, so she got in first.

'Now you listen to me, Billy Seaton. Jack has just done a wonderful thing for me and your Dad – he's offered help when certain members of this family turned their backs. Now everybody's entitled to their own opinion and that's fine, but if you want to continue to live here, you'll keep a civil tongue in your head when you're talking about Jack.'

Billy held his hands up like a cowboy giving himself up to the sheriff.

'All right, I surrender. Helped you out with the getting rid of Trevelyan Street, has he? Had a word with the landlord? The old pals' act?'

Bella looked across at her husband.

'You might as well tell him, Bill. I don't like secrets and he'd find out soon enough.'

'Jack's helped us buy the two shops, if you must know.'

Bill waited for the penny to drop.

'Buy them?' Billy couldn't believe it.

'And how much has you loaned you for that?'

'Never you mind – it's a business arrangement, that's all.'

Billy didn't like the sound of that one little bit. Business arrangements meant there was a winner and a loser and he knew whose side his money was on.

'Business, is it? We all know Jack always had a good head for business. What's he charging you?'

'What do you mean?'

'Interest. What rate is he charging you?'

'Nothing,' said Bella. 'I went to see him to ask for money to help with fixing up Trevelyan Street but he said we'd be much better off buying both shops. He loaned us the money for nowt. What was the phrase, Bill?'

'Interest free.'

Billy still wouldn't have it.

'Let's see the loan agreement, then – I'll just check the small print.'

But Bill was now the one looking smug.

'There is no small print because there is no loan agreement. He told your Mam that he trusted us completely.'

'That's right,' said Bella. 'He said we were to pay him back as and when we could afford it.'

Billy was so shocked he had to sit down next to his Mam.

'We are talking about the same Jack Ford, are we? The one who blew up a precious country house so he could build an access road? The one who conned the council out of that land? The one who never did anything for anyone else but himself?'

'I told you, Billy – a civil tongue.'

'I'm sorry Mam, but I'm shocked. I really am. Perhaps he's changed. He must have done.'

'Here,' said Bella as she handed him the deeds to the properties.

'See for yourself.'

Matt had arrived in Bremen safe and sound and was waiting in the Telegraph Station for Jack's response.

Ford wrote: Proceed A G Weser Works Contact Franz Lohmann stop Be honest stop Remember Marne stop Jack

He gave the message to the lad and hoped to high heaven that Matt didn't blow it. It wasn't that Matt was unreliable but he could get flustered – especially when he was under pressure. Jack consoled himself that, at least Matt would definitely remember Marne. That was where they'd saved Morty Black.

The War was nearing its end and the Americans were pouring into the Western Front at the rate of ten thousand men a day. Jack had already volunteered to join the North Russia Expeditionary Force and was awaiting his transfer orders. There was a night patrol and Jack, Matt and Paddy Boyle had found themselves separated from the rest of their platoon when they ran for cover during a shelling. Paddy Boyle had come prepared and the three of them shared a bottle of brandy and settled themselves down in a slit trench to watch the fireworks overhead.

As he sipped his Scotch in the comfort of the hotel room, he remembered it like it was yesterday. If he closed his eyes he could even hear the shells fizzing through the air and exploding over a mile away behind their own lines.

It had been Matt who'd noticed it first, the German voice between the shell fire – an officer, barking instructions.

Ford smiled to himself, you could always identify an officer's voice - no matter what language he spoke. There was something about the delivery that separated him from the men and even the NCOs. It was full of hubris – even if that hubris was coated in fear.

The fog had been terrible that night, and it was made worse by the cordite that drifted over no-man's land - as if the devil was enjoying a smoke. But Ford had used the field glasses given to him by Captain Manners and in the ragged holes that appeared in the drifting grey curtain, he saw a small squad of German infantry marching a man back to their own lines at gun point. The man was clearly wounded and he had his hands on his head.

'I make it four plus the officer,' he'd said. 'What do you think, lads?'

'You're the Sergeant. What do you think?' Paddy Boyle had never been big on taking responsibility.

'I think, either we can go over there with the bangs and the bullets and get our man. Or we can stay here and drink some more brandy.'

'Bloody hell – let's get on with it.' Matt had known they would be killing Germans as soon as he'd heard the officer's voice. He also knew that Ford liked to drag these things out just for sport.

Paddy had stayed in the trench to give covering fire, while Matt and Jack had gone out into the darkness, separating so they could attack from two sides. What with the fog and the noise, they caught the squad completely by surprise and it had been over in seconds. The final act of slaughter had been committed by Ford himself - shooting the officer while he was aiming his pistol at the head of his prisoner. The poor man was so shocked at what he'd just witnessed that he couldn't speak but Ford had known he was an American from the uniform.

'You can drop your arms now, Yank, unless you're worried your head will fall off.'

The man was Morty Black. Matt and Jack had carried him between them – a Morty sandwich – back to their slit trench. He'd been shot in the leg – the fleshy part of the thigh – and could barely walk, never mind run. As soon as Paddy saw the three of them running back through the mist, he opened fire over their heads until all three were safely below ground level.

They'd finished off the brandy while they were waiting for the barrage to quieten down and Morty had said he didn't know how he could ever repay them.

You were wrong about that, though, Ford mused to himself, you haven't done a bad job as my stockbroker – I reckon you've found a way.

Morty had been lucky that night – not only because Matt had heard the German officer and Ford had managed to spot them. He'd been lucky because the Northumbrian Fusiliers weren't even supposed to be in Marne at all. Ford's Company had been drafted in at the last minute to offer some battle-hardened training to the new American recruits that had been thrown in at the deep end – war weary Geordies who had been ordered to pass on their skills. If Matt could remember that, maybe he'd be able to save his job and, more importantly, Sarah Headley's house.

Come to think of it, Sarah could do her bit, too.

Billy Seaton couldn't possibly keep that kind of news to himself – Jessie had to be told. And because his sister and his mother weren't exactly on the best of terms, he had to be the one to tell her.

'Don't make jokes, Billy – it isn't funny.'

'It's no joke, sis – it's true. I've seen the deeds with my own eyes.'

'But Jack? How?'

Jessie had to sit down. She was beginning to feel sick.

'Mam went down to London to see him.'

'Mam? London? Don't be ridiculous.'

'I'm telling you – she went down to see him, at The Connaught, no less.'

'Oh my God. And she begged Jack Ford for money? How could she?'

253

'It doesn't sound like that the way she tells it. According to her, she went to ask him for a loan to help with the rent. When she got there, he'd been badly beaten up. She looked after him for a few days and he advised her and Dad to buy the shops while they could get them at a good price. And on top of that, he's lent them the cash to do it – interest free.'

'Poor Arthur. He's going to come out of this very badly.'

'That's not all.'

'What now?'

Jessie had hardly even begun to process the fact that yet again, Jack Ford had managed to inflict more misery into her life.

'The people who beat Jack up.'

'What about them?'

'Mam said they were Russian.'

Jessie put her hand to her mouth as the word, 'Russian' echoed around in her head. And then she started to panic.

'Jack's on to us, isn't he?'

Billy backed off.

'What do you mean, 'us' – don't drag me into it.'

'I will drag you into it Billy Seaton, you seconded Les's motion at the CLP. And you knew all about that document.'

'That's right, I did,' said Billy, 'But I didn't steal it from a Member of Parliament.'

The bickering went on for a few minutes more until Billy realised that his sister was becoming hysterical.

'Look – we don't know that Jack's on to us, do we? He's probably been snooping around on behalf of Charlie Needham. Let's face it Jess, Needham could hardly do his own dirty work, could he? Not in his position.'

That made sense. Suddenly a wave of relief washed over her.

'Yes. Of course, you're right. Jack was probably asking too many questions – he never could let anything lie – and he's upset them. He's been warned off, that's all.'

'All the same, I think you have to put things right,'

Jessie didn't understand.

'What do you mean? If it's like you said, then what is there to worry about?'

Sometimes Billy was amazed at his sister's naivety. He was going to have to spell it out.

'Look, you stole that paper from Needham and dropped it through Mallow's letterbox. Mallow is going to use that information and it's going to hurt the man who has just loaned a huge sum of money to your parents.'

Jessie still didn't get it.

'But, it will hurt Needham mostly, and Jack hasn't known him all that long.'

Billy took a deep breath – it was either that, or tear his hair out.

'You still don't follow, do you? Les is going to use that document to gain profile in the Party AND in the union. He's going to stir up a hornet's nest with Bukanin and then, you can bet your life he's going to run for Secretary. With that kind of momentum, the chances are he'll win and then...'

The penny had dropped and Jessie finished the sentence for him.

'And then Matt Headley will be out of a job.'

She stood up then and walked to the window.

'Jack's best friend. Oh, that's horrible. I can't bear it. Jack will never forgive me.'

Billy put his arms around her.

'It's not Jack you need to worry about, Jess. It's Mam and Dad.'

She didn't want Billy to go with her but he insisted and she didn't have the energy to argue. She had stolen the document to bring Jack down a peg or two, embarrass him in front of his new friend. She knew she had done it out of malice because while many were starving, some were still getting fat. How could Needham even be a Socialist? He was born into privilege: a house in London and a vast mansion in Northumberland. Privately educated no doubt, and thousands in the bank. There were many more of them now that Labour had to be taken seriously as a party of Government – all looking to jump on the bandwagon. This had been her justification, still was her justification as they walked past the Town Hall, under the railway arches and up to Palmerston Street where Les lived in his Tyneside flat.

'Do you think you can persuade him?'

'I don't even know that I want him to be persuaded,' she said. 'But I do know I've got to try.'

Billy banged on the front door and they heard Les's work boots clumping down the stairs to answer it.

Tyneside flats were small terraced properties with a self-contained dwelling on the ground floor and another one above. Their front doors were separate and adjacent to one another so the ground floor door opened onto a hall and the door to the upper one led straight to the staircase.

Les opened up and the first face he saw was Billy's. The face softened into a smile when Les realised that Jessie had also come to visit.

'Come in, come in.'

They followed Les up the steep climb which led straight through to a simple sitting room. Les didn't have much but what he did have was looked after. The furniture, the tea service, the clock, the tablecloth, had all belonged to his mother who had died of TB twenty years earlier – even the companion set had been hers. The place smelled of mothballs and carbolic. Actually, so did Les Mallow.

He didn't get many visitors so, long ago, he had learned to be comfortable in his own company. He was a great reader now – thanks to Jessie – and he was in the process of assembling the one new thing in the residence which Billy clocked immediately.

'What's this Les? Are you building a crystal set?'

Les never wanted to appear profligate.

'It was being thrown out – so I picked it up. All it wants is a little solder – I'm fettling it up.'

Jessie and Billy had known Les a long time. He was a deep thinker and quick conversations were not his forte. They had come to see him and would have to endure the formality of tea in his – or, rather, his mother's – best china cups. He had a chipped enamel mug for everyday use.

'I'm sorry there's no biscuits or cake,' he said. 'I don't bake for myself. There's no point.'

He was being blunt, open and honest but whenever he referred to his domestic situation, people generally felt as though there was more than a touch of the martyr about Les.

'Don't worry Les, we'll get straight to the point.' Billy felt that he should say something to give Jessie a nudge – they'd been there twenty minutes already and no-one had said a word beyond the ritual tea preferences and the weather.

On cue, Jessie cleared her throat to speak.

'We want to speak to you about the meeting the other night, Les. The CLP.'

Les smiled and leaned back in his chair with a rare look of satisfaction.

'I want to thank you for that – you as well, Billy. I couldn't have managed to get that proposal through without your support. But I hope you don't mind me saying that I believed it would be forthcoming. I had every faith in you.'

'The thing is, Les,' Jessie was feeling agitated now and triumphant Les and his munificence weren't helping at all.

'The thing is we know all about that information you were talking about and we want you to return the document and, if you would be kind enough, say nothing more about it. To anyone. Ever.'

Mother's clock ticked increasingly loudly as Billy and Jessie waited while Les processed the request.

The look of satisfaction was gradually replaced by a scowl of grave concern.

Billy couldn't bear the waiting.

'You got that information by mistake, Les. It was genuinely made with the right motives, but it should never have fallen into your hands in the first place. We're dreadfully sorry about this, of course. But we need it back.'

Les looked at Jessie, then he looked at Billy and his bottom lip quivered in readiness for speech.

'Is the information inaccurate?'

'Not as far as we know,' said Billy.

Les shrugged, unmoved and slurped his tea. Jessie leaned forward to look him in the eye.

'It was me, Les. I stole it. Then I posted it through your door.'

He put his cup down and sighed.

'Did you, Jessie? I'm sorry you did that. You shouldn't have taken it.'

'I did it because of us. Because of the Movement. You understand, don't you?'

Les nodded.

'So why do you want it back?'

He was like a slab of granite – cold and hard.

Billy tried again.

'It's complicated, Les. It's a family matter. Something has

happened that Jessie couldn't possibly have known when she took that paper from Needham's coat. That's the reason we need it back.'

Les was silent again. The sound of the clock was like the workings of his brain steadily weighing up what he was being asked to do against what he knew, had to be done.

Eventually he said, 'The complication you mentioned – that's Jack Ford, isn't it?'

He was looking directly at Jessie.

'In a way.'

'In a way?' he repeated. 'That's three words for yes.'

'You've come here to give me one reason why I should hand over that paper. But I've got thousands of reasons not to do so. I'm sorry Jessie, Billy. I wouldn't have done it anyway, but when your one reason is Jack Ford – it's just impossible. I have to say no.'

'But Les –'

He held up his hand to stop her.

'I hate saying no to you, Jessie. But Bukanin is coming here and he is going to see that Privy Council note. He's going to see exactly what some of our elected politicians want to do to people like him and people like me. The needs of the many, Jessie. That's what sacrifice is all about. Think on that.'

Jessie and Billy didn't speak until they got to the bottom of Palmerston Street.

'Well, what now?'

'I seem to have made rather a mess of things, Billy. I think it's about time I faced up to Mam and Dad.'

Tom and his father were sat at the table when Billy and Jessie came through to the kitchen.

'There's more stew if you're hungry,' said Bella.

'No Mam, all I want is a word with everyone.'

'I know why she's here,' said Bill. 'Billy's told her about the business with Jack. Haven't you?'

But it was Jessie who got in first.

'Yes, Dad. Billy has told me and I'm glad. I'm glad you've got the help you need.'

'By you've sharp changed your tune.'

But Bella could see her daughter was already on the bottom. There was no need for Bill to start kicking her.

'What is it then, pet?'

'I think you'd better sit down, Mam,' said Billy.

When they were all sitting, Jessie swallowed hard, took a deep breath and out it came, right up to and including the point where she pushed Needham's document through Les Mallow's letterbox.

'Well that's bloody marvellous, that is,' said Bill. 'Did you hear her, Bella? Princess Principle? I don't know where the hell we went wrong. Three children and three thieves. A pitman, a doctor and a schoolteacher and not one of them is honest.'

'I haven't stolen anything,' said Billy.

'Oh yes you have. You've borrowed money and not paid it back – that's as good as stealing in my book.'

'Oh, be quiet the pair of you, I'm trying to think.'

'What's there to think about? She has stolen, Bella.' He drew the word out for as long as possible.

'Stolen from a Member of Parliament. That's going to look good in the Gallowshield Gazette.'

Bella could see from the look on Jessie's face that there was more to come but she didn't want Bill to hear it.

'Billy, Tom, take your father out for a pint. I want to talk to our Jessie.'

'But I don't want to go out, Bella. I want my children to tell me when they're planning their next armed robbery.'

Tom stood up.

'Come on, Dad. We'll leave the lasses to it. I don't get out so often these days that I can afford to turn down the opportunity.'

When they were gone, Bella folded her arms and sat back in her chair.

'Right young lady. I understand that you've done a terribly wicked thing just because you were jealous. But I don't know exactly what it means for Jack. I think you owe me an explanation.'

Jessie took her time and Bella listened. And all the while that Jessie talked, Bella held Jessie hands in hers – feeling the softness of her daughter's skin against the smooth, dry hardness of her own.

Jessie looked down at her feet the entire time and tears dripped from the end of her nose onto the fender, where they formed a tiny black puddle that bled into the hearth.

When it had all come out, Bella pulled Jessie to her feet and wrapped her arms around her.

'You know hinney, you think Jack's got everything, don't you? Well he hasn't. No wife, no children, no love. You've got Arthur, Dolly's got our Tom and all Jack did was walk away. All that poor lad's got in the whole wide world is a pocketful of money and a couple of mates. And you've done your damnedest to take them from him.'

'I know Mam,' she said. 'I wanted to hurt him.'

'I know you did, bonny lass. That's why it's you I feel sorry for.'

Sarah Headley didn't make a habit of going into pubs and she'd never even considered going inside one on her own but the telegram from Jack had been perfectly clear. She was to go to the Bluebell, ask for Geordie Milburn and make sure he made a telephone call.

'It's Mrs Headley, isn't it?' The landlord seemed relieved to see her.

'Is Matt not well? We haven't seen him since Sunday.'

Sarah explained that Matt had been called away for work. Did he know a Geordie Milburn?

Geordie was a giant of a man with hands like shovels and a grin as broad as a dinner plate.

'I've been expecting you, Mrs Headley. Matt said there'd be a message from Jack.'

'We're to telephone him, Geordie – at his hotel in London.'

The dinner plate smile crashed to the floor.

'But I don't know how to work the doings, Mrs Headley.'

'I'll work the doings, Geordie, don't you worry about that,' said Sarah. 'You come with me. There's a telephone kiosk over the road.'

Getting the two of them in there was proving to be impossible. Because of Geordie Milburn's sheer bulk, no matter who went in first, Sarah ended up pinned to the sides unable to move her arms or navigate her hands to the receiver. In the end, she went in alone to get Jack on the line.

'Well done Sarah. Did you get the money I wired across?

'Yes Jack. What's it for?'

'Good. When I've finished with Geordie, give it to him. Put him on now.'

She had to leave the kiosk altogether in order to let Geordie inside – even then he couldn't close the door because of his thirty-six-gallon backside. Standing behind him, holding the door open, Sarah could overhear everything that Geordie said, but it didn't matter one jot. She got precious little insight into Jack's plan.

'Aye, Jack. How many? Aye. Right you are, marrer. St Katherine's. Aye. See you then.'

Sarah could hear Jack shouting at the other end.

'Put the phone down now, Geordie. Just put it down.'

Geordie dropped the phone where he stood and left it like a hanged man dangling from a noose.

Sarah went back in again.

'Jack? Jack?'

But he'd gone so she replaced the receiver and went outside.

'Do you know what you're doing then, Mr Milburn?'

'Aye missus,' he said.

'Jack told me to give you some money,' she said as she handed him a well-cushioned envelope.

'Come on, you can use a little bit of that to buy me a drink.'

Twenty minutes later, Jack received another call from Gallowshield. This one was from the Royal Saracen Hotel.

When Bella told him about Jessie he said nothing but in a strange way, he felt relieved. He would never have put Les Mallow down as a thief: a manipulative, loathsome, resentful, coward, yes. But not a thief. And he remembered when they'd all had supper that night after the meeting that Jessie had been less than charitable towards him. Probably served him right but that was no reason for Needham to lose his seat and Matt to lose his job.

'Can you help, Jack? Can you stop it?'

'We'll see. Depends how greedy Mallow is.'

'I thought you should know, though and...well..'

'What is it, Mrs Seaton? What's wrong?'

'Well if you want your money back, we understand.'

'Certainly not. That's a business arrangement between you and me. It wasn't you stabbed my friends in the back, was it?'

'No, Jack.'

'And it wasn't Jessie either. Not really. Mallow and Bukanin are the enemy Bella. We have to remember that.'

She went back into the lounge bar to join her daughter.

'What's this?'

'It's sherry Mam. It's what ladies drink in hotels like this. What did he say?'

Bella took a sip of her drink and pulled a face in disgust.

'You know what, our Jessie? The minute you brought that man home I should have left your Dad and took him for myself. You're in luck. He still loves you – more fool him. Now get me a proper drink, this is like supping malt vinegar through a lemon.'

# CHAPTER 18

It was five miles from The Connaught to St Katherine's Dock but the roads were clear and the taxi took less than half an hour. At three-thirty in the morning it was still dark – at least two hours before dawn. Seeing the deserted streets reminded him of the times he'd spent with Rose Milne. With any luck, she'd be in Northumberland now – recuperating at Adlington Hall. She and Jack had walked back from the Ham Bone on early mornings like this, often enough. And they'd laughed as the late-night revellers had crossed paths with the early starters making their reluctant way to work – the porters, the bakers, the market traders. She was in the best place now, though. She had a chance – the Needhams would see to that. Rose Milne was too fragile for London life. Sooner or later it would have broken her. Now she was in a different world – a world of fresh air and fresh thinking. If Rose could leave Lansing Bell and London behind her, she'd be all right.

It was raining that fine, incessant fret that is silent as it falls and soaks right through to the skin. It was foggy, too, and the murk was becoming thicker as the driver followed his pointless headlamps East through Blackfriars and down towards the river. Jack got off at the bottom of Cartwright Street and walked from there. He pulled up his collar against the weather and checked his pockets. Everything her needed for a pre-dawn raid: tabs, lighter, cash, torch, wallet and Webley Mark Vl Revolver – courtesy of Captain Manners. He struck a match to light a cigarette. His hand was shaking. He watched the flame flicker in the gloom and cursed himself for not having a steadying glass before he left the hotel. You're out of practice Jack, he thought to himself.

He counted off each warehouse as he passed the double gates. He found the sixth entrance and gave a tap on the metal doors with his stick.

A voice came from the inside. It was Finn's.

'Who's out there?'

'It's me, Finn. Jack Ford - open up man – I'm catching me death, here.'

Jack heard the chain being unlocked and the grating of the gates as they slid open.

'Come in lad – you found it all right, then. Have a nip to keep the rain out.'

Jack didn't hesitate for a second and took a swig from the flask.

'Best Jamaican rum,' said Finn. 'Any amount of it three doors down.'

'Damaged in transit, was it?'

Finn smiled back at him.

'Six hundred cases came in with a load of molasses. Sadly, one or two crates slipped out of the net. River damaged, sadly.'

'The ones that got away, eh? By, that hits the spot.' He wiped his mouth and took another.

Finn lit his paraffin lamp and held it proudly above his head.

'Welcome to the Ivory House,' he said.

Through the feeble light of the faltering lamp, Ford peered into the yellow gloom. The building was so vast that Jack couldn't make out its perimeter walls which were shrouded in complete darkness but what he could see, appeared utterly bizarre. On the floor, were great piles of elephants' tusks pointing determinedly out at various angles as if they were indicating spots of particular interest. There were hundreds of them, all carefully positioned leaning against one another in neat triangular shapes like wigwams in a cowboy film

'Thousands and thousands of pounds worth of ivory,' said Finn, shipped straight here from India and Africa and destined for all corners of the civilised world.'

'Good God,' said Ford. 'No wonder you keep a padlock on that gate.'

Finn was quick to point out that usually the building was patrolled by the River Police all through the night.

'As I said, you have until five thirty, then the bobbies will be back – and I promised them everything would be here, just as they left it.'

'Don't you worry bonny lad. It's not as if anybody could slip one of those into his back pocket, is it? Might do themselves a serious mischief – some of those tusks are taller than me.'

As Ford spoke they could hear vehicles pulling up outside and Finn hauled back the gates.

'I'll get them to back in,' said Ford, 'Then they can drive straight out when we're done.'

There were three trucks in all – each carrying a dozen men. Although they were all ex-Army vehicles, one of them was now engaged in furniture removal, another belonged to a greengrocer and the third was a mobile butcher's shop. Jack shook each man by the hand as they hauled their stiff bodies out of the back of the vehicles, stretched their limbs and lit their tabs.

'What's to do, then Jack?'

Geordie Milburn approached him and held out his hand.

'Hey Geordie lad, you're a sight for sore eyes. I bet you haven't stopped grinning since you left Gallowshield.'

Jack took Geordie outside to show him the lay of the land.

'No sense in everybody getting wet.'

They stepped out of the little door at the far end of the warehouse and out onto the quay. The mist was still thick and the idling engine of the SS Krasnayar ground out a low, rhythmic drone just twenty-five yards from where they stood. Further away down river, there were fog horn chants from other vessels – rude and regular.

'If I'm right, they'll have a lass with them. She's what we're after, Geordie. They'll be trying to put her on that ship there, the SS Krasnayar. She's not too keen on the idea.'

'Damsel in distress is she, Jack?'

'Something like that. Howay.'

The Krasnayar towered above them as they approached the gangway. She was building pressure for departure but even so they could hear the Thames lapping away at her under-belly.

Jack lowered his voice to a forced whisper.

'She has to leave by five thirty to catch the tide. Hear that?'

A church clock was striking four.

'If they're not here within ninety minutes, they're not coming.'

'Won't bother us, Jack. You've already paid us.'

Then Geordie thought for a moment.

'You won't want it back, will you?'

Jack put a hand on his shoulder.

'No fear, bonny lad. Wisht!'

He gestured for Geordie to be quiet. Ford pulled his friend into the shadows and pointed at the bow of the ship.

They could see one crew member on watch. They watched as he finished his smoke and flicked the tab end over the side. As the sailor walked across to the starboard side of the ship, Jack signalled that they should move further in. They moved with long, soft strides along the ship's flank and took up a position under the metal gangway right by the water's edge.

There was virtually no breeze but still the Krasnayar creaked and moaned in the misty darkness.

Jack pulled Geordie closer so they could see each other's faces. Then he got hold of the metal ladders with both hands and shook them. Geordie nodded. Then, Jack released the gangway and made a cutting action at his throat. Geordie nodded again and this time accompanied the nod with his familiar grin.

There were footsteps above them as the crewman ambled to the stern and the two men on the dock waited until he passed overhead and turned, then they made their way across the quay to the bollards where the car would be forced to park up. Jack went through the mime once more. Dockers weren't the only ones to use sign language. Soldiers used it, too.

Jack winced as he walked back to the warehouse. He hadn't moved this much since he was attacked and his ribs grumbling about the early morning exercises.

'You all right, Jack?'

'I'll be fine, Geordie.' He reached into his coat pocket for the tablets that Nurse Chivers had left for him. 'It'll be just like the old days.'

Jack split his forces into two platoons: one to halt the enemy's advance, the other to prevent a retreat.

Two men, Reggie Pattinson and Carver Jameson, volunteered for the sentry raid; while Tommy Wright, a time-served riveter, put himself forward to be hammer man along with his mate, Mac Bovil.

Jack reckoned it would take eight men to manage the lift and that would leave half-a-dozen to make sure the objective was captured.

When he'd been through every detail, Jack went through

it again. When nobody had any questions, the two platoons dispersed without a murmur and every man took up his position.

Thick fog, cloud cover, ice cold, miserable fret and the element of surprise - Jack couldn't have ordered better conditions if he'd picked them from a menu.

His men were virtually invisible in their thick black, woollen work coats and blue overalls, caps pulled as far down over their faces as practicality allowed.

The waiting would have been intolerable had it not been so familiar. They had all done this many times before and what's more, they had done it together. They were good at it, too. They must have been because each and every one of them had survived it all.

There was a flash from the look-out's lantern. Jack signalled to the raiders. This was it.

Reggie and Carver weren't the quietest but they were by far the fastest. They were up the gangway like a couple of whippets following a chop. They hadn't even reached the upper deck before Tommy Wright and his riveter's mate, Mac Bovil, set about the gangway.

Jack didn't see Reggie and Carver's work but he heard it. There was one yelp then a muffled mumble and the slight sound of shoe heels being dragged along the deck. At the same time, there was one clanging crack from Tommy's two-handed hammer on to the iron punch held by Mac in precisely the right position on the foot-long hinge of the gangway.

'Hold, Tom!'

Reggie and Carver were sprinting back along the deck, they grabbed the gangway, jumped down to the half platform, took two steps and then leapt on to the quay. Carver's feet had barely landed on terra firma when Tommy's great arms swung again and wielded the mighty hammer once more. Mac held the punch rock steady and it forced out the bolt that was holding the ladder together. The bottom half crashed to the ground and while the top was still attached to the ship, it was satisfactorily out of reach of anyone less than twenty feet tall.

As Jack spoke he could see the headlights of a car swoop around the bend and approach road's end at the bollards. The whole thing had taken less than a minute.

'How's the lad?'

'Gagged and tied to the wheelhouse, Jack. We didn't even have to belt him.'

Jack nodded.

'Wait here boys, but prepare to advance.'

Jack walked slowly and steadily towards the car. The fog was still thick in places but it was becoming patchy in the slight breeze which had blown up as dawn approached. He watched as the front doors opened and two men got out. Then, through a gap in the mist he saw another male passenger get out of the rear and pull a female out after him. They started to walk towards the ship and towards Jack. The man and the woman in front and two men behind. When they had walked twenty yards, Jack decided that was more than enough.

'Stop!'

He yelled it – just as if he'd been talking to raw recruits. He was standing still now, thirty feet away from them.

He heard some chatter in Russian and then there was a louder voice.

'Get out of the way, Mr Ford. This is our business.'

Ford tried to concentrate as he peered through the smoky air. He recognised the bearded face.

'It's Igor isn't? Call me Jack. Hand her over and bugger off.'

The fat man laughed and spat on the ground.

Igor spoke in Russian and drew a pistol, they moved off once

271

more.

Ford could see now that Irena was blindfolded, her feet were slipping on the cobbles. Her hands were tied behind her and Igor had her firmly by the arm.

'Squad!'

The Russians stopped again as Ford shouted.

'Advance!'

Ford took a step back and looked to his right. He heard his men long before he saw them. They marched in total unison, work boots beating out a steady drum pattern on the gritty quay.

'Jack, what's happening?'

That was Irena, calling out and Igor slapped her and cursed her in Russian.

Jack drew Captain Manners' pistol from his pocket and walked over to Igor and his men. He could see over Igor's shoulder that his second platoon were already carrying out their orders.

'It's like this, friend. You've got a gun and I've got a gun. You have men and I have men.'

Igor yelled at the top of his voice and fired his gun in the air.

'Don't bother, marrer. Your crew can't get off the ship.'

Ford was up close to him now and was shoving his face up close against the Russian's.

'Tell your men to let her go.'

Igor spat out another instruction and held the gun to Irena's head.

'Perhaps we go tomorrow.'

They edged back to the car, then ran the last few strides, bundling Irena into the back. Ford heard the starter being pressed and the car lurched into gear. The engine revved hard and then it kept on revving.

Platoon Number Two had successfully lifted the back of the vehicle manually and dropped it onto axle stands.

Ford ordered his men to surround the car and seconds later thirty-odd fellers formed a ring around it. Igor and his friends were not going anywhere and the three men inside the car were exchanging confused looks.

'They're stuck lads. I think maybe we should give them a push.'

A dozen of the men got hold of the car and started rocking it from side to side until it looked as though it would tip right over. Inside, the Russians rolled around like marbles in a biscuit tin and Igor appeared to be the one bearing the blame for the embarrassing predicament they found themselves in.

Jack raised a hand and his men stepped back.

'Had enough, Igor? Or do you want to stay on the shuggy boat until the police turn up.'

The rear passenger door opened and Irena was thrown to the ground.

'Let them down, lads.'

He went to her and helped her on to her feet, pulling her blindfold off as he did so.

'Welcome home, bonny lass,' he said.

The makeshift company did a March Past as they headed down the bank and along the quay. The crew of the SS Krasnayar were lined up all along the upper deck handrail – all thirty of them. Ford could have sworn he saw the captain wink at him as he went by.

As the last of the trucks pulled out of the warehouse, Ford thought to himself that it had been a flying visit, but the lads hadn't lost any of their touch. They'd done well, worked as a team, used their individual skills to enhance the overall effectiveness of the unit and achieved their objective without a drop of blood being spilled. They were damned good soldiers – each and every man. And it was a crying shame that the country had little or no use for their abilities in peace time. At least Finn made sure they could congratulate each other properly as they re-lived the adventure on their long journey home. Two cases of rum were split between the three trucks – that would see them at least as far as Watford Gap. After that they could fund their own celebrations – ten quid a man was bloody decent money for an hour's work.

Jack and Irena's first stop was St Mary Abbott's hospital. His ribs were screaming blue murder and he'd swallowed the last of his painkillers. Nurse Chivers gave him a good scolding for not taking care of himself and she tied the fresh bandaging extra tight around his torso for good measure.

'The tighter, the better,' she said as she secured the knot.

'That's what I say when I'm out drinking.'

'And there's far too much of that than is good for you.'

Then it was Selfridges and Harrods for clothes shopping and lunch at Simpsons. But all the while Irena was looking over her shoulder.

'I can't help it, Jack. These people are butchers and they don't like to lose.'

'Neither do I,' said Jack.

But she was right. As things stood she was a runaway alien and the only way she could be truly free was to gain political asylum and a legal identity.

'I'm taking you to stay with a good friend of mine up north. He lives in a large country house, miles from anywhere. He's got powerful friends, too. You'll be safe there until we can sort things out.'

'Are you going to bring all your women here to stay with us, Jack? If you are, I'll have to tell Charles to build another wing.'

There wasn't a hint of sarcasm in Beatrice Needham's question – only mischief.

'No need for that, most of the women I've known would be just as happy in a tent at the bottom of the garden.'

'You are a truly dreadful man, Jack – but, of course, that's why they all love you.'

Mrs Needham picked up the tray of cups and saucers and Jack brought the coffee and the milk.

Irena and Charles were deep in conversation about asylum and Rose Milne was sat by the fire with the two oldest Needham children, Julian and Clarissa.

'How is Rose doing?'

Beatrice considered the question.

'She's fragile.'

Ford could see that Rose was withdrawn. She'd hardly spoken during supper.

'Mentally? Physically?'

'Yes – in equal measure, I would say. The children all adore her but she's dreadfully quiet – as if she was somehow disconnected from the world. Not even Mary can coax a smile out of her.'

That was bad news, the five-year-old could get a laugh out of sliced liver. Ford studied Rose from across the room. The hand gestures and facial movements seemed to be following conversation easily enough but it was if they were operated on strings, ever so slightly out of time. And although she was present in body, her eyes told the story of an absence of spirit – an absence of light.

'Jack, come over here and bring that coffee pot with you.'

Charles and Irena were looking pleased with themselves.

'Look here.'

He showed Jack a document with a long list of Russian names.

'This is a list of the Russian aristocracy now living here in Britain. Most of them have ended up in Berlin or Paris but we've had quite few as you can see. The point is this, almost all of them have now been granted citizenship so they have exactly the same rights as you and I. More importantly, Irena knows several of these families. That means they can vouch for her true identity. On top of that, of course, you and I can support her application through the Home Office protocols. I really can't see any reason why she shouldn't be allowed to stay here on a permanent basis.'

'You'll be writing one of your letters then, will you Charles?'

'Oh yes, Jack. I shall relish the opportunity. And with a bit of luck and a following wind Countess Irena Goliksyn will soon become one of His Majesty's subjects.'

At the sound of those words, Irena crumpled and Beatrice was there before the first tear fell.

'It's all over now, darling. You're here and you're safe. Home and dry.'

She cradled Irena's head in her lap and gestured with a flick of her head that it was time for the men to go elsewhere.

They sought refuge in Charles' study and plundered his store of whisky.

'Here you are, Jack. I think you roundly deserve it after your efforts today.'

But Jack just shrugged his shoulders.

'All I did was put the plan together. The lads did all the donkey work. The whole thing went like clockwork, thank God.'

'So that's Phase One of the operation completed successfully. I hate to be selfish Jack, but what are your thoughts about Phase Two?'

The next morning, Julian drove Jack through to Gallowshield and he dropped off his bags at the Royal Saracen before going in search of Matt Headley. He'd had no word from his friend for two days and if they were going to stop Bukanin and Les Mallow, Matt would have had to have won a major charm

offensive with the Germans. Jack would have described Matt
as many things – loyal, steady, ponderous, generous, reliable –
but never charming. Turning into Lavender Avenue, he consoled
himself with the thought that Sarah may well have taught her
husband a thing or two in that department. And even while she
was in his thoughts, the lady herself came into view, closing the
garden gate of her house before walking up the road.

Jack called after her and when she turned and recognised him,
her anxious face relaxed into a genuine smile of relief.

'Oh, it's you, Jack. Thank God - what a sight for sore eyes. I'm
just off to meet Matt, his ferry's docking any minute.'

'Can I walk along with you?'

'You can count on it. I'm not letting you out of my sight until
you explain everything that's gone on.'

They walked on together past the pristine gardens of the
avenues, across the park where the bowlers smoked and grunted,
over the little railway bridge beside the old school where the
bairns gathered to plot rebellion and on to the new road that led
down to the river. He could tell from the pinched look around
her eyes that Sarah hadn't been sleeping well and she was pale
– even for a lass from Tyneside.

'Are you all right, Sarah? You look worried?'

'Worried? I've been beside myself, Jack.'

'That's a neat trick.'

She stopped and turned and challenged him, then.

'Don't start.'

'What?'

They walked on again.

'You being you. Cracking jokes, making light. There's nothing
funny happening here, Jack. This is serious. I've been so scared.
So frightened.'

She swallowed the last word as her gloved hand came up to

cover her mouth and the tears started to flow.

The wall around the school yard was only three feet high with a six feet iron fence drilled into it. Sarah perched on the wall and leaned back against the railings. She'd pulled the plug out now and the tears wouldn't stop until they'd all drained away.

Ford gave her his hankie.

'I do know, Sarah,' he said.

'I do know it's not a laughing matter. It's just my way of dealing with it, that's all.'

She lifted her eyes above the level of the hankie and glared at him.

'Well it's a stupid way.'

'Not half as stupid as trying to hold a conversation with a hankie in your mouth.'

She didn't laugh but she did resign herself to nod as she took out her powder compact and surveyed the damage with the little mirror that lived in the lid.

'Look at the clip of me. This is all your doing, Jack Ford. What on earth will Matt think?'

Jack was going to make another joke about Matt and his capacity for thought but decided against it. Sarah was angry at him – that meant she felt better.

Instead he played it straight and true. He told Sarah everything. He started with his friend Lohmann and how he'd helped him after the war. That's why he'd sent Matt to meet him and made the introduction.

'What can this Mr Lohmann do?'

'Well he's not going to turn down an order for a dirty great ship, he needs it as much as we do – if not more. But he could perhaps give Gallowshield a bigger part of the deal.'

'Enough to beat Les Mallow?'

'That's up to Matt. It's his own job he's fighting for as well as everybody else's.'

Sarah had been dabbing away at her face while Jack talked and even though she was still dissatisfied with the result, she resigned herself to the make-do-and-mend result and the two of them walked on.

'But couldn't you have gone with him, Jack? You were a great team, you and Matt. You knew Mr Lohmann.'

'I would have gone if I could, Sarah. But there was something else I needed to do.'

She looked at him and a loud gong sounded in her head.

'Geordie Milburn!'

Sharp as a tack.

'That's right,' said Jack, 'Geordie Milburn and the thirty blokes just like him.'

He told her about the Countess and about Igor and the Russians; about her plans for escape and how she'd been imprisoned by Bukanin's men.

Her eyes were like pudding bowls when he described the scene at the dockyard.

'Poor lass. Where is she now?'

'She's at Charles Needham's house in Northumberland. And mind, Sarah – that's just between you, me and Matt. Nobody else.'

'I won't tell a soul, Jack. This isn't gossip, this is real people's lives. I know when to keep my gob shut.'

'I know you do, pet – I wouldn't have told you otherwise. There's something else an' all.'

'Go on?'

Jack hesitated but he'd come this far and, like Sarah said, people lives were at stake. Sarah had earned the right to know the lot.

'While Matt was on his way to Germany, I got a phone call

from Bella Seaton.'

'Oh, aye? What has she got to do with all this?'

'Nothing at all. She just wanted me to know that it was her daughter, Jessie, that took the paper from Needham's coat pocket and gave it to Les Mallow.'

There was a slight pause in Sarah's stride and Jack saw the muscles in her jawline ripple as she clenched her teeth.

She said the name very softly.

'Jessie Seaton?'

'Aye. Well, Jessie Ashton, now.'

'Your Jessie Seaton?'

'It was a long time ago, Sarah.'

'Obviously not long enough, Jack. My God, what a mess.'

The posters began appearing as soon as they passed the locked gates of Lewis Bishops Shipyard and they continued at regular intervals all the way down to the riverside. Even the ferry terminal had one on the notice board. Under the headline 'Hands Across The Water', there was a picture of smiling Russian Trade Union leader Mikhail Bukanin addressing the adoring crowds at Clydebank.

'Don't you think he looks a bit like Lord Kitchener, Sarah.'

'No, I don't. I think he looks like trouble.'

Jack read the advertisement.

'The North East Trades Union Council is honoured to give you the opportunity to meet Mr Mikhail Bukanin, hero of the Russian Revolution at Gallowshield Mining Institute, 7.30p.m.

Saturday 30th September. Tickets 1s.'

Somebody had gone around earlier and pasted a large 'Tonight!' sign right across the poster from corner to corner.

'You don't want to be like that, bonny lass – he's top of the bill.'

'He was Jack, look – here comes our Matt.'

Sure enough, Matt was first off. He saw Sarah and Jack in the waiting area and gave them a wave before striding down the gangway.

Sarah ran forward to hug him as he came through the ticket barrier and she was still clinging to him like a well-cut coat as they re-joined Jack.

'Well, Matt. What fettle?'

The big man gripped Jack's hand.

'What say we take a walk up to The Blue Bell and I'll tell you all about it.'

The pub had only just opened when they walked in the door and the smell of old tab smoke and stale beer was overpowering.

'Are you sure you don't want to wait for me at home, pet? Jack and I won't be long, I promise.'

'No fear Matt Headley. You're stuck with me, like it or not. I want to know everything.'

'Best get on with it, bonny lad – I've had the same trouble with her,' said Jack.

The landlord was caught on the hop. He hadn't found time to put the collar on his shirt, yet.

'Pint Matt, Jack – oh, and Mrs Headley. How nice to see you, again. That's twice in three days.'

Matt's face was like thunder and Jack could barely contain himself.

'What the Hell's he talking about, Sarah? He's chatting to you as if you were a regular.'

Sarah looked right past him.

'Port and lemon please, Mr Hind.'

And then to Matt.

'I had to come in to find Geordie Milburn, didn't I?'

'Did you? What for?'

'That was the instruction in Jack's telegram.'

'Was it? Telegram? Oh right. I see. Right.'

'Come on then, Matt. Cut to the chase. What happened?'

'Well first off, I was bloody sea sick, which didn't help but I found me way to Bremen all right. Mind you I had a right carry on getting a ticket. If it hadn't been for that Polish lass...'

'What Polish lass?'

This could take days and Jack knew the clock was ticking.

'Never mind, Sarah. Spoke English, did she Matt?'

'That's right, Jack. Anyway, I got that telegram you sent and read the bit about Marne.'

'You remembered it?'

'Of course, I remembered Marne. That's where we rescued Morty Black.'

Sarah was baffled by now.

'Who?'

'Never mind, pet. The important thing is that I also remembered the training we had to do so I knew what you were driving at, Jack.

'I walked to the yard and asked for Mr Lohmann only to find that he was expecting me.'

'He got my letter?'

'Yes, Jack and he was so grateful to you for helping them out in 1921. He went on and on about it.'

'So, could he help us now?'

'It took a while to agree on some numbers but there is an offer on the table.'

Sarah was fit to bursting.

'Well? What is it?'

To be truthful Matt wasn't exactly sure whether he'd got a good deal or a bad deal, so he blurted it out in a rush.

'He'll take another two hundred of our fitters for six months on a work and training contract.'

'Two hundred?' Jack was amazed.

'It was the best he could do – he only agreed to that because I wasn't pushing for any other trades. He won't have welders, sparkies or chippies. Just fitters.'

Sarah looked from Matt to Jack and back again.

'By lad, you've done well. Bloody well,' said Jack.

'Have I, I mean, do you think so?'

Jack shook him by the hand.

'I couldn't have done any better myself and that's a fact.'

But Sarah still wanted reassurance.

'Will that be enough, Jack? Will two hundred six month jobs in Germany put an end to Mallow?'

'Who knows bonny lass, but it's a start and it's better than I'd dared hope for.'

But Matt still wasn't looking thrilled.

'There's something else, Jack.'

'Oh, aye. What's that?'

'I know who the customer is. Lohmann told me.'

Jack grinned at him.

'It's the Russians, isn't it?'

'Well yes. How did you know?'

'I didn't – not for certain. There was something that Manners said, months ago, about the Germans under-cutting everybody and even building ships for rebel nations. But there was something else an' all. Do you remember when Tom had a snoop around the 1917 Club?'

'I'll never forget it,' said Matt, 'I was look-out.'

'That's right. When Tom came back he brought me a bottle of beer he'd picked up from a crate under Bukanin's bed.'

'I remember that, too,' said Matt.

'That beer was made by Brauerel Beck and Company.'

'So?'

'It's a brewery based in Bremen, Matt. That was a little thank you gift – probably from Lohmann himself.'

'But that's bad for us, isn't it? With Bukanin and Mallow and the meeting tonight. Mallow and the Russians will be all in this together.'

'Depends how you present it, Matt. Bukanin has come here on a recruitment drive, right? But he hasn't a clue that we know he's done a deal with Lohmann. In fact, nobody knows.'

Matt still didn't see how that helped but Sarah had been hanging onto every word.

'You could use that against him, couldn't you Jack?' she said.

'If I have to. But I've got plenty of other stuff to be going on with.'

# CHAPTER 19

J ack slipped out of the Royal Saracen Hotel at half past five
and walked along to the Mining Institute. If he was going to
have a heart to heart with Mr Bukanin, he would need to find
somewhere private to talk and Fitzy was just the man to provide
the accommodation.

'Well of course, there's a boiler room, Jack. Follow me but
watch your step.'

They went through the door opposite reception and down the
spiral staircase. The steps were metal, narrow and very steep
and slippery.

'You've got to watch yourself down here in the dark mind. You
could come a right cropper.'

'Thanks Fitzy, I'll try not to have too many before the meeting.
At the bottom of the stairs was a single door that led straight
into Fitzy's lair.

'It's bit cramped mind, Jack.'

'If it happens there'll only be the two of us. This'll do nicely
Fitz. I'm grateful.'

'No bother at all lad. I'll be upstairs when you get here. You
just tip me the wink when you want to come down and I'll unlock
the door for you.'

Bathed, changed and ready he walked into the hotel bar at seven o'clock for a quick one before the main feature. A quick look around told him everybody else had had the same idea – well the Royal Saracen was the nearest watering hole to the Institute.

Ford already knew Bukanin was staying in the hotel that night so it was no surprise to see him and his comrades drinking vodka at the table by the fire but he was surprised to see Jessie Ashton and Billy Seaton sitting with Les Mallow in the corner by the window. Just as Jack was wondering why Billy looked so sheepish and Jessie so dejected, Matt and Sarah arrived.

'Well the gang's all here,' said Ford. 'What time do you think the show starts?'

'Right now, by the look of it,' said Matt.

As he spoke Les tried to get up, Jessie put a hand out to try to reason with him but as far as Jack could see, Les had that determined look on his face. He walked straight over to the Russian's table and introduced himself.

'I think Les is about to show his hand,' said Matt.

'In public? With witnesses? Surely, he wouldn't have the nerve,' said Sarah.

'He'd be daft enough,' said Ford. 'But Bukanin isn't. Hey up – they're on the move.'

Bukanin stood up and left the bar with Les leaving his drinking buddies to tussle over responsibility for the next round.

'They'll be going up to his room and Les will hand over that document as sure as night follows day.'

'Right,' said Sarah, 'I'm going over to give that Jessie Ashton a piece of my mind.'

'Whoa there. Don't spoil it, Sarah – we're only half way through Act One. We haven't even got to the interval yet. Just relax and enjoy the show. Drinks?'

Matt worried, Sarah fumed and Jack wondered what he was

going to say to Bukanin.

Five minutes later, Bukanin returned to the bar and the Russians got up to leave. Mallow, looking particularly smug, went over to Billy and Jessie who immediately turned her head away from him.

They all trooped out of the hotel and turned right down the street towards the Institute. A crowd had gathered by the great oak doors as people queued to get in. There was Press there too and the flash bulbs were popping with gusto just ahead of Jack as the snappers went to work on their esteemed Russian visitor.

'When we get inside, Matt, take Sarah to the seats. I'm going to try to get a word with Bukanin before it starts.'

'You'll never get him alone, Jack. Not with all his flunkeys with him.'

Jack winked at him.

'You never know your luck.'

They all had VIP tickets, except for Jack who hadn't bothered to get a ticket at all, and walked straight past the waiting crowd and into reception. It was then that Jack charged through to Bukanin's side.

'Could I have a private word, Mr Bukanin?'

Bukanin looked at him.

'The name's Ford. Jack Ford.'

Two of the comrades were trying to edge Jack away.

'I'm sorry, Mr Ford. I'm running late. I must get on.'

He pressed ahead and the comrades edged more enthusiastically.

'I have an important message from a Mr Lohmann,' said Jack.

Bukanin stopped dead in his tracks.

'It will take just one moment. There is a private room just through this door.'

Bukanin sighed.

'Very well. I will give you one minute.'

Ford nodded at Fitzy who unlocked the door and descended the narrow steps, Bukanin followed accompanied by his largest comrade and Jack brought up the rear.

As he closed the door behind him he saw Sarah throw a 'fingers crossed' sign in his direction. He caught a glimpse of Jessie, too, in the throng. She had rather a puzzled look on her face.

Fitzy opened the boiler room door and Bukanin and Ford went inside. Fitzy and the comrade stayed on sentry duty.

'Well, Mr Ford. What is this message from Herr Lohmann?' Jack became businesslike.

'He says to tell you how much he is looking forward to doing business with you.'

'Really? What sort of business is he referring to, do you think.'

'Building you a ship, Mr Bukanin.'

There was silence then as Bukanin mulled over the possible repercussions of that information becoming common knowledge in a depressed shipbuilding town like Gallowshield.

Bukanin took off his hat and put it down on Fitzy's work bench and started to undo the buttons on his coat.

'It's very hot in here, Mr Ford. I prefer the cold. Tell me, how did you get to know about this arrangement?'

'It's a small world, Mr Bukanin and Lohmann and I have done business before. He's a good man.'

'He's a capitalist, Mr Ford. But he's the cheapest capitalist we could find.'

'Tell me, Bukanin, why are you here? What's the purpose of your European tour? I'd have thought you would have had plenty to get on with back home.'

Bukanin laughed – a deep, throaty chuckle.

'There is much work to be done at home and abroad, Mr Ford. You see this?'

Bukanin looked down and patted Fitzy's old wooden work bench.

'I was tied to a bench like this for twenty-five years. I made farm tools for the peasants, Mr Ford. I made the spades and the scythes and the pitchforks and the chains that broke their backs when they went to work. They didn't own their tools, Mr Ford, their landlord did. He also owned their houses and their cows and their seeds and their carts – even their wives and their children. Today, no man owns anything and every man owns everything. That's why I'm here, Mr Ford – to show what can be done if people say they've had enough.'

'You're a bit like St Paul the Evangelist, aren't you? Spreading the good news.'

'If you like. But if I'm going to spread the word effectively, I need to help make my country great. That means we need new roads and hospitals and factories...'

'And ships,' said Ford.

'That's right. And ships. We did a deal with Lohmann because we had no choice. Freedom is a wonderful thing, Mr Ford but to grow, we need to modernise at a price we can afford.'

'The Germans aren't very popular around here, Mr Bukanin. People sacrificed a lot during the war and they have long memories. Now they can't get work, their bairns are shoeless, their wives are sick and their houses are cold. As soon as I tell them who your new friends are, they'll tear this place apart and you with it.'

'Why would you do that? Politics?'

Jack leant forward and pushed his face right up to the Russian's.

'I don't care about your politics Bukanin or anybody else's for that matter. And you're no apostle, either. Your men beat me to a pulp and left me for dead in a London street. You kidnapped a friend of mine, locked her up and if I hadn't got her away she'd have been well on the way to St Petersburg right now to face a firing squad. Does that sound like the promised land to you, Bukanin?'

Bukanin protested then.

'That is not us. That is the Cheka – the secret police – they go everywhere with us. They do what they like.'

'Then so will I Bukanin. So will I.'

Ford walked to the door. He had his hand on the handle when Bukanin spoke.

'What is it that you want, Mr Ford?'

Jack stopped and turned.

'You must want something, otherwise you would have just ruined my speech or gone to the police. What will it take for you to remain silent?'

The sunken lecture hall at the Mining Institute was rammed full – the staff had given up checking tickets when Jack and Fitzy forced their way up the stairs past the men who were queuing with their union banners and their Labour Party memberships. The police were there too, but they kept a discreet distance from the throng – no sense in teasing the beast, better to let it cheer and stomp and let off steam in a confined space.

'This way, Jack.'

Fitzy led him through an unmarked door and along a passage way which ended in the wings of the lecture theatre. Fifteen feet away from him in front of the waiting crowd was the top table – the organising committee for Bukanin's visit. There was Les Mallow, looking down at his welcome speech and making last-minute adjustments with a well chewed pencil. Next to him was his henchman-in-chief Malcolm Poskett and on the other side, Billy Seaton looking proud as punch that the good ship Socialism had finally docked in Gallowshield. His sister was in the front row of the audience and just behind her sat Matt and Sarah – desperately trying not to look anxious.

Jack straightened his tie and marched slowly out onto the floor. In his left hand, he carried a piece of paper. He stopped at the top table, and leaned forward in front of Mallow.

'Sorry to interrupt Les, but before you get underway, I've got an important message for Mr Headley.'

Mallow didn't speak. His eyes were fixed on the document and the House of Commons portcullis emblazoned at its head. When Jack was certain that Les had seen enough he walked out to the crowd, excused himself to Jessie before leaning over her to talk to Matt.

'Mr Bukanin sends his regards, Mr Headley. When he's finished his speech he'd very much like to invite you to make your announcement – if that would be convenient.'

'Thanks Jack. Tell Mr Bukanin, that I would be delighted.'

Sarah beamed.

Les Mallow didn't join Bukanin for drinks in the lounge bar of the Royal Saracen after the rally but Matt and Sarah were there, and Jessie and Billy. The toast was International Socialism but as far as Jack was concerned, the whisky tasted just as good.

Jessie eventually plucked up the courage to approach him.

'Where've you tethered it then?'

'I'm sorry?'

'The great white steed. Is he tied to the lamppost outside or have you left him in reception?'

'I'm no knight in shining armour, Jessie. You know that better than anyone.'

'Aye, I do. But you do a bloody good impression of one, Jack – enough to con the masses.'

He put an arm around her.

'Look at that.'

The bar was packed and there was a great throng of people around Matt and Sarah Headley all raising their glasses in celebration of the man who'd travelled to Germany to win jobs for Tyneside.

'I'm not conning the masses, Jessie. I leave that to the politicians.'

And then his voice softened.

'Are we friends again?'

She was looking at him but he could tell she was trying hard to find an answer to the question.

'You hurt me too much for us to be friends, Jack. I can't seem to get past that, I'm sorry. I tried revenge and look where that got me. Let's just say we know each other well, and call a truce.'

Jack was about to reply when he saw a breathless Julian Needham run into the bar.

'Mr Ford – you need to come to Adlington. Rose is very ill.'

'What's the matter? Has she seen a doctor?'

Julian shook his head.

'Our local quack is delivering a baby over at Otterburn.'

Jack turned to Billy Seaton.

'Fancy a night shift, Dr Seaton?'

They had to stop at the Seaton house to collect Billy's bag but then Julian put his foot down and they raced through the half-light of the town and out into the gloom of the Northumberland countryside.

'Tell me about the patient, Jack.'

Jack had to shout to make himself heard over the straining motor.

'Her name's Rose, Rose Milne. Been suffering from depression. Charles Needham brought her up here from London to recuperate.'

'From the depression?'

'From the drugs she's been taking to keep the depression at bay.'

Billy had seen a lot of drug addiction in Edinburgh where he'd done his medical training.

'What was she taking, Jack, do you know?'

'She used to take a sleeping draught regularly – something called Neonal - but she also took cocaine. As much as she could get her hands on. That's why Charles brought her out of London – to get her away from the stuff.'

As they sped along the Scotland Road, the full moon guided them like a giant paper lantern suspended from a clear sky. Jack recounted the tales of the Ham Bone Club and the all-night parties that Rose hosted with Lansing Bell. He described the profound loss Rose felt at the death of her mother and her growing addiction to anything that would take away the pain.

'She used to say it was the only thing that brought some pleasure into her life. Then one day I found her unconscious in the bath.'

Jack told Billy about the young doctor and the nose bleed.

'A doctor can only go on the evidence presented to him, Jack. It's not his fault.'

No it wasn't, thought Jack, but it wasn't Rose Milne's fault either.

The car very nearly took off over the little hump backed bridge and a spray of gravel shot out from under the tyres as it pirouetted to a standstill outside Adlington Hall.

One look at Charles' face told Jack that the situation was grim and Billy went straight up to Rose's bedroom.

'Bea just found her collapsed on the bed, Jack. There was blood seeping from her nose and mouth – even her ears. A terrible, terrible mess.'

They sat and talked and drank and Jack suddenly remembered

Bukanin. He dug in the inside pocket of his jacket and handed the briefing memo back to Charles.

'While I remember, put this in the safe, Charles. Tonight's not the night for celebrating.'

Charles took it and raised his glass.

'You're right, Jack. Tonight's not the night, but you're one Hell of a friend.'

No sooner had Charles re-locked the safe than Beatrice and Irena appeared at the door.

'I'm sorry. She died a few moments ago.'

It was Irena who spoke. Beatrice went straight to her husband.

Jack and Irena left Charles and Bea comforting each other downstairs and went up to find Billy.

'You can come in, Jack. The ladies have been marvellous. They've cleaned her up as best they could.'

Rose lay on the bed as dead as dead could be. She looked tiny in her stillness, her form so small it barely raised the bedclothes.

'Bloody waste,' said Billy.

'I'm sure you did all you could, lad.'

'Oh she was well on the way when I got here – hardly breathing. My guess is she'd a heart attack. There was a massive haemorrhage, too. She must have misjudged her medication.'

'What do you mean, her medication? She wasn't taking anything. That's why Charles brought her here, so she could get all that stuff out of her system.'

But Billy was certain.

'She was definitely on something, Jack. Her pupils were dilated and she was completely unresponsive. She was breathing, yes, but not conscious. Out of it.'

Jack started opening the drawers of the bedside cabinet and searching through them.

'If she was on something then it must be in here. She wouldn't risk hiding anything elsewhere in the house because of the children.'

The three of them began to look through Rose's belongings but it was Irena who found the gift basket. It was tied with yellow silk ribbon and placed out of sight in the bottom of the wardrobe. Inside were bath salts, perfume, rouge and a powder compact.

'This isn't face powder,' said Billy, licking a sample from the tip of his little finger. 'It's cocaine.'

There was a card attached, it read 'To my darling Rose, this is to make you feel good as new again. Love LB.'

'Who's LB?' asked Billy.

'Lansing Bell,' said Jack. 'Her best friend in the whole wide world.'

Best friend or not, Lansing Bell didn't attend the funeral. Beatrice Needham arranged everything and mourners gathered at Adlington Hall before following the horse-drawn hearse on the mile-long journey up to Camber Village. The Needham family was out in full force – even little Mary steadfastly strode up the steep hill hand-in-hand with her father. Bella had come too, to accompany Billy Seaton. The churchyard was up on a hill overlooking Tynedale with views stretching almost as far as Gallowshield itself.

The vicar's surplice flapped erratically about like a flag on a pole on a windy day, he read the words well enough and the coffin was lowered into the ground.

The setting was picturesque and the solemnities appropriately observed but there was an insignificance to the whole proceedings which did nothing but deepen the sadness.

'It's odd,' said Jack, 'I've seen a lot of deaths but I haven't been to that many funerals.'

'Is it odd?' Asked Irena, 'I am the same.'

As they walked back down to Adlington the wind blew stronger and she pulled him even closer.

'In St Petersburg, after you left, there were battles in the streets. I had to step over the corpses to queue for bread.'

There wasn't a trace of emotion in her voice – no revulsion or pity, just a frankness born out of familiarity.

'That woman there with the doctor. Who is she?'

'That's Billy's Mam, Bella Seaton.'

'She loves you, like a son.'

'Get away – she's got two sons and a daughter of her own.'

'So what? She still loves you. She can't help it.'

'How do you know?'

'By the way she looks at you – it's obvious.'

'We've been through a fair bit together – that's all.'

Bella came over then and Billy introduced her to Irena. Jack could see she was desperate to gather everything she could possibly glean about the Countess.

'By lad, a proper Countess, eh? And you met in Russia – well, I wouldn't fathom it. And Jack, Bill says to tell you all's going well with the shops. That one in Trevelyan Street will be open next week.'

'I'm glad Mrs Seaton – that's really good news.'

'Thanks again lad. We'd have been lost without you.'

Later, when they were alone he told Irena about Jessie and about the shops and how he'd loaned the money to buy them.

'You did this? But why?'

'Because I could.'

'But you're taking a risk. You might not get your money back.'

'I've already got it back.'

She looked puzzled then.

'How come? Explain.'

'It's perfectly simple. I loaned them eight hundred pounds to buy two shops that I already owned. I got them thrown in as makeweight in a big land deal I was involved with two years ago. There were six altogether. All I've got to do now is work out how to get rid of the other four.'

Irena's eyes were out like organ stops when he'd finished. Then she started to laugh.

'You won't stop it, you know.'

'Stop what?'

'The revolution.'

'I don't want to stop it. I just want to delay it long enough for us to get to America.'

# CHAPTER 20

'Of course, I want everybody there – it's a celebration. And anyway, Irena says if the children aren't coming she's cancelling the whole thing.'

'But why not have it at Adlington? After all, it's me who should be thanking you. You got me out of one hell of a scrape, Jack.'

'It's always questions with you, Charles, isn't it? If we hold it at the Hall, then you'll play host all night and Beatrice will do all the work. It's all booked, The Royal Saracen, tomorrow night at seven o'clock. Now please don't argue. We'll be back in plenty of time and we'll see you there.'

The train pulled away leaving Charles Needham still protesting on the platform. Jack and Irena wandered down the carriage to their seats. Irena had almost begun to relax during their stay at Adlington but now they were heading back to London for their meeting at the Home Office and the tension was beginning to return to her face.

'Look again.'

'Everything is in the case. I checked the papers before we left.'

'Please Jack.'

He knew she wouldn't let up until he complied. He opened the case.

'It's all here: letter of introduction, application form, sponsor identification, supporting statements – the lot.'

She nodded her satisfaction.

'What if it's not enough, Jack?'

'Then we'll get them whatever it is they need – stop worrying.'

They ate on the train then went straight on to Westminster to meet with Senior Assistant Principal Secretary Sidney Bowen.

Jack handed over the letters as requested and Mr Bowen went through each one in ponderous detail pausing only to utter the words 'Very good' and 'Excellent' in a husky basso profundo voice with every turn of the page.

Eventually he picked up the papers and straightened them in a neat pile by tapping them on the desk.

'So, Countess Goliksyn, you actually want to become a British citizen, is that right?'

'What kind of a question is that?' said Ford. 'Why else would we be here?'

Bowen smiled benignly and Ford instantly became even more irritated.

'My dear Mr Ford, most Russian emigres have no desire whatsoever to become British citizens.'

'Really? Why not?'

Irena knew immediately.

'They believe that one day they will return to Russia,' she said. 'They do not think Bolshevism will last.'

Bowen's benign smile was this time accompanied by a patronising tilt of his perfectly coiffured head.

'Absolutely correct, Madam. And where do you stand?'

'Unlike my compatriots I have seen Bolshevism first hand. I have seen the control they have over the people. I have no desire to go back. I am lucky to be alive.'

There was that frankness again – a no-nonsense honesty that

even pompous Bowen could not resist.

He emitted a nervous cough and looked down to fill in yet another form.

'Right, yes. This form declares you to be a desirable alien – that is, someone we would welcome as a resident here in Great Britain and Ireland. Your financial guarantees are in order and you are free to obtain employment here if that is your wish.'

'It is but not just yet.'

The cough again.

'Quite. Because of the, shall we say, esteemed calibre of your backers, because you are known to other Russian aristocratic families and because your well-being is underwritten, you will not be considered a potential burden on the state. It is therefore highly likely that you will be granted Nationalised Citizenship. Until those formalities have been concluded, we can make you an offer of permanent residency from today. Would that be satisfactory?'

The Countess was more than satisfied – she was even prepared to treat them both to a smile.

She celebrated with a shopping trip to Bond Street - Jack had other matters to attend to but they were back at The Connaught by teatime.

'I'm so grateful, Jack.'

'Don't tell me that when we're in bed. It makes me sound like some kind of monster.'

'You are a monster,' she said. 'That is one of the reasons I'm so grateful.'

'Thanks a bunch. Do you want your champagne?'

He reached over and handed her the glass.

'I don't want you to feel like a prisoner.'

'I don't,' he said. 'Not in the least.'

'Not now – but you might. You might feel it is your duty to stay with me so I can stay in this country. I don't want that.'

He looked at her – and took in the sight of one of the most naturally elegant and graceful women he had ever encountered.

'I know what you mean. It's hard work, but I think I can cope.'

But Irena Goliksyn wasn't just mesmerizingly beautiful, she has hard-headed and competent, too.

'When we're tired of each other, I promise to find a rich man somewhere else.'

'We've only just got back together again and you're already on the look-out for another feller. You're unbelievable.'

'When we're tired of each other, I said.'

'And how long will that take?'

'Who knows? Certainly not in the next hour or so.'

She reached for him again and the glass had to be returned to the bedside table. It was ten in the evening before he stirred himself.

'Come on. It's time to get ready.'

After bathing they had supper in their room before enjoying a drink in the hotel bar. The doorman ordered the cab and they were outside the Ham Bone Club just after midnight.

'Now remember your promise to be a good boy.'

'Yes, Miss,' said Jack as he escorted her up the stairs.

There was no Rose on sentinel duty – just a slim, greasy-haired youth in an expensive suit haphazardly throwing their entry money into a pot. He was too far gone to even count it.

Inside the jazz was warming up and band was good – American and they were half way through a muscular rendition of Hard Hearted Hannah The Vamp Of Savannah. The dance floor was heaving and that familiar, heady fug was hanging over dozens of gyrating bodies.

Irena was obviously fascinated and would have stood transfixed just watching the entertainment had Jack not spotted Lansing

Bell by the bar.

'Come on – I recommend the whisky. It's from Croydon.'

Lansing Bell felt his world fall out of the pit of his stomach when he turned to see a grinning Jack Ford approaching. He was ever-so-slightly relieved when he saw that a tall, glamorous woman was holding on to his arm.

'Jack Ford. An unexpected pleasure, I'm sure.' He managed to say the words clearly enough but even over the noise of the band, there was no disguising the tremor in his voice.

'How are you, Lansing? Fit and well?'

The last three words were delivered with just sufficient venom to leave Lansing in absolutely no doubt where he stood.

'Oh, you know. We try to carry on. I miss Rose terribly, of course. She was such a joy. A true delight.'

'Wasn't she just,' said Jack.

Irena could see Jack's simmer was about to erupt into a rolling boil so she delicately intervened.

'Good evening. I'm Irena, what a fascinating place, this is.'

'I'm sorry. How rude of me,' said Jack. 'Lansing Bell, this is Countess Irena Goliksyn.'

Even through his fear, Lansing's eyes lit up at the sound of the title.

'A Countess? How marvellous. Welcome to our little Ham Bone Club.'

He exchanged just enough meaningless chit chat not to appear rude before scuttling off to be self-important elsewhere.

While Jack ordered the drinks she said, 'Nasty little man. I'm glad he's gone.'

'Let's just find a quiet corner and enjoy the music. I shouldn't think we'll have to wait too long.'

It was just after two in the morning when the club descended into the full blown hedonistic behaviour that all the guests had come for. And when the band had finished and the exhausted bodies had paired off to disappear in dark corners and underneath tables, Jack asked Irena if she had ever seen anything like it in St Petersburg.

She shrugged.

'I think it's too cold there,' she said. 'And people are usually too drunk to manage anything else.'

'Time to go,' he said.

They stepped over the bodies and collected their coats from the bored-looking woman in dark red taffeta. Arm in arm they walked down the corridor and straight out into the darkness. Rose's stool was there but no-one was around to wish them good night. It was Autumn now and there was a slight frost just forming as they briskly made their way across the yard.

'Excuse me, just one moment.'

Ford walked over to a car that was parked on Great Windmill Street.

Two men got out, they exchanged a few words then they walked straight past Irena and straight for the club. One of them was carrying a camera.

'Friends of yours?' she asked when Jack returned.

'Just two fellers I met recently. Interesting pair. They're avenging angels, you know.'

It was just after three when they got back to the hotel and the only thing left to do was sleep.

They were in no rush to get the train the next morning – in fact it was almost mid-day before Jack was woken by an over-zealous room maid. Irena was a completely changed person on the journey back North, she had lost that gaunt, hunted look and the smile initiated by Sidney Bowen of the Home Office became a frequent visitor to her features.

Jack had organised a private dining room for the celebration dinner at the Royal Saracen. As well as the Needham family, Sir Horatio Manners would be there and Matt and Sarah Headley, too.

'I must make sure there is ice cream for the children. And not too many rich sauces. I will talk to the chef.'

Jack was delighted to see something of the air of the old Countess returning, but at the same time spared a little thought for the chef, Francois, whose parents ran a fish and chip shop in Tynemouth and christened their son, Harold.

Nevertheless, Francois ne' Harold managed to excel himself and the high note of the evening was a baked Alaska in honour of Countess Irena and utterly demolished by the Needham family, adults included.

Even Matt was in awe of their ability to consume desserts. He drew on his cigar and swilled the cognac around in the bottom of a ridiculously large balloon glass.

'I have to say, Jack, it has been a tremendous evening and you've been extraordinarily generous but I don't really understand what it is you're celebrating.'

'What do you mean?'

'Well, it's me and Charles and the Countess that should be doing the celebrating. He's escaped a political scandal, she's escaped the Russians and I've escaped the dole queue. What have you got out of this?'

Manners was earwigging from further down the table.

'Are you going to tell him Jack, or will I?'

Jack rubbed his hand across his chin. Matt would find out soon enough, anyway and this was as good a time as any.

He looked closely at his old friend.

'Well you know this new company that Sir Horatio is heading up at Lewis Bishop?'

'The one that's building parts for the ship?'

'Yes. What about it?'

'I'm the sleeping partner.'

Matt took another swig of his cognac. Then he drained his glass and refilled it.

'You? But why the Hell, didn't you say so?'

'Because it's a secret, Matt. I'm just an investor, that's all. I didn't want to complicate things what with my history in the union and all that carry on. We decided it was far better if nobody knew.'

'I see,' said Matt. 'So, if that deal had broken down, you'd have lost a lot money.'

'Possibly,' said Ford, 'But thanks to you, bonny lad, I'm going to make some money instead.'

Matt nodded.

'By, you always come up smelling of roses, don't you Jack. Still, I don't begrudge it – as long as the lads get the work.'

'There's something else. You might as well find out now.'

'What?'

'The training jobs at Lohmann's yard in Bremen.'

'What about them?'

Ford pulled a document from his inside pocket.

'They have to come through our company as well. All two hundred of them.'

'What?'

The colour drained from Matt's face as he scanned the procurement contract from the Russian Government. Ford pointed to the clause and it was signed Mikhail Bukanin and J Ford.

Manners could see a look of panic flashing across Matt's eyes, his cheeks were beginning to turn pink and tiny balls of sweat were appearing on his forehead.

'Don't worry Headley – the men will get the full rate. We'll just be charging the Russians a bit more to cover insurance, travel, accommodation and other minor overheads.'

Matt looked Jack square in the eyes.

'You bugger, Jack.'

Ford looked hurt.

'What are you getting all worked up for, bonny lad? You know you can always trust me.'

The next day was Sunday but, despite his banging head, Jack dragged himself up early.

'I'm just popping out to get a paper pet,' he said. But Irena was still dead to world. He pulled on his clothes and went out of the hotel via the rear door. He made his was along the station concourse past the Telegraph Office where he had first spotted Irena with Igor. Next door was a small newsagent and tobacconist's where the man was still unwrapping the string from the bundles of papers that had just arrived from the London train.

'Have you got a News of the World?'

Ford didn't even wait for his change. He ran back to the hotel and hardly paused for breath until he was sat on the edge of their bed flicking through the pages.

He didn't have to look far. On page five was a picture of an extremely startled Lansing Bell cuddling Sir Broderick Hogg under a table at the Ham Bone Club under the headline, 'London's Den Of Iniquity – Drink, Drugs and all that jazz!'